YOU'VE GOT THE WRONG GUY

A Mystery Novel

MICHAEL JAYMES

TWISTED KEY
p u b l i s h i n g
2024

First Printing: 2024

ISBN 978-1-63911-125-1

Twisted Key Publishing, LLC
www.twistedkeypublishing.com

Ordering Information:
Special discounts are available on quantity purchases by corporations, associations, educators, and others. For details, contact the publisher at the above listed address.

U.S. trade bookstores and wholesalers: Please contact Twisted Key Publishing, LLC by email twistedkeypublishing@gmail.com.

TABLE OF CONTENTS

For my brother, Dave, whose transformation inspired many aspects of this story.

CHAPTER 1
BENTLEY RINK

I slapped the soda can puck with my makeshift hockey stick, passing it to Jamal, a twelve-year-old boy wearing jean shorts held up by a tightly pulled belt. He received the puck with ease and rocketed a shot past the sandy-haired defender. It rattled off both trash can goalposts before heading in.

"It's good!" shouted Timmy through a traffic cone, sitting cross-legged on the sidewalk. "Wildcats take the lead. The synergy between Jamal and CJ is unreal today."

Kids of every age and size cheered from the sidelines, their voices echoing off the brick apartments of Bentley Street.

Ronny, sporting a collared shirt and khaki pants, joined Jamal and me in the center. "Nice rip!"

"Yeah, nice shot, little man," I said.

Jamal and I high-fived with our hockey sticks—his made out of copper pipe inserted into a block of wood, mine being a push broom with one end of the brush and all the bristles removed.

Jamal, Ronny, and I were always on the same team, which Timmy had named the Wilkes City Wildcats.

The opposing team included three other boys, all twice the size of my teammates. The sandy-haired boy was Kaleb with a *K*, something he clarified whenever he introduced himself. Davie was a fill-in, a nervous player who avoided any physical contact. Marcus was Jamal's older brother, always playing shirtless. By far the best in the streets, he had a real carbon fiber hockey stick, the rest of us using whatever the boys put together from the dumpsters.

Next to Timmy sat the prize pot, a jar full of pocket change. This week, the jar nearly overflowed.

Kaleb tossed the flattened Coca-Cola toward the center. Marcus and I took our positions for the faceoff. His dreads hung before his gaze, sweat sparkling in the afternoon sun on his dark skin. For sixteen, Marcus was a big kid, taller and probably stronger than me.

"Looking tired, old man. Need a sub?"

I gave a sly grin and turned my flat-brim cap backward. "Big words for someone who's about to lose."

We slapped sticks before fighting for possession in traditional street hockey fashion. The puck flew to the side, and the game commenced. The boys bodied one another, pushing and passing the puck around the street, taking turns firing shots on either end.

Marcus gained control and bulldozed his younger brother to the ground. Next in the line of defense, I battled for possession. Marcus slapped my shin with his stick to get past me—a low blow, but there were no rules in the streets.

He took a shot that whizzed past Ronny's face. The audience parted like the Red Sea as the smooshed Coca-Cola flew down the alleyway behind them.

Hoots and hollers came from the crowd as our announcer gave an update. "Bulldogs tie it up with a lightning play by Marcus!"

Jamal held back tears from having the wind knocked out.

"Don't be such a wuss!" Marcus barked from his side of the rink. Davie and Kaleb laughed beside him.

"That was a foul!" Ronny shouted.

"Go cry about it! You have a player twice our age," Davie retorted.

This was true. At twenty-seven, I was a decade older than the rest of them. What started as hopping in to score a quick goal turned into playing every Friday after midday Uber rounds.

Marcus shut anyone up if they complained about me. He never admitted it, but I presumed he liked the challenge. I wasn't better than the other boys, but my size made up for my lack of skill.

Ronny and I helped Jamal to his feet.

"Marcus wins every week," Jamal pouted.

Mocking came from behind me as I spoke. "Don't pay attention to them. We got this!"

An onlooker from the alley tossed the can back into the street, and another faceoff took place in the center. I shouldered Marcus away to protect the puck, sending it to my left. Jamal took another shot, but Kaleb swatted it away.

"Ronny!" called Mrs. Hopskey from a third-floor window. "Supper time!"

"One second, Mom!" he replied, focusing on the fast-paced game, saving a wicked shot from downtown in the process.

"You heard it, folks," Timmy said. "That was the supper bell. We're in golden goal territory. Who's got the ice? Who's gonna clutch up? This one's coming down to the wire."

Jamal passed the puck, and I took a slapshot of my own. It clashed with the garbage can and bounced away. Davie sent the puck out of the box. Marcus drilled me with his shoulder to steal possession. He had a clear shot, but somehow Ronny made another miraculous save.

I called for the puck. Davie guarded me, but I sent the flattened can through his wobbly legs, leaving Jamal in a one-on-one position against Kaleb.

He reeled back to send a power shot past the goaltender. Surprising us all, Jamal faked the shot, sending Kaleb sailing in the wind.

With the goal wide open, Jamal finished it with an easy tap-in.

"I can't believe it! Jamal has put a shot between the iron. We're calling it there! Wilkes City Wildcats have defeated the reigning champs. My name's Timmy, and we'll see you next week at Bentley Rink."

Cheers of praise surrounded us as Ronny and Jamal leaped with joy. We achieved the impossible; we defeated Marcus.

After the boys collected their winnings, we said "good game" to the other team. Marcus blamed his sub for the loss, leaving without another word.

"Wanna play another?" asked Jamal and Ronny.

"You know I'd love to, but—"

"Ronny, let's go," his mother demanded. "Your macaroni's getting cold. Jamal, honey, come have dinner if you'd like."

I gave Mrs. Hopskey a wave. "Maybe next time, boys. Go get some dinner."

The crowd fizzled away as I returned the hockey sticks behind the dumpster for safe keeping. The lingering figure from the alleyway was gone, too. Thinking little of it, I turned up the street, and headed for the corner building, The Pizza Bar.

Chapter 2
The Pizza Bar

Smoky cherry blossom-and-rain incense burned in the corner beside Mr. Zhang's bonsai tree. The weightless haze wafted through the air, dancing to the tune of the shamisen. It was the same smell and music Mr. Zhang had chosen since I first entered The Pizza Bar.

"Music and incense raise aura," Mr. Zhang told me. "Happy people buy more drink; more drink make me more money."

The Pizza Bar was unlike any other bar or pizza place. It was owned and run by a short Asian man, but the cuisine was as American as it gets. It was a bit of a cultural whiplash the first time I'd eaten here.

"Pizza popular; beer popular. Easy to make and sell. Don't break what work."

Mr. Zhang was born and raised in China. He said he came to Wilkes City to start over, but due to him never speaking of family, I believed he was running from the past. I couldn't blame him; I was running from my own demons.

One might say it was a coincidence, and another may say it was divine intervention—either way, our paths led us both to Wilkes City. It just so happened that he opened The Pizza Bar shortly after I began my hunt for an apartment, and I had become a regular. Despite his difficulties with English, we quickly became acquaintances, eventually ending up under the same roof. That was four years ago. I couldn't fathom why he trusted a twenty-three-year-old kid, but he hadn't kicked me out yet.

"What's rocking, Rodman?"

I slapped Nate on the back, nearly causing him to spill his beer as I vaulted into the empty bar stool beside him. His caramel curls shook like a shaggy dog.

"Didn't mean to scare you," I added.

"Where were you, man?" he asked as he knocked off my black flat brim. "I'm already on my second beer." He cut me off before I answered, analyzing my dust-covered jeans. "Let me guess: street hockey?"

I pulled out a handful of change that rattled on the dark cherry counter next to my hat.

"Winnings were big today. They had over $30 in the prize pool."

"You know, I think it's charitable of you to play with the neighborhood kids, but you can't take their money, CJ. That's like—"

"Stealing candy from a baby?" I laughed.

"Exactly!"

"Relax, I only took enough to buy a beer. Besides, Jamal insisted I have a share of the prize."

He held back a smile as he rolled his eyes, half-hidden by an overflow of hair. Some would say his *hipster* hairstyle made Nate Rodman look immature, but he was the most sophisticated person I knew (which probably wasn't saying much since the sum of my acquaintances was an old Chinese man with broken English and a bunch of neighborhood rugrats).

He spent more time in the library than anyone else in Wilkes City. I'd tease him about it occasionally since it was a bit *old school*. Besides, what purpose did it serve when everything was online? But I suppose that's what he liked about it.

"Hey, guys!" came a familiar voice from behind us.

Sophia's long espresso hair fell gently down her petite frame, contrasting with her yellow, polka-dot blouse. Her dimpled countenance was enchanting, powerful enough to lighten anyone's mood.

"Sorry, I'm late. You didn't eat without me, right?" Sophia added with a knowing grin as she slid in next to Nate.

"No worries. You haven't missed anything. Hockey pro over here just showed up."

Sophia leaned past Nate, her irresistible violet eyes locking with mine. "Oh, I see you're still picking on the neighborhood kids?"

"I'm not picking on them! They literally beg me to play."

"Sure, they do," Sophia teased.

"Seriously! I love spending time with them."

Her thin lips curled into a giggle, causing flutters of warmth to wash through my face. "I guess it's nice they have someone to look up to."

When Mr. Zhang entered from the back room, we ordered a tray of pizza and a round of Dunkel beers (my favorite). He topped Nate off and placed dark, frothy beers before Sophia and me, returning a few minutes later with our pizza.

"CJ, where rent money?" asked Mr. Zhang as he laid the pie in front of us. His eyes were icy, his wrinkles full of annoyance.

"Here's some of it." I pushed the pile of change toward him. He didn't find it funny. "I left my wallet in my car."

He thumped my shoulder with his little finger as he spoke every word. "No more excuse. You suppose to pay week ago. You lucky you not on street."

"I know, I know. I have some cash on me today. I'll bring it in later."

Mr. Zhang walked away, muttering words in his natural tongue. The only word I recognized was *jiàn rén*, something I heard him say often, but I never knew what it meant. Nate said he thought it was a swear word.

"Hey, turn this up," Sophia said, pointing at the TV.

I grabbed the remote from behind the bar. We chowed down and listened intently to the silver-haired woman in all gray on the TV hanging from the corner.

"...have not yet released any information on suspects. All we know is that blood was spilled on the corner of Eagle and Cornwallis, and the action was caught by a local's front door security camera, showing that the luxury chauffeur company, Private Rides, was on the scene. Their involvement in the crime is uncertain, as Jonas Tooly, owner of Private Rides, is still under investigation. An anonymous source has informed us that the chauffeur company will suspend all drivers for the time being until this case comes to a close. Stay tuned for more updates after this short break. I'm Haley Thompson, and you're watching WCN."

"George Morris is up to no good again," Nate said as a long string of cheese dripped from his lip.

I washed down a mouthful of pizza with beer before responding. "Every time something bad happens in Wilkes, you blame that guy."

"Because he *is* behind it all."

"*Every time*?" interjected Sophia. "You guys make it sound like we live in a city of crime."

"Well, it's not Heaven!" spat Nate.

"Still, Sophia has a point. Besides, doesn't the guy own the old paper warehouse or something?"

"Ask me, and it's just a front," said Nate between chews. "Anyone who crosses Morris ends up dead."

"Nathan! Can you please stop talking with your mouth full? It's disgusting," Sophia said in her motherly tone.

Nate and I laughed. It was an inside joke that Sophia always kept us in check.

I still didn't understand why Sophia hung out with us. Sometimes, she sat quietly listening, only speaking to remind us of our manners, while Nate and I would go off on meaningless tangents. Other times, she made a point of standing her ground between our vacuous disputes. Nate's big brain was beyond her; my ignorance and cheesy jokes stooped far below her standards. In my opinion, we needed her for balance more than she needed us for company—our personal mediator to keep things civil.

"Hey, did I ever tell you guys I applied to Private Rides?"

"What, did you bomb the driving test?" Nate bantered.

"No. Actually, I got the job. It was back when I first moved in with Mr. Zhang. I was going to leave Uber for the pay, but I didn't know wearing a suit was part of the criteria, which is bogus if you ask me."

"Not bogus; you're just narrow-minded," Rodman scoffed. "Surveys argue that enforced dress codes raise work ethic."

"Says the guy that has no taste in fashion," Sophia replied.

"What? You don't like this sweater?"

"Looks like something out of my grandfather's closet."

Sophia was right. Nate had an odd sense of fashion. Some days, he wore striped sweaters from the 70s and a pair of Walmart sweatpants. Other days, he wore collared shirts (but still with sweatpants). His attire fell somewhere between a hippy preacher and a street bum.

"Nate, you're telling me you'd want to wear a suit in a place where it's nearly eighty degrees year-round?" I asked.

"I wear sweaters year-round."

"You also work from home at a desk," Sophia interjected.

I sipped my beer. "Besides, they have soundproof backseats and private glass in their vehicles. Passengers never see their driver, so I don't know why formal attire was a requirement. That's why I decided to stick with Uber."

"Too bad Uber pay not good," said Mr. Zhang, cleaning a glass behind the counter.

"All right, all right." I took a few bites of crust before jumping out of my seat. "I'll make a few runs now, and when I return, I'll have my wallet."

"You just got here!" Sophia crossed her arms and pretended to pout.

"You heard the man. I have bills to pay. I'll be back in a few hours if you guys still want to hang."

"Is money all you talk about, Mr. Zhang?" Nate asked.

Mr. Zhang lowered his head, looking over the top of his oval glasses. The shine of his baldness nearly blinded us. "Talk about money less when CJ pay on time."

"And maybe one day I will," I replied with a wink. "Catch you guys later."

I shot my friends with finger pistols and headed out the door.

CHAPTER 3
CINDY LOU THE MALIBU

There was nothing quite like the smell of the city on a Friday night—pizza, garbage, and sweat. Wilkes City wouldn't be what it was without it—and for that, I loved it.

Windows down and radio on, I cruised through the suburbs and onto the main drag. I slapped the shifter into third and steered Cindy Lou into the left lane, then the right, then back to the left, bobbing through traffic like a sewing needle. The deli, Mr. Italy, Stop 'N Shop, and a string of other small restaurants and apartments blurred past me. I waved, like always, as I sped by Ricardo's Rum and Ribs, doing as the neon sign above the bar said. *If you can't stop in, at least wave as you pass.*

"*Take me to the land!*" I sang, spinning the volume knob a few notches, just shy of causing my ears to ring. My fingers drummed on the steering wheel to the rhythm.

I checked my mirrors, smoothly pulling into the left lane as I stopped at a red light. Idling motionless stripped me of the breeze, causing me to melt into my pleather seat.

I reached into the center console for my emergency deodorant, applying it generously under my black v-neck.

"*Take me to the land of rock 'n roll!* Whew, sing it with me, Cindy!"

As I sang into my deodorant stick microphone, I noticed a mustached man in a suit and tie staring from the right lane. I grinned and offered him a thumbs-up; he frowned in response. Once the light turned green, I stepped on the gas, leaving the man and his mustache in the dust.

Cindy interrupted the song as she gave me my next instructions.

"Take the next left onto Mulberry Street; then, your destination will be on the right."

Cindy's tires shrieked with enthusiasm as I took the sharp turn, blazing past the Route 20 turnoff, the very highway I had arrived by years before.

As I approached Blue Ridge Lodge, I came to a slow, lowered the music, and pulled in leisurely.

A woman, who looked to be in her thirties, raised her hand. Her hair was pulled into a tight bun, her skirt and blouse a matching blue. All she was missing was a stewardess hat, and she could have been mistaken for a flight attendant.

"Are you CJ?"

"Yep! And this is Cindy Lou the Malibu." I fondly patted Cindy's silver exterior.

She gave a nervous smile (maybe she didn't like the name).

Once she was comfortably seated, I rolled up the windows and turned on the air conditioning. With my Uber app synced to Cindy Lou's touch-screen navigator, her voice came over the speakers with instructions. I shifted her with a smooth and gentle touch as I got back on the road.

Trading glances with the rearview mirror, I struggled to catch my rider's eyes. She sat quietly buckled in her seat, with her face glued to her phone.

My father's words echoed in my mind.

Rule 1: Make eye contact before speaking.

I tried again to no avail.

Sorry, Pop. Rule 1 isn't going to work this time.

"So, Mary, heading to dinner?"

Her eyes wandered up to the rearview. "How did you know my name?"

"The app tells me," I said, pointing to my phone magnetically attached to the dashboard next to Cindy Lou's touchscreen.

"Oh, right."

"The Jigger's a pretty popular place," I added. "Big crowd on a night like this. They always have dancing and live bands on Fridays."

"So I've been told."

"If it's your first time, I've heard from other passengers that their house reuben is to die for."

"I'll keep it in mind."

She was less than enthusiastic, but after breaking the ice, I switched to my pitch anyway.

"Well, in case you want to look nice for your special date, or perhaps you want to surprise them with a gift, I have a lovely collection of jewelry, as you can see." I gestured toward the back of my seat, where a plastic seat organizer with see-through zipper compartments of jewelry hung neatly. "Find something nice, and name your price."

Mary glanced at the organizer, but her eyes quickly found their comfort with the screen of her phone.

I doubted she'd buy anything anyway, but I miss 100% of the shots I don't take, right?

The rest of the trip carried on without another word. After she was gone, I refreshed the Uber app.

"Can you believe it, Cindy? No tip. *Psh*! I didn't even go over the speed limit!"

I parked in front of The Jigger for a few minutes, waiting for a notification of another rider. I usually made twenty-five an hour on Friday nights, but Mary was only my fourth ride in three hours. It was almost 9:00 PM, and I only made thirty bucks.

While aimlessly watching a sea of people cross the road ahead of me, large knuckles knocked on the passenger window. I pressed the power window switch on the armrest.

"Sorry, can I not park here?" I asked, assuming by his black polo and wayfarer sunglasses he was a bouncer from The Jigger.

"Is this an Uber?" His voice was like a brute, monotone and gruff.

"Uh... yeah, but you have to order through the app."

"Will you take cash?"

I considered the question. "I mean, I don't typically take cash. Where do you have to go?"

He pulled out two Jacksons and held them through the window. "1256 New Binghams Street."

Well, I can't pass up $40 for a quick drive.

I took the money and nodded toward the back. "Hop in."

The giant climbed into the car testing its suspension as I shut down the Uber app. I entered the address into my phone, which synced to Cindy Lou's navigator.

"How much for a watch?" he asked, eyeing the organizer behind me.

Heck! This guy's about to pay for the night!

"Name your price."

He unzipped a compartment and pulled out a fake silver Casio with a blue bezel. He dug into his wallet and held three more Jacksons between the front seats.

"You've got a deal!"

The next few minutes passed quietly. I wanted to carry a friendly conversation with my passenger, especially since he was a buyer, but something about him put me on edge. He sat stiffly in his seat, not uttering another word since his purchase. New Binghams was on the other side of town, and with Friday-night traffic, it took longer than anticipated. To pass the time, I counted the Chevys, but it didn't relieve the tension.

I'd glance back at the man at every red light—which felt like every freaking block. With most riders, I could read them like a book. This guy was different. His shades covered his eyes, masking his gaze. His burly beard covered his mouth, disguising any emotion. The only thing I could tell about him was that he probably worked in security, which I only assumed from the black shades, hat, shirt, and cargo shorts.

Maybe he lacks any taste in fashion like Nate.

"What's your name?" he asked suddenly, interrupting my thoughts.

The question caught me off guard. Something about his monotone voice made me uncomfortable. The question felt penetrating, which was weird, as I've had plenty of passengers ask the same thing. I mulled the question over for so long I failed to realize the light had turned green. The blaring horn from behind gave me a cordial reminder to keep moving.

Get a grip before he asks for his money back and wants to get out.

I took a sip from my water bottle before responding. "Tom," I lied. "And yours?"

"Joe." He then added, "Did you see the game last night?"

I shook my head.

"Wilkes Wizards won. Ricky Samone nearly pitched a perfect game."

"I don't really watch any sports," I admitted.

"Really?" Finally, a flicker of emotion entered his voice. "I would have guessed you're an athlete from first impression."

The compliment helped me relax, and I couldn't help but smirk. "I used to ride a bike a lot. I took long bike trips with my father, sometimes riding a hundred miles in one direction before quitting to stay somewhere. But I don't bike anymore. These days, I play street hockey with some neighborhood kids."

"What made you stop?"

I found myself parched again and took another large gulp of water before clearing my throat. "My father died."

"Sorry to hear that."

I shrugged my shoulders, clicking on my turn signal. "It was a long time ago."

I crinkled the plastic water bottle in my free hand to fill the moment of silence. Speaking about my father made me fidgety.

"Do you have any other family, Tom?"

I didn't like the way Joe said my name (or my fake name), pausing before the pronunciation and exaggerating the single syllable. His friendly demeanor masked the all-too-familiar tone of a cop.

Could he be a cop? Undercover? No! He bought a watch. Can't be. Now I'm being paranoid.

I kept my composure as I answered. "The only family I have is my older brother. Between you and me, sometimes I feel like *I'm* the big brother."

I chuckled at my own joke, but Joe sat motionless, causing my laughter to die stiltedly.

"Have you always lived in the city?"

"No, I moved here after my father passed."

"Have you ever thought of going back?"

"Where? To my old home? Ha! That place is full of regrets and memories that I don't need to be worrying about."

"Regrets?"

We were reaching territory I wasn't ready to share with a stranger. I went to take another sip of my water, but at this point, it was empty. He led the conversation and I was playing to his every whim. I needed to pull this back somehow. It didn't help that—

I slammed my brakes, my heart leaping into my throat.

"Watch where you're going, you lunatic!" the man in the crosswalk screamed, flipping me the bird.

I expected Joe to freak out like any sane person would. Surely, he'd want to get out at this point. But there he sat, awaiting an answer, still as a statue.

Another one of my father's rules reverberated in my mind.

Rule 6: Control the conversation.

I decided not to answer as I slowly accelerated.

"So what about you, Joe? Do you live in the area?"

"For the time being, yes," he answered in monotone.

"Do you travel a lot?"

"Yes, I suppose I travel more than most."

Seeing that he didn't want to give details, I tried another question. "Do you have a home or a place to go back to?"

"My home is where I lay my head at night."

"So your home, *for the time being*, is Wilkes City?"

"Correct," he said after a pause.

I raised an eyebrow as I observed him in the rearview mirror, wondering if he was watching me.

"Okay... what about work? What do you do?"

"I'm a freelancer."

"Oh, that's cool! I can always respect a man that works for himself."

I monitored the mirror again to see if he accepted my compliment, but this guy was hard to crack. He refrained from emotion with stoic composure.

"So... you enjoy watching baseball?" I asked in a vain attempt at conversation.

"No," Joe replied in his low voice.

"But you mentioned the game from last night."

"It was on the news this morning." Joe extended his arm and pointed to the right. "Do they have good chai?"

I shook my head as I looked out the window at a corner café. "Never been there."

"This will do. You can pull over here."

The abrupt response caught me off guard. "We're still six minutes from your destination."

"That's okay. I could use the exercise."

I pulled over by the curb next to the café.

"Thanks for the watch," he said before closing his door.

He tapped the hood before walking away, giving me a brief smile. I stared in confusion with my jaw hanging open.

"That was weird, don't you think, Cindy?" I retrieved my wallet and pulled open the center to make sure I wasn't delusional. "Well," I chortled, "at least I made a hundred bucks."

It was 9:30 at this point. The night was still young for a Friday, but the unsettling feeling Joe left in the vehicle robbed me of any avarice I had left. I no longer smelled the invigorating scent of the city, desired the breeze from the open windows, or felt alive from the thrill of the drive.

I texted Nate to see if he was down for more drinks.

My phone chimed a few minutes later.

"Be there in ten minutes."

I shook my arms like an inflatable tube man, trying to shake off the sticky uncomfortability that lingered in the car. I put on my hat, threw down the windows, and cranked up the music, leaving Eastside behind me to head back to The Pizza Bar.

Chapter 4

Ignorance Is Bliss

I pulled up behind The Pizza Bar, parking next to Rodman's yellow 2022 Ford Mustang. The tinted windows, the Mustang decal on the back windshield, the sparkling custom rims, the 12-inch subwoofer in the trunk—she was a beauty! I envied his car, but I couldn't stare. I didn't want Cindy Lou to think I was cheating. Besides, Chevys are better.

"Took you long enough," Nate said as he emerged from his car.

"Sorry. I was on the other side of town."

"I'm teasing." He pushed a yarny lock of hair behind his ear. "Sophia texted me and won't be here for fifteen minutes. Wanna take a walk?"

That was always Nate's response when we had time to kill. "They're good for mental health," he would say, rattling off a dozen different books and surveys that backed up the claim.

We walked down the street behind The Pizza Bar, Nate's flip flops slapping with every step, passing Bentley Rink along the way.

"Flip flops with sweatpants?"

"What?" he innocently replied. "My feet sweat."

The trash cans were still set up as goalposts, ready to be used for next time. The boys cared for this portion of the street. The area was swept clean of debris, while garbage and rubble littered the surroundings.

The dim yellow light from apartment windows guided our way down the dilapidated sidewalk. Most of the street lamps on Bentley Street were out, except for one behind us at the corner near The Pizza Bar's parking lot, which was on its last leg. The brick buildings on either side of the vacant road left dark, narrow alleyways in between, some only large enough for a child to squeeze through.

Voices came from one alley. Shouting came from a window above. Music blared from a distant rooftop. My stomach was riddled with snakes from hearing voices and activity but not seeing a single soul in sight, like ghouls in the air. That summed up Southside; never asleep, but never really awake either. We were the sleepwalkers, the daydreamers, hidden in the shadows of Wilkes City.

"Get any good tips tonight?"

I walked with my hands in both pockets of my jeans, kicking a rock as we went, attempting to avoid the litter along the path.

"Kind of. Had a weird rider today, but he bought a watch, so whatever."

"Still selling that counterfeit crap?" Nate rolled the sleeves of his striped sweater as he spoke, revealing toned forearms. "I keep telling you, CJ, that stuff will catch up with you."

"Law can't catch me," I sang.

"Says every criminal before they're behind bars."

If only Nate knew.

We turned onto Jabinsky and stopped at a street lamp another block down that was too fancy for the area. I hung on its aluminum pole, leaning out and swinging around it freely.

"I'm not making a killing doing it anyway. And I'm pretty sure my riders know it's fake."

"Which makes it worse," Nate argued. "What's the saying? To him who knoweth good but doesn't do it, it is sin."

"You quoting scripture at me?" I scoffed. "I thought you weren't religious."

Nate put a finger to his chin. "Maybe. I forget where I read it." He pulled out his voice recorder. "Look up 'to him who knoweth good' quote."

I laughed. "Why do you still use that dinosaur?"

"It's faster than pulling out a pen and paper or finding an app on my phone." He slipped it back in his pocket. "Anyway, my point is, just because you both know it's wrong doesn't make it right."

"I think that this is a scenario where two wrongs do make a right."

"So if we both agreed to murder, then it'd be okay?"

I stopped swinging around the pole. "Okay, Rodman. You don't have to bring mortality into this."

Before Nate could continue his side of the debate, his phone chimed. He didn't have to say who it was. We both headed back from where we came.

"All I'm saying," Nate began, "is that if you're not careful, your actions will suffer the consequences in due time. You can't run from past decisions forever. If you're going to keep doing it, at least accept the reality of the matter."

His words reminded me of the past, something I did everything possible to avoid pondering. Then came one of my father's rules.

Rule 17: Your feet move faster than your mouth.

I shrugged, kicking a new stone I found along the sidewalk. "What can I say, Rodman? Ignorance is bliss."

We made our way back to The Pizza Bar, but I stopped short before heading inside.

"Be right in," I said to Nate as he held the door. "Can't forget my wallet this time."

I hit the unlock button on my key fob as I approached; Cindy Lou's blinkers flashed in response. I grabbed the handle, only to freeze in place before opening the door. In the dreary flickering light of the lonely parking lot, a Post-it note had been slapped to the windshield.

Dear Crispin Jiles,
Return what you've stolen...
or else.

CHAPTER 5

SOMEONE KNOWS MY NAME

I turned on the spot, gravel crunching beneath my feet. Bentley Street was quiet, only lit by the ominous yellow lamplight at the corner.

How long has this been on my car? A few minutes? Hours? All day?

I scanned the perimeter, unable to move, paralyzed by the feeling of being watched. I didn't want to see anyone, and yet I searched anyway.

First, I thought the sticky note was placed during my walk with Rodman.

They were waiting for me to leave. No, we would have heard someone behind us.

I considered my Uber riders from that day, which wasn't much to go on, as I drove a dozen passengers that morning, followed by another half dozen in the evening, and none of them knew my full name.

No, it would fly off. I would've seen it.

I wondered if one of the neighborhood boys was playing a joke on me, but it didn't seem like a joke. And they didn't know my name either.

"Who in Wilkes City knows my name?" I whispered.

Everyone knew me as CJ. If someone knew my full name, they knew me from before Wilkes City... which only meant they knew my past.

I hadn't heard anyone use my full name since my father died. The note felt personal. The thought knocked the breath out of me, and I leaned on Cindy Lou for support. I didn't want it to be personal. It couldn't be personal! But there was nothing else that came to mind.

Someone knows my name. Someone knows my past. Someone knows what I've done.

Chapter 6
Big Deal

Back inside The Pizza Bar, the atmosphere had shifted since a few hours before. It had nothing to do with my friends, the music, or the aroma in the air—it was the sticky note I had shoved in the pocket of my jeans. I hadn't said a word since I re-entered. I hadn't even taken a sip of the beer Mr. Zhang placed in front of me.

Nate and Sophia, who had taken little notice of my arrival, continued to chat about irrelevant topics, and Nate, as always, integrated his big-brain concepts.

"What does someone's 'moral compass,' or whatever you called it, have to do with buying name-brand clothing?"

"Well, Maslow's Hierarchy of Needs simply proves what is important in one's eyes, which I would directly tie to one's choices in comfortability. Why does someone pay for a more expensive plane ticket? Because it promises a more comfortable trip. Why does someone buy more expensive shoes? Because companies tell us they provide more comfort in appearance, fit, or performance. Why do people order Uber? Because it's the convenience factor of having someone else drive you. People like being comfortable, ultimately thinking comfort is proportionate to happiness."

"Yeah, you lost me at *plane tickets*... basically left me at the airport for that matter." Sophia gestured with her hand, showing Nate's rant-plane take off over her head. "Besides, I'm sure that CJ drives plenty of people around who *actually* need a ride and don't just use Uber because they're lazy. And haven't you used Uber before? So you're calling yourself lazy?"

"We all have a comfort addiction to some degree; we do things we're not necessarily proud of saying out loud." Nate folded his arms over his chest and spun in his barstool. "What do you think, CJ?"

I missed most of the conversation, only looking back at Nate because I heard my name.

"CJ? Are you okay?" Sophia leaned onto the bar to see past Nate, her dark waterfall of hair dropping over her arm.

I gave a fake smile. "Yeah, I'm fine; just thinking."

"About?" Nate prodded.

I waved him off. "Don't worry about it."

"No, no, no," Sophia shook her head. "It's written all over your face. Something's bothering you."

My Adam's apple struggled as I swallowed the lump in my throat. "I..."

Crap! Why did I start? Shut up!

"Well?" Sophia asked.

Knowing there was no escaping this, I continued. "I received some sort of threat."

With furrowed eyebrows, they pulled back their heads like they sniffed something repulsive.

"But I doubt it's a big deal," I added quickly with a nervous laugh. "It's nothing. Forget about it. I don't know why I said anything. Don't worry about it."

"Why are you laughing? This happened in the parking lot?" asked Sophia.

"Did someone try to rob you?" Nate added.

I rubbed the back of my neck, my other hand crumbling the note in my pocket. "Please, really, guys. It's nothing to worry about."

"Then what is it?" Sophia dropped a hand on the counter in annoyance. "I don't understand why you're making a big deal of this if it's really nothing."

"I'm the one making a big deal of it? *You're* the one still pestering me!"

Sophia scoffed. "Don't point your finger at me. You're not acting yourself. Obviously it's a big deal if you're being threatened."

"And I *obviously* don't want to talk about it, so will you drop it?"

"Okay, okay, let's calm down." Nate's voice was low and controlled, settling the tension.

Everyone took a moment to breathe, sipping our beers and staring anywhere in the room except at each other.

"CJ," Nate finally said, "we just want to make sure everything is okay. You're not one to usually keep anything from us."

I bit the inside of my lip, continuing to rub the back of my neck, scratching the short brown hair that protruded from my hat.

"You know you can trust us," Sophia said with a softness in her voice that wasn't there before.

The thought of them knowing my real name went against everything inside of me. In the four years of living in Wilkes City, I had managed to keep it locked away. The old man was buried six feet under. They were making me dig him back up.

My father's words came to mind with a blistering chill.

Rule 19: Vulnerability is equivalent to failure.

A shaky breath escaped my lips as I slowly pulled my hand from my pocket.

"I found this stuck to my car."

CHAPTER 7
THIEF

"Return what you've stolen," echoed Nate as he read the words, passing the note for Sophia to read. "Never knew your first name was Crispin."

I shifted in my seat uncomfortably, pulling off my hat and wrinkling it between my hands, staring at the eight-bit rooster logo between the front eyelets.

"This must be a mistake, right?" Sophia asked. "You wouldn't actually steal anything, right, CJ?"

I didn't answer.

"Do you know who it's from?" Nate asked.

My head wanted to implode. I had to tell the truth, but I couldn't find the words. "I-I-I don't know... because I've—"

"CJ, you wouldn't!"

An anvil dropped on my chest as disappointment flooded Sophia's freckled face.

"When was the last time?" Nate asked.

"A few months ago," I muttered in shame.

"Is this something you do often?"

Tears pricked the corner of my eyes, but I didn't dare make eye contact with Nate.

"It used to be."

"What do you mean *used to be*?" Sophia cried. "Have you stolen from us?"

"No! Gosh, I would never! I can't believe you would think that."

"I don't know what to think, CJ."

I folded in my chair, staring at my sneakers, wishing to crumble away and disappear.

"It was a mistake, okay? I haven't stolen anything in years."

"Except for a few months ago," Nate corrected.

"Well, yes. But it was small! And I know I shouldn't have. I don't know why I did it. I'm not struggling to pay rent or anything."

"Someone say rent?" Mr. Zhang's voice came from the kitchen. His little, round face popped out of the swinging door. "CJ, have my money?"

I pulled out my wallet and paid him.

He held the money up and shook it in the air. "Next time, you pay first day of month."

He dropped the money in his grease-covered apron and returned to the kitchen.

"It's probably connected to the most recent time, don't you think?" asked Nate.

"I don't know."

"Tell us what happened."

I ran my hands through my messy hair, scratching my scalp with untrimmed nails. I took a quick glance around but only saw a man sitting in the corner, picking at his lips and reading a book. He sat far enough away that I didn't believe he'd hear me.

The words fell out of my mouth in a fumbling ramble. "I stole from a pawn shop. The owner caught me and yelled at me. I apologized and handed back a watch I'd taken."

"Okay, so you got caught, and you said 'sorry.' How is this connected?"

I took a sip of my lukewarm beer before answering. "Because I only returned *one* watch. I had five in my pocket."

Sophia slapped the bar. "CJ! What were you thinking?" she said in a mother's voice. "You know better!"

"I know. It was stupid."

"Where are the watches now?" Nate asked.

I threw up my hands. "Gone to who knows who. Sold them to riders like my other jewelry. I felt guilty afterward and gave some money to one of the neighborhood families anonymously as punishment. I guess God didn't think that was enough."

Sophia got up from her seat to use the bathroom, leaving behind the lingering stench from the conversation. This broke all the rules of "bar talk," spoiling our Friday night. We'd gone months without an awkward conversation, let alone a confession.

Nate pointed behind him at the bathroom. "See? People flee uncomfortability."

"What?"

"The conversation we were having? I was just talking about comfort-addiction before you mentioned the—" He stopped short. "Never mind."

I suddenly felt cold, folding my hands and holding them close to my chest, staring at the lager in front of me. Nate's fingers galloped on the table rhythmically. My heart matched the pace—fast... too fast! I wanted to scream. I wanted to cry. I wanted to disappear. I *tried* to disappear. But someone found me. Somehow, someway, my past scraped its way back into my life.

As if he heard my thoughts, Nate said, "Seems weird for someone to threaten you over a few watches, don't you think? Could it be connected to something else? Anything bigger?"

The question pushed me further into the past. I couldn't look Nate in the eyes. I'd never told him about my old life, nor did I have the intention. That went against the entire purpose of moving to Wilkes City. The past was supposed to be forgotten, never to be spoken of, let alone thought of, ever again!

"CJ?"

"No," I quickly stated, realizing I hadn't answered.

"You don't have to lie to me, you know."

"I'm not lying, Rodman. Believe me. If I knew who this was from, I wouldn't have said anything in the first place. It doesn't make sense to me either."

"Could the note be a mistake? A joke?"

"I don't know."

"Then why are you so afraid?"

"They knew my name, Nate," I said in a low voice, barely able to choke out the words that sent shivers through my goosebumped skin. "If they know my name, they know other things about me."

Nate's beady raven-like eyes locked onto me. "What do you have to hide?"

Sophia returned with a fresh scent of bergamot perfume, probably hoping to clear up the atmosphere from the reeking topic.

"Okay," she said confidently with an upright posture. "This isn't so bad. It was petty theft anyway, right? You made a mistake, and now you have to resolve it. The watches from a pawn shop can't be worth that much. Just go back and pay what you owe. Simple as that."

"I don't even know if it was from him," I replied.

"Doesn't hurt to make things right anyway," Nate said. "No one else you have an unsettled debt with, right?"

"He means other than Mr. Zhang," Sophia added in hopes to lighten the mood. My friends got a kick out of it; I barely smirked.

"Not that I'm aware of. It's not like I've ever really lived with a target on my back," I lied.

"Don't beat yourself up, CJ. Nobody's *targeting* you. This isn't a death threat. It was only a few watches."

I nodded, trying to accept the reassurance from Sophia. Her words were tender, but Nate's gaze was cold. He was still thinking. I turned to my beer to detach from his stare.

"So, who'd you steal from?" Sophia asked.

"The guy from Common Trades up on Kindler Street."

"Interesting," Nate said slowly. "Been there a few times myself. Bought a painting once. Jeremiah never struck me as someone who'd threaten anyone."

Exactly why I stole from him, I thought.

No one said anything. I pulled back the note and stared at the chicken-scratch letters, too embarrassed to look at my friends—the only friends I had.

"Well," Nate paused to take a final gulp of his beer, "I never knew you to be a thief, but heinous crime is often shadowed by a friendly smile."

His complexion glowed with grace, but his eyes were full of questioning.

"Is that supposed to make me feel better?"

He shrugged as if the comment were meaningless. "I don't know. I read it in a book once."

Sophia rolled her eyes. "How much do you owe?"

"I'll have to ask."

"Who cares what you owe? Let's be thankful the cops aren't involved," Nate said.

"Yeah, I guess."

I thought about the time I was arrested with my father at the age of sixteen. "Don't worry, son. They have nothing on us. Keep your mouth shut, and we'll be just fine."

I never told anyone in Wilkes about before, not even Mr. Zhang, who graciously never did a background check on me. All I told him was that my mother and father had passed, and I came to Wilkes City for a fresh start. There was nothing else to share. I didn't have to say my mother left us, and I never heard from her again, or that my father died robbing a gas station. I didn't have to tell anyone that the reason we always rode bikes was because we couldn't afford a half-decent car. I didn't have to tell them that thievery was a part of my old lifestyle. No one had to know. I was a changed man! Right?

It was one small slip-up, I tried to reassure myself. *One mistake that crept its way back into the present. The note must be from Jeremiah. My friends don't need to know anything else. I'll sweep it under the carpet tomorrow like it never happened, and we'll forget about it.*

I felt like an alcoholic who had claimed to be sober but decided to have one final drink when push came to shove. Adam told me stories about my mom, memories from when I was too young to remember. She hid shooters in old socks or underneath folded sheets no one used... like she wanted to be caught. She was too ashamed to ask for help. Her guilty conscience put the evidence in plain sight, bound to be found when life decided the time was right.

My head pounded from the stress, and I got up from my seat. "I think I'm gonna call it a night."

"Aw, come on, man. This is the second time you're leaving us early. It's Friday night. It's not that big of a deal. This note is such a little thing. Let tomorrow bear your worries."

"Thanks, Rodman, but I'm just not feeling it."

"What if the next drink's on me?"

I didn't respond. His words were friendly, but Nate's not stupid. I knew he wanted to dig for more answers.

As I walked past my friends, Sophia touched my hand. A flicker of compassion glided over her face. Usually, a simple touch of our skin sent shockwaves of ecstasy racing through me, but it had little effect.

"Maybe see you tomorrow?" she asked.

"I'll let you know."

"And you're going to see Jeremiah, right?" Nate questioned.

I don't have a choice now.

"Yeah, I'll talk to him."

"Text us when you do," Sophia said.

I nodded as I walked away.

"And CJ?"

I stopped at the swing door of the kitchen.

"We don't hate you. You know that, right?"

We locked eyes one last time. He no longer searched my thoughts. His words were genuine.

"I know."

I headed through the door, past Mr. Zhang, who was cleaning the kitchen for the night, and into the back hallway, taking the stairs to my apartment.

They don't know everything, but they see me as a thief. They definitely hate me. I should've kept my mouth shut.

Rodman's words echoed in my mind.

...heinous crime is often shadowed by a friendly smile.

Then came my father's voice.

Rule 3: Don't forget to smile.

CHAPTER 8
A WEREWOLF

"Nope, you've got the wrong guy."

"You have to be kidding me!"

Jeremiah folded his arms, confused by my outburst. The skin of his forearms was barely visible underneath thick gray hair. Even his sausage fingers were covered in wool. I always thought he must be a close relative to a werewolf.

"And if I needed to contact you, I wouldn't be playing games and leaving notes on your car. I mean, look at me," he said with a belly laugh. "I'm sixty years old. My blood pressure is higher than gas prices. Do I look like someone who is running around leaving notes for people?"

I threw back my head and let out an agitated sigh. "No... I just thought—"

"Thought what?" he asked, stroking his beard. "What's this note say anyway?"

He squinted his wrinkled eyes; the cogs were spinning.

"Never mind, I gotta run. Thanks for everything."

I ran for the exit before he asked another question, accidentally bumping into a man applying lip balm, knocking it to the floor.

"Sorry," I said without looking back.

Once outside on the corner of Kindler, I stood in the sun, surrounded by the buzz of morning traffic. It was a hot day—a bad day to wear jeans.

I pulled out my phone and sent a quick text to Sophia and Nate. I debated lying to them, but it didn't seem worth it. I wasn't looking to go back to my old ways.

"Was wrong about Jeremiah. Not sure who the note's from."

I always knew in the back of my mind the Post-it note wasn't from Jeremiah, but it would have made everything easier. I wouldn't have to worry about the idea that someone had followed me cross-country to Wilkes City.

Typical Sophia responded in less than thirty seconds.

"Did you still pay him back?"

I ignored the text. She made it hard not to lie.

Not coughing up a few hundred when the old man's oblivious.

Pulling out my wallet, I stretched its mouth to see the Benjamins withdrawn earlier that day between Uber runs. Dozens of excuses came to mind for why I needed them.

I could use this for next month's rent.

When was the last time I treated myself?

What if sticky note guy shows up and wants cash?

I could invest this into more merchandise.

Cindy Lou could use a tune-up.

My father's words were the cherry on top.

Rule 16: Give to the wise; take from the ignorant.

Before making a decision, a teenage girl ran by and took my wallet.

"Hey, stop that kid!" I gasped, pointing toward the long-haired blonde running in neon high-socks and pink sneakers.

The few bystanders near the bus stop mindlessly swiped their thumbs on their phones, barely acknowledging what took place. I darted after her, regretting the jeans more than ever.

We zigzagged down different streets I had only known from the seat of my car. Down one alley and out another, I began to gain ground. She wasn't faster than me, but my tank was dwindling. I used to love the rush from running, but that was when *I* was the one being chased.

She slipped through the Wilkes Center Street Mall entrance to hide among the crowd, but her bright apparel made her easy to pick out. I ran through families and couples, even bumping into Jamal and his friends at one point (probably spending their winnings from the day before). A few angry voices came from behind, swallowed by the loud clopping of our feet echoing through the mall's tile-floored food court.

The distance between us was small. I swatted at her cosmic purple backpack but only grazed it with my fingertips as she headed for the JCPenney. Pushing between clothing racks, I bellowed like a bagpipe, gasping for air. The gap lengthened, and I was ready to give up. It was hopeless. I lost her. She hid somewhere among the sea of clothes.

"Hold it right there, young lady!"

I floundered breathlessly toward the voice, falling through the last rack to the feet of the pink-sneakered girl, her wrist seized by a woman standing by the exit to the parking garage with a birthmark the size of Alaska. I put up my hands to thank the heavens for allowing this mall cop to be on duty.

With my wallet still in the thief's hand, there was no need for explanation.

"Thank you, ma'am!" I praised between breaths as I got to my feet. "You're... a lifesaver."

"This isn't the first time I've caught this one. Is it, Nancy?"

Nancy stared at the floor, her lips pursed to one side. I would have done it myself at her age... except I would've gotten away.

I decided not to press charges and made my way back to my parked car on Kindler Street. I opened the door, but before getting in, I put both hands in my pockets, checking for the third time I had my keys, phone, and wallet.

Feeling my wallet, I thought about the money in it—the money I exerted so much energy for that wasn't even rightfully mine. I looked back at the Common Trades front sign. Half the bulbs in the sign title were dead.

I let out a sigh and shut the car door without getting in. "I'm sure the old werewolf needs the money just as much as I do."

I went inside, explained my debt, and repaid Jeremiah. He forgave me for my honesty before adding, "...and don't come back."

It wasn't harsh in the slightest. I deserved it, but I didn't care. It felt good to be honest.

CHAPTER 9

BAD BLOOD WITH A WOMAN

Three Benjamins lighter, I made my way to the north side of Wilkes City, or, as Rodman called it, Privileged Parkway. The five-mile-long residential strip had homes the size of cruise ships. Every few blocks, there was another gated entry to a community beyond the houses on the main road.

I drove through this area frequently. These people gave the best tips and sometimes bought jewelry. Lawyers, doctors, executives (like George Morris), and a list of other occupations dominated this part of the city, but a few shady corners had been inhabited by hustlers—like my brother.

I hadn't spoken to Adam other than a few phone calls on holidays since I moved out four years ago. Half the time, he didn't answer, and half the time, I didn't leave a voicemail.

The last time I visited, the conversation ended with an argument (although I couldn't remember what it was about). Stupid things always seemed to drive a wedge between us, so petty they're not worth remembering, so impactful they kept us separated.

We were thick as thieves (literally) growing up, but when we moved to Wilkes City, we had polarizing intentions. He wanted to get back into living by Father's T.B.S.P of Rules—Take or Buy, Sell and Profit. I thought the acronym was just B.S. and searched for new opportunities as soon as possible.

It wasn't the motto he lived by; it was the habits he prescribed. Drug use became an evident problem, one that Adam said he could manage, but I wanted no part of it. He may have been living by Dad's motto, but he had certainly forgotten one of the golden rules.

Rule 14: Never keep for yourself what can be sold for a profit.

When I reached his home, I found his black Corolla parked in the front. He still hadn't replaced the dented fender from backing into someone a few years ago.

What, he's too lazy to use his gated driveway?

I stared up at the two-story white house, wondering if I should leave. He was the only person in the city that knew my full name. I couldn't imagine him blackmailing me or even thinking of such an idea, but I could see *him* being blackmailed. It matched the lifestyle. Maybe he used my name. It was a long shot, but what other option did I have?

Going against my presumption that this would be another dead end, I adjusted my rooster hat, matted down my white v-neck, and knocked at the door.

I waited about thirty seconds before impatiently knocking again. I checked the time: noon.

"Probably sleeping," I muttered to myself.

I jiggled the handle and found it unlocked. I used to tell him all the time to lock the door.

With his lifestyle, he should really be more careful.

I cracked the door and yelled inside. "Adam. You home? It's me, CJ."

No response.

I took a step inside the ground floor. It was a small living area and kitchen. A mudroom extended from the kitchen, leading to the backyard. I had only been here a few times since moving, and like before, the front room appeared relatively clean.

I climbed the stairs to be met by the mess, quickly smelling the all-too-familiar scent of vape juice, urine, dirty laundry, and essential oils. He always thought that lemongrass helped with the smell; it didn't. He used to hire a cleaning maid. I guessed she had stopped coming. I didn't blame her.

Adam slept in blue plaid boxers on the couch. The TV was the only light in the room. Blankets held up by tacks shaded the windows. I turned on the lamp and squeezed between the couch and overflowing coffee table to sit next to his head.

Cheese doodle dust sprinkled his chest and fingers, the bag spilled on the floor next to a bong. He looked uncomfortable with his skinny body sprawled in every direction. I wished he had cleaned up. I wondered if I could have helped him more.

I gave him a shake, but he didn't move. I shook him again, more aggressively this time, and he came to life, shooting up with a gasp for air as if he were drowning.

"What time is it?!"

"Uh... a little past twelve."

"Shoot! I'm late for my shift. LaNysha's gonna kill me."

I recognized the name. I knew my brother was having one of his "foggy moments."

"Adam," I called as he ran to his bedroom. "You don't work for McMurray anymore."

A moment passed before his head whipped back around the entryway, sniffing and wiping his nose. He stared at me, puzzled, for a few long seconds before buckling over and laughing.

"You right! You right! What was I thinkin'?"

He continued laughing before licking his cheese-covered fingers clean, then running the same hand through his greasy, unintentionally spiked hair and walking over to a home bar in the corner.

"Man, CJ, my head's always in the past. My bad, man. Hey, what you doing here? I haven't seen you in a while, have I? Or have I? I don't remember. Wanna drink? I got some good liquor options. Or somethin' stronger?" He tapped his nose. "Nah!" He swatted at the air. "Just messin' with ya. How ya been, man? Still doin' the drive-around-town thing? Pick up any ladies while you're at it? I met this smoking Brazilian girl the other day who..."

I stopped listening as my brother put a vape in the side of his teeth and went on speaking a mile a minute. He poured us drinks in hazy glasses that hadn't been washed in centuries.

He slapped my back as he sat down, spilling whiskey on my shoulder.

"Well, cheers, brotha! Man, you quiet. Come on, now! Tell me what's new."

I pushed aside take-out containers to set the glass on the coffee table. "I'm not here to catch up, Adam. I'm here to ask if you have any unsettled debts."

He pulled back his neck as he downed his shot, picking up my glass to enjoy a second. "Debts? What d'ya mean?"

I pulled the sticky note from my pocket and tossed it on his naked lap. "I found this on my car the other night. I wondered if maybe they were looking for the wrong Jiles. You didn't use my name for anything, right?"

Adam analyzed the note and tossed it back at me. "Nah, man. It's prolly nothin'," he answered, followed by the second shot.

"Come on, Adam. I'm not playing around. I don't need your decision-making to mess up my life."

"Relax, CJ. I didn't use your name for nothin'. You got nothin' to worry about, lil bro. It's probably just someone messing with you. I mean, who leaves a note on a car? Soundin' like some high school girl drama to me. Well, how would I know? I never finished high school. But I bet it's a girl, man. It's always the females. You got bad blood with a woman? I've had plenty try to mess with me in the past. Believe me! I bet it's an ex. There was this one girl, whew! She was H-A-W-T, hot, but you wouldn't believe the kind of stunt she was tryna pull on me the next—"

I cut him off. "It's not a girl, Adam. I don't know who it is."

"How do you know? Sounds to me like you don't know squat."

His nonchalant composure always got under my skin.

"You're sure it has nothing to do with you?"

"Like I said, I haven't used your name for nothing. Doubt anyone 'round here knows I have a lil' bro. Prolly 'cause you a no-show these days."

"And who's fault is that?" I spat.

He took a long draw from his vape and spoke with a bellowing voice through the fog. "Ain't my fault if that's what you sayin'. Still haven't told me where you livin' these days. I'd come visit every now and again if I knew."

"Sure you would. You don't answer your phone."

He chuckled to himself. "Ah! I'm always losin' that thing. Or it's dead. Come to think of it, where is my phone?" He checked the couch, one hand feeling between the Navy blue cushions, the other scratching a pink rash on his scrawny ribcage. "Never mind that. Hey, wanna grab lunch? I'm starvin'! My buddy owns a place on Main, and they got incredible hoagies, and I mean, the best! He had that critic guy come one time, you know the one—he's always on Wilkes's social page, crooked smile, and fedora—anyway, he said they are to die for! And if he said it, you know it be true!"

I shoved the note in my pocket and stood. "Forget it. I knew this would be a waste of time."

"Aw, come on, my man. You just got here."

"Yeah, and now I'm leaving."

He followed me down the stairs and called for me from the front door. "Why you so uptight these days, CJ?"

I didn't respond. In my opinion, I wasn't uptight at all. Rodman and Sophia thought I was the wild one, but they hadn't met my brother.

As I got in the car, I heard my brother calling to someone across the street. "What you lookin' at, diphead? Mind your own biz!"

"Always causing a scene," I said to myself.

I looked out the passenger window across the street to see a familiar face staring back.

Probably an Uber rider.

I gave a slight wave before waking Cindy Lou.

I took one last look at my brother, his half-naked body hanging in the doorway. His hair was a wildfire in every direction. He'd lost weight since I last saw him; his ribs and shoulders protruded from his tightly drawn skin. He was paler, too. He was out of place living on a street like this. I couldn't imagine the soccer moms and grass-watering dads enjoyed having Adam in their opulent community.

Something about the way he looked seemed normal. I couldn't picture a cleaner version of Adam. How could such a thing exist? I wished for it, but part of me said that would never be so, not after what had happened... what he saw... what I missed.

"Take care of yourself," I whispered before turning back the way I came.

CHAPTER 10
CRISPY JESUS

After finding a place for Cindy Lou to rest, I climbed the stone steps to Wilkes City Public Library.

The library was truly a sight to see. Beyond the front desk where ole Miss Sherry checked out guests, thousands of books lined the rotunda's walls. White runners went down each aisle between shelves, contrasting with the copper-colored linoleum floors. At the center of the room, a staircase led up to another floor. The upper level wrapped the room's walls as a balcony, leaving open space in the center that allowed the heavenly tilework of the dome above to be seen from the ground floor.

Usually, I'd take a moment to appreciate the artwork, but I felt empty.

I walked up the stairs and rounded the left side with a hand on the mahogany banister. Nate's voice came in earshot; he and Sophia sat among the leather loveseats opposite of me—Nate's favorite spot. I could only assume he was ranting at Sophia about something he read.

"It's not out of the question. The possibility of another dimension is tangible. We just haven't found a way to reach it with the state of our technology."

"Whatever you say, Nate," Sophia replied. She chewed bubblegum (which was not prohibited, I might add), sitting with her legs crossed in a caramel-colored chair, flipping through a Platinum Fashion magazine as Nate gazed in admiration at an old cloth-bound book on the center table.

"The Superstring Theory clearly explains the possibility of six other dimensions beyond the four we know of today." His voice raced on as he pointed to different lines on the page, using his other hand to make flamboyant gestures of excitement. "I mean, back in the day, Einstein was looking for a connection between electromagnetism and gravity. Now we're beyond that, seeing that there's a bonafide possibility there is one unified theory that can unlock the answer to tapping into alternate dimensions operating under the same governing theory."

Sophia noticed me approaching. Her maroon painted lips mouthed the words, "Save me."

I didn't truly feel like saving Sophia. It was too playful, too free-spirited. How could

I enjoy time with my friends when I had an unknown bounty to repay? But it was Sophia; I'd do anything for her, even if that meant pretending everything was okay.

I turned my unease into fake energy and bounced to a seat.

"Oh, yeah?" I said in a loud enough voice to get Nate's attention as I sat down across from them. "And what are you going to do about it?"

Nate's face lit up when he saw me. He looked like a turtle in his jumbo-sized green sweater.

"You know me, CJ, I just like reading about this stuff. I'm a nobody when it comes to actually finding results. But isn't it riveting? Hypothetically, these alternate worlds could be mirrors of our own. Doppelgangers can actually be real—mirror images, identical to ourselves, living a completely different life in a completely different world. Who knows how much further along they are than us!"

"Or further behind," I suggested.

"I think one Nate is enough for me!" Sophia laughed.

"Oh, come on! You can't get enough of me!"

I'd lie if I said their banter didn't cheer me up, but it only lasted a moment, as reality reared her ugly face back into the conversation.

"I think something a little more fascinating is hearing how CJ's day went, don't you think?" Sophia said, closing Nate's book before he could protest. She then faced me, her violet eyes full of inquiry. "No luck with Common Trades?"

"No." I shook my head. "He didn't know what I was talking about when I asked if he left me a note."

"You still paid him back though, right?" Nate asked.

I left out the convicting pursuit of the teenage girl. "I wasn't going to, but I knew it was the right thing to do."

Sophia reached across and put a hand on mine. "I'm happy you did the right thing."

I wish she didn't pull away. The fiery feeling of her hand was desperately craved. I needed something to hold onto, *someone* to hold onto. I felt stupid for allowing such a small thing, a sticky note, to be a burden.

They remained silent, so I continued. "I then thought maybe there was some sort of mix-up with my brother, and maybe he had unsettled debts or something to do with this."

"And?" Nate asked.

I flopped my head to the side, staring at the whiskey stain on my shoulder. "Another dead end."

"That's good news, right?"

"How is that good news?"

Rodman raised his hands as if to say, "Isn't it obvious?"

"You went to the two most probable sources of the note, and they both turned to naught. That should draw us to the conclusion that it really is nothing."

I laid my head back and stared at the towering wall of books behind my friends. "I don't know. It doesn't feel like a joke."

"Well, is there anything else you can think of that you've done?" Sophia paused, pulling on the hem of her white skirt before continuing. "Anything else... you've stolen?"

I shook my head. "As I said, I haven't stolen anything in years."

"So, was stealing something you used to do often?"

I bit the inside of my cheek. "Kind of... just small stuff. It was a long time ago."

"Ah! If it was petty, as you say, then there's nothing to worry about," Nate snorted.

He mocked me through his doublespeak. Sophia was ignorant to the disguised prodding in Nate's comments, but

I wouldn't give in. I couldn't tell my friends of the life I lived.

"I mean, they did use his full name, Nate. Doesn't that mean they know CJ personally?"

He put his finger to his chin. "Possibly, but CJ doesn't give his full name to anyone." Turning to me, "I didn't know CJ stood for Crispin Jiles until yesterday."

"Exactly!" I blurted. "Isn't that weird? I never give my full name, which is why this note is getting to me."

"If it's really getting to you, why not go to the police?"

There are plenty of reasons I can't go to the police, Rodman, as I'm sure you already know! I've gotten away with too many things over the years for them to be sniffing around.

"I doubt they'd do anything," I answered, and Nate thankfully agreed without further questioning.

"What about the kids from hockey," Sophia said. "Would any of them pull a prank on you?"

"Again, they don't know my full name."

"Maybe they looked you up?"

"Any social media I used to have just had *CJ* or some childish handle like *@Crispy_Jesus* or *@CranberryJuice*."

"Crispy Jesus?" chuckled Sophia.

"Cranberry Juice?" laughed Rodman.

"Ha, ha, ha, yeah, have your laughs. Cut me a break; I was fifteen. I don't even use those accounts anymore."

Sophia noticed my irritation and collected her composure.

"Well, what if I look you up? There's gotta be something online that gives your full name or some form of information, right?"

Sophia pulled her laptop from her bag. As soon as she lifted the lid, I slapped it shut.

"No! Don't look me up!"

"Woah, cowboy," Rodman remarked. "What? You have other usernames you don't want us to know about?"

"Shut up, Rodman!"

They both laughed, but it wasn't funny to me. Nervousness prickled the hairs on my neck.

"Please, don't look me up. I'm not on social media anymore for a reason. I moved to Wilkes City to put my past behind me. I don't need to be reminded."

Their laughs faded into silence as they pondered my request. I locked eyes with Sophia. Her violet stare bore into me. She knew there was more to be said, but she didn't press.

"All right, let's just assume they got your name from online somehow." She put her laptop away as she spoke. "Maybe that means they don't know you personally. Maybe they have the wrong guy or something."

Nate nodded in agreement. "I'm telling you, CJ. You crossed your *x*'s and dotted your *i*'s. You probably have nothing to worry about."

"I'm not one to correct you, but isn't the saying, 'crossed your *t*'s and dotted your *i*'s'?" Sophia asked.

"Same difference," he said to Sophia, then turned to me. "My point still stands. If there really is a problem, someone will come talk to you. Don't let it get to you. You haven't been yourself since this happened."

Nate's fake optimism wasn't reassuring in the slightest, but I hoped he was right anyway.

"I guess I should let it go."

But I didn't.

CHAPTER 11
THOUGHTS OF A CALICO CAT

I was rarely home before dark on a Saturday. I usually drove weekend partiers and late-night flight arrivals home.

Jamal and Ronny begged me to play street hockey. I turned the boys down and didn't budge. My legs were tired, and the day's stress was overbearing.

I wasn't myself. I didn't know if it was just the note anymore. Maybe it was my brother, too. He was the only family I had left, and I shut him out. Like my father did to me, I pushed him away. My visit was strictly business, and I hated it. I thought about calling him, holding my thumb over his name in my contacts as I stood in the gravel parking lot, but I disregarded the idea, telling myself he probably hadn't found his phone yet anyway.

As I headed inside the back entrance of The Pizza Bar, I didn't stop to say anything to Mr. Zhang. He knew something was wrong; he offered me a slice of pizza (for free, which he would never do). These days, the only questions he ever asked were about rent.

I declined his offer and slumped upstairs to my apartment. My stomach felt empty, but pizza was unappealing. I had this odd sensation of desiring food but not having the energy or motivation to eat it. It was similar to the limbo of my headspace—grateful nothing had turned up from the note but still feeling the ominous presence of the sender.

I went straight to bed. It wasn't even 6:00 PM. I told myself I should go back to doing Uber rides, but once I lay on my futon, there was no way of getting up. I was fatigued physically, mentally, and emotionally.

I lay in bed with my cat, Marrie, contemplating the note, flipping it between my fingers as I digested the day's events.

"What do you think, Mar?"

She answered with a purr, rubbing her head against my chest.

"Yeah, I don't know what to think either."

She meowed a few times.

As if I knew what she said, I replied. "But they don't know about... you know." I sighed.

Marrie continued to meow, bounding to the window. This time, I knew exactly what she said.

"Fine, but promise me we'll talk later."

I opened my window to the fire escape, and out she leaped. I watched as she elegantly pranced from the second floor to the dumpster below, then onto the parking lot. I found her there four years ago when I moved in. A stray I accepted as a roommate, she came and went from my window ever since.

Marrie had very little to worry about. Even before I fed her, she found a way to scrape by. I wondered if she ever had thoughts or concerns about ordinary things in life. Did she worry about relationships, an occupation, or sticky notes coming from anonymous senders?

These were the meaningless thoughts that plagued my restless sleep—thoughts of a calico cat that I saw as a companion, the only companion that knew my darkest secrets.

CHAPTER 12

RETURN

Sunday and Monday passed slower than switching traffic lights, most of the time unproductive. I made a list of people and places I had robbed before moving to Wilkes City, or at least the ones I remembered, but the moment I pondered the events, I shut the laptop and left the honey-colored desk for the comfort of the living room TV screen.

I stayed on the couch those two days, only getting up for instant ramen, coffee, or the bathroom (it was COVID 2020 all over again). My friends had seemingly forgotten about the note since they hadn't texted me, or maybe they were re-evaluating our friendship since discovering my past of larceny. Meanwhile, I was having mental meltdowns at the thought of someone knowing my name.

I woke up Tuesday morning with a kink in my neck. Maybe it was from the stress, or maybe it was from sleeping on my ugly periwinkle couch (probably both).

I pushed away my blanket and went to the connected kitchen for a fresh pot of coffee, walking the six steps with my eyes half-closed. While waiting, I noticed Marrie didn't follow. She'd usually be sunbathing by the corner plant next to the living room window, jumping to my side when I came to the kitchen, meowing and rubbing my leg. Her absence was just as much a reminder as her actual presence to feed her breakfast.

Although she wasn't home (out for a stroll, I assumed), I went to the bedroom and filled her food dish anyway, leaving it by the open window of my bedroom awaiting her return.

Before I left the room, the yellow note's edge permeating from the closed laptop caught my eye. A slight breeze wisped through the room, sending tremors down my spine and ringing to my ears as the note called for me in the faintest of whispers, echoing through every cavern of my mind.

Crispin Jiles. Return what you've stolen, Crispin Jiles. I'm coming for you, Crispin Jiles. I know your name, Crispin Jiles.

I left the haunted room, retreating to the spluttering coffee maker for comfort, clutching my throat as I found it hard to breathe. I wanted to clear my mind, but the note attached to every thought that lingered. Every ounce of me wanted to believe it was meaningless, but with the life I lived, how could it be?

I'm overreacting. It's just a stupid note! I told myself.

But it wasn't just a stupid note; it could unmask everything I worked so hard to escape. All my life, I had run from my problems, and now something was in my way, a road sign saying I hit a dead end and must turn around.

I stared at the picture of Adam and me hanging before the hallway, the only picture I had of us taken right before I moved out. I wondered if he was in trouble too, but we didn't know it yet.

I couldn't let something happen to him, no matter how much we butt heads. I failed him once; I wouldn't fail him again.

With my thoughts already retraveling that dark, forsaken trail, I grabbed my mug of coffee and went back to my desk, returning to the days my father was alive.

CHAPTER 13
CIGARETTES AND CANDY BARS

I sipped my morning coffee, its aroma awakening my tired senses as I stared at my laptop with the crinkled note stuck to the top corner.

The first name on my list was Mark Smallock, a foreman who hired my brother and me when I was fifteen. It was our first larceny operation after my mother left and the money ran dry. My father found the job on Craigslist. The advertisement details were clear in my mind:

Hard workers needed. Garbage removal from warehouse. Lunch included. Eight-hour days.

We shoveled muck off the floors into black bags, then carried them to the dumpster outside. It was back-breaking work, definitely not worth the measly fifty bucks.

Mark was a nice man. Tall, bald, and respectful—none of the traits of most construction workers. He was a Christian guy with a Spanish wife who made us pozole every day. We only worked for him for about a week, just long enough to find out where he kept his money.

I highlighted the name and hit DEL. I couldn't picture him hunting me down, especially since it was twelve years ago.

A few names down was Pete Caldwell. He owned the Always Open Mart a mile from where we lived. Adam and I had been buying candy bars and soda from him for years. He liked us, always making small talk when we came on hot summer days. He didn't feel the same about my father, especially after he held poor Pete at gunpoint for a pack of cigarettes.

"I have two kids," he said.

That was the last robbery we did in Gainesville, the first time I had ever seen a man's eyes filled with genuine fear, the first time I saw my father's gun, and the last night we spent in the house I grew up in.

I sipped my coffee and poked the backspace. I didn't think someone would look for me over some cigarettes and candy bars.

Once we were on the road, biking to and through different towns, the places we robbed blended together. I had a hard time remembering the names of locations or people. My list had vague details on different locations like "Curly-haired woman who wouldn't shut up" and "Big brown store we got chased out of." All I remembered was moments, fragmented memories.

Like the times we spent collecting plastic bags along the road, which we used to steal from stores, praying that an alarm wouldn't go off when we walked out the door; or the times we would walk into fast-food chains, where my father would lie that he had been there thirty minutes before and they had messed up his drive-through order so we'd get a free meal; or all the pawn shops we'd break into to fill our backpacks and bring to the next town to sell.

There weren't any large robberies. My father said only a fool would try to rob a bank. It went against the rules.

Thinking of the rules brought back our last conversation.

We biked all day, baked under the hot sun, and finally arrived in a small town. Our bike caddies were empty. We were hungry and hadn't had a drink since the day before—except for my father, who had finished the last of his beers.

Night had fallen. We were walking toward a small gas station storefront, our bikes left in the corner of an empty parking lot across the street. Father had finished going over a few of the rules, his war cry, before sending in his troops.

"I'm tired. Can we wait until tomorrow?" I asked, scuffing my feet along the asphalt.

"Rule 5: Business shall be done in private," Father replied.

I groaned, tugging on my backpack straps. "Why do we have to follow these stupid rules?"

Father stopped in his tracks, his shadowy figure towering over me. Time stopped as his bloodshot eyes drilled into mine.

In an instant, he struck. His fist met between my eyes before I could react. My feet took flight. The blow sent me backward enough to make me slide a short distance as I hit the ground.

"The rules keep us alive, you little brat!"

Tears fled the scene as they washed down my cheeks. My nose filled with the all-too-familiar metallic scent of blood.

"Look what you made me do, Crispin. Now I have to do *your* job." Father turned to cross the street toward the store. "Why can't you listen like your brother?"

I cradled my face in pain and curled into the fetal position. Adam stood by my side in the eerie darkness, his body turning red from blood clouding the vision of my right eye.

The memory was vivid—his teenage complexion, shaved head, hazel eyes, carrot nose, dimpled chin. We looked nearly identical back then, often mistaken for twins.

He reached out a hand to me, bidding me to my feet, but I neglected the invitation.

"Leave him," our father shouted from the other side of the street.

Adam held out his hand for another second, but when I didn't accept, he left me.

I didn't know how long I sat there. Seconds? Minutes? It didn't matter; it didn't change the outcome. The next thing I knew, I heard a gunshot.

I lifted my head in shock. I never heard my father pull the trigger.

Waiting anxiously, no one came out. Something was wrong.

I ran across the abandoned street, ripping open the stickered glass door. Just ahead of me lay my father on the dirty tile. He gripped a six-pack in his hand. His black handgun lay at my feet. A crimson pool seeped from his worn bomber jacket. Adam stood paralyzed behind the lifeless body, shoulders lifted, ears covered, eyes stretched.

A heavyset man in overalls and a trucker hat stood behind the counter on my left. His shotgun shakily pointed toward Adam. No one said a word. We were mystified.

Somehow, I kept a stoic composure. Thoughts no longer controlled my actions; it was instinct.

I cautiously bent down and lifted Father's gun. The man watched me but didn't take his aim off Adam. He tried to say something, but only a gasp left his quivering lips.

I beckoned Adam to come, but he didn't move. He didn't even look at me. He locked his eyes on the body between us.

I stepped into the growing puddle, wiping my face to clear my vision. The blubbery man aimed his gun toward me. His tomato face covered in sweat, he let one word escape his lips, no louder than a whisper.

"L-L-L-Leave."

I nodded shakily. Reaching out my hand to Adam, I quoted my father's words.

"Rule 18: Leave while you still can."

His face was still downcast; he didn't respond at first.

Slowly, he put out an arm, stiff as a board, taking my hand to cross the divide.

I shook my head and sipped my coffee as the memory sent shivers through me.

A sick part of me said it had to happen. Father had to die. If it weren't for that night, I would have never had the courage to turn from my ways.

But was it really courage? I wondered. *Or was it fear?—fear that I should have obeyed; fear that my father's death was my fault; fear that stopped me from taking Adam's hand; fear that not being there with Adam made him the way he is.*

Fear gripped me; it hunted me; it clawed at my brain, and it felt closer than ever before.

I went to take another sip of coffee, hoping the bitter taste would cleanse my creeping thoughts, but the ceramic mug was empty.

The list led to no conclusion other than reminding myself that everything was my fault and I probably deserved this.

I had to get out and clear my head. It was Tuesday, and I hadn't made a dime Uber driving over the weekend. Part of me pathetically dreaded going outside. I attempted to leave the day before, only to find myself sitting on the couch staring at the door, rubbing my feet on the area rug as if static electricity would make me move. In the end, fear had won the battle, and I stayed home.

But this day would be different. Wallowing in my apartment made me a captive to my thoughts. Even worse, Marrie hadn't returned since our Saturday night conversation. It was normal for her to be gone for a few days at times, but the lack of her company made me lonely. The company of strangers was better than this.

I pulled the sticky note (which wasn't very sticky anymore) from the laptop and shoved it in my pocket. I didn't want to have it, but I couldn't leave without it for some reason.

When I got out to Cindy Lou, I inspected her body for any new mysterious notes. I found nothing.

Maybe Rodman and Sophia were right, I thought. *Maybe there's nothing to fear.*

Other thoughts begged to differ.

I fired up Cindy Lou's engine, turned on the Uber app, and drove down Bentley Street, hoping to leave my worries behind me.

CHAPTER 14
MARYANN THE CARAVAN

I clinked my beer bottle with Nate's as the evening sky slowly faded into a purple hue, the fresh smell of cut grass filling the air. "I guess you were right. Nothing to worry about."

I used to wish I had a backyard with a barbeque grill and white picket fence on the outside of the city. Then I realized I probably wouldn't take care of it the way Nate took care of his.

His gray t-shirt hugged his biceps. Grass stained his toned legs and gray sneakers. He stank of gasoline and dirt. Seeing or smelling Rodman this way was odd. I had forgotten how strong of a build he had due to him always swimming in a sweater.

I adjusted the flat brim on my head and sipped my beer, releasing a happy sigh as I sank into my seat. "Nothing like an orange shandy after a hot day."

"It is interesting," Nate started between sips, "that you're not on edge about it."

I shimmied in my camping chair to face him. "What do you mean?"

He placed his beer in the netted cup holder. "Well, a week ago, you acted like your life had met its inevitable end. Now you're back to the freewheeling CJ. Don't get me wrong, I like this side of you, but you seem to have forgotten the weight of the matter." He pushed blond locks behind his ears as he spoke. "I once read about anxiety, how it often has a stranglehold on a person, and a coping mechanism that many use is believing a fictitious reality that their problems do not exist."

I turned to the sky with furrowed eyebrows. Dark clouds slowly passed over the waning moon. "Are you saying I'm avoiding the problem?"

"Not exactly."

"Come on, Rodman. I feel good. I even played street hockey with the boys before heading over." I leaned back, reminiscing the clanger of a shot I ripped earlier that day. "Worst that came of it was having my wallet stolen."

"Your wallet was stolen?"

"Yeah, some kid stole it when I went to Common Trades, and I had to chase her through the mall. Got it back, though. She made a mistake trying to head for the parking garage. If I were her, I would've gone to a changing room or something."

I laughed. Nate didn't.

"It's beside the point," I added. "Things are back to normal."

"I'm just saying you shouldn't be so quick to believe the note was meaningless."

I turned back to Nate and tipped forward in my chair. "Just a week ago, you were telling me to forget about it."

Nate chuckled to himself like an old man laughing at the innocence of a novice. "Oh, come on now, CJ. You know as well as I do that my comments were goaded."

"What do you want from me, Rodman?"

Eyes half-closed, he peered at me with a smirk. "It's not what I want from you, CJ. It's what *you* want for yourself."

I shook my head. "I don't follow."

"Remember when we went to buy Cindy Lou, when your soccer mom van bit the dust?"

"Maryann the Caravan," I corrected.

"Right. Remember staying the night at that motel with the loose door guard?"

"Oh, yeah!" I laughed at the memory. "When the door slammed, the door guard flopped shut. I had to let you back in after picking up sushi."

"Exactly! That's our relationship, CJ. It's like we're talking to each other on either side of that door. You open the door to me, but you keep the guard latched. You don't actually let me in."

My smile faded along with the illuminance of the moon.

"I'm not asking you to let me in, CJ. And I'm sorry for pestering you about it. That's not my choice. You have to flip that latch yourself." He paused, considering his words. "I don't know all the details going on inside. Just know that you don't have to be afraid. I'm not going anywhere."

I nodded slowly. "Thanks, Rodman. Maybe when I'm ready."

Nate grinned. "Whenever you're ready."

We locked eyes, and Nate raised his eyebrows in expectation.

"What? You mean now?"

"Ha! Okay, okay, sorry, I'm done teasing."

We both laughed together and went back to looking at the sky. The clouds slowly passed, and speckled stars around God's fingernail became clear.

"Man, Rodman, why do you always gotta use analogies to hit me where it hurts?"

He emptied the last of the amber bottle above his head.

"Jesus spoke in parables when he taught. Maybe he was onto something."

"And you say you aren't religious."

Nate shrugged his shoulders. "Says the guy that used 'Jesus' in a username."

The laughter died down, and the sounds of the night took over—crickets in the yard, traffic in the distance, a tweeting bird here and there. The clear night was pleasant, but one question still clouded my mind.

"Rodman? Without getting into details, do you think there is any way that the note isn't meaningless? You know... like it's a real threat?"

He closed his eyes, deep in thought. "Do you honestly not know what it could be about?"

"I made a list a few days ago of people I've stolen from in the past. Honest to God, man, it's all been petty theft. We never stole anything big. It was just enough to scrape by."

"We?" he asked.

"My brother and I. Well, and my father."

Seriousness filled his blue eyes, a lock of hair falling before the one, barely visible in the dim light. "I don't know how to answer. Revenge is a scary thing. Even the little things can drive a man mad. But if you ask me, the note's wording seemed specific. I think you'd remember what it was. Since you can't, I'd say not to worry about it and hope nothing comes of it. And if it was urgent, I'm sure they would have reached out again by now. Maybe they've got the wrong guy."

I leaned my head back in the fabric chair, letting out a sigh of relief. I thought the same thing, but hearing him say it made me feel a lot better.

"Just be watchful. You never know," he added. "And call me if you need anything."

"Thanks, man. I will." I finished my beer and stood up to stretch. "I should head home before I end up drunk, sleeping on your couch."

"Already?"

"I have a few Uber days to make up, so I'm trying to wake up early."

"Sleep here. I thought you loved my couch."

"Yeah, until I wake up the next day with a kinked back."

"I guess I'll have to finish the rest by myself," he said sarcastically.

"Don't have too much fun without me," I said, shooting him with finger pistols as I left.

CHAPTER 15

SLEEPING ON THE COUCH

I cruised the dark streets with joy, windows down, tunes cranked, and singing at the top of my lungs. I was back on top! The fear that haunted the days before was gone and forgotten.

I wished Cindy Lou a good rest as I headed for the back entrance of The Pizza Bar. Just before heading inside, I stopped at the dumpster in the gravel parking lot and pulled out the sticky note I had been carrying in my pocket for a week.

"'Dear Crispin Jiles, Return what you've stolen... or else'," I read. "I guess I don't need to worry about you anymore."

I tossed the note into the dumpster, releasing the heavy load from my shoulders.

Before heading upstairs, I stopped in the kitchen to say hello to Mr. Zhang, who busily rolled out dough on the white counter. Voices and deep laughter came from the bar on the other side of the swing door. I was happy to hear he had a few customers other than Nate, Sophia, and me on a Friday night.

"What's shaking, Mr. Zhang?"

The landlord didn't reply. He didn't even lift his bald head to acknowledge me.

"Sounds like you've got a good crowd out there."

Still, no response came.

"Mr. Zhang, is everything alright?" I walked over to stand next to him, eyeing the half-tray of pepperoni by his side. "Any leftover pizza I can snag on my way upstairs?"

"Yes," he replied.

I reached to grab a slice, but he swatted my hand away.

"But you no get any."

"Aw, why not, Mr. Zhang? How about that free slice you offered me the other day?"

"You piss me off today. You do not listen."

He smacked me with his dish towel as he passed me to grab a can of sauce from the kitchen caddy in the corner.

"Ow! What do you mean I don't listen?"

The old man mumbled things in his Mandarin tongue before answering. "I knock on door, tell you be quiet, you no listen. Noisy all day long. I have headache. Leave my kitchen."

"Noisy? I wasn't here."

Mr. Zhang pulled his dish towel off his shoulder and hit me again.

"Leave now."

"Okay, sorry. Geez!"

I walked the hallway past the back entrance of The Pizza Bar and the stairs descending to Mr. Zhang's basement apartment, staring up at my door.

"Noisy," I mumbled. "I wasn't home."

The wooden steps creaked as I climbed the stairs.

"Just be watchful," Rodman had said.

Was someone in my apartment?

I reached for the door handle, stopping halfway, my fingers dancing in the air.

What if they're still in there? No, are you insane? No one's here. But if they were, why? Were they coming to hurt me? Were they waiting for me to leave?

I put my ear to the door, waiting intently.

This is ridiculous.

I attempted to turn the door handle.

Locked. Just how I left it. The old man is hearing things.

I unlocked the door, cracking it open slowly. I stared into the darkness of the small apartment. The green glow of the digital clock on the toaster oven was staring back at me. I stood in silence, waiting, listening, but heard nothing other than the bellowing laugh of a man at the bar.

But I felt something. The hairs on my forearms stood up from a slight draft.

And I smelled something. My nostrils flared as I sniffed the air.

Is that... fish?

I reached over to hit the light on the wall, freezing in place from what I saw. My eyes fell directly on the center of the room where my periwinkle couch was on its back, and the coffee table was upside down, its glass top shattered, glittering on the green area rug pulled from its place.

A moment of déjà vu penetrated my mind—a flashback vision flickering between reality and my mind's eye. One moment, I saw the coffee table; the next, I saw my father. One moment, I was in my living room; the next, I was back in the small convenience store with white vinyl tile.

I rubbed my eyes multiple times before the scene faded; all that remained was reality. To my left, the kitchen was a disaster. The small, two-person dining table was the only thing seemingly untouched. Someone pulled the refrigerator away from the wall. The door was open, with drawers and food tossed to the floor (explaining the draft and smell of fish). Every cabinet was open as well, some completely emptied, with shattered dishware masking the counters and sink.

To my right, along with the couch and coffee table, everything was out of place. The TV was face down on the floor. The unread books from my shelf scattered the room. The corner plant's clay pot lay broken on its side, leaving speckled dirt where Marrie would lie.

Even with the disaster of the room, one thing stuck out more than the rest—a sticky note slapped to the wall.

I didn't dare to go and read it. I didn't dare to enter. The only thing I could do was turn off the light and shut the door.

I pulled out my phone and called Rodman.

"Hey, about sleeping on the couch..."

CHAPTER 16
STRIKE ONE

Sophia met us at The Pizza Bar the next morning. I didn't want her to come, thinking it may be dangerous, but we were overdosed with curiosity, and I knew we could use an extra hand with cleaning.

The pungent smell hit like an airbag as we ascended the stairs. Nate used the neckline of his oversized Christmas sweater to cover his nose. Apparently, a warm upstairs apartment with raw eggs, fish, and chicken left out doesn't bode well.

"Gross," Sophia said.

"Putrid," Nate added.

I opened the door to find the ransacked apartment the same as before. Sophia sucked in a sharp breath, putting a hand on my shoulder.

"I'm so sorry this happened."

"I'm just glad I wasn't home."

Nate walked past us with bravery. "I think they intended for you not to be home, CJ."

"How can you be sure?"

Rodman had spotted what I saw the night before. He pulled the note from the wall, then shook it in the air. "Second note, plus the searched apartment. They want to stay discreet."

"*Searched*?" Sophia cried as she stepped inside, shaking her hands wildly. "How do we know this was a search? It's like a college party gone wrong! It'll take ages to clean this place."

"It's a way to send a message," Nate answered. "Part of this person's tactic, I suppose." Then, turning to me, "They're trying to push you to do what they say."

"More like break me."

Nate handed me the note, and I read it aloud, choking on the written words.

Strike one, Crispin Jiles,
I gave you a chance, but you
have forced my hand.
Return the cases, or I'll visit
your friend.

Sophia stood in the kitchen with her hands on her hips and tears on her cheeks. "Whoever did this is psychotic," she yelped. "And now we have to worry about one of *our* places looking like this?"

I didn't know what to say. This was all my fault. My past caught up, and it was taking my friends with me.

"Friend," Nate muttered. "Interesting."

"What?" I asked.

"They say *your friend* as if to speak of someone specific. As if you would know who they referred to."

"So? That could be either of you, Rodman."

"Maybe... most likely me, I'm guessing," he replied.

Sophia darted her eyes at Nate.

"What? There's no question I'm a little closer to CJ. If anything, you should be thankful. You're probably last on the list to get hurt."

"Oh, whatever!" she pouted.

"I found the first note after our walk that one night," I said. "Maybe they saw me with you?"

"Possibly," he answered. "But they don't use my name. They only use yours, CJ."

"What's your point?" I replied.

"My point is that they don't know who I am." Nate poked at the note as he spoke. "This person... this blackmailer, extortionist, whatever you want to call them... they may know *your* name, but they don't seem to know who you're associated with by name."

"Which brings me back to the same conclusion as before that this has to do with my freaking past, and I can't think of who it could be!" I threw my hat across the room, rubbing my temples in distress, sinking against the door frame until I sat on the floor. "This can't be happening to me."

Nate squatted down next to me. "We'll figure this out, CJ."

"This is insane," I said in a low voice to him. "I just wish this never happened. I'm so sorry you guys are being dragged into this."

Nobody replied. What were they supposed to say? They obviously weren't going to say how they felt because I'm sure they weren't too grateful for our friendship at this point.

Sophia tied her dark chocolate hair into a ponytail and went under the sink to grab cleaning supplies. "CJ," she hesitantly started, whipping a garbage bag in the air, "we suggested before that maybe this doesn't have to do with you."

I bumped my head against the door frame behind me. "I honestly can't think of anything it *does* have to do with, but I don't know anymore."

Nate took the note from me to study it. "It says 'cases.' Does that ring any bells?"

"Cases," I whispered as I thought to myself. "What kind of case? I can't think of any cases I ever stole. Although, I did *fill* a suitcase with things once."

"Maybe a camera case," Sophia suggested.

Nate scratched his bristled chin. "I think 'cases' is like 'friend.' It's specific. They wouldn't say it unless he meant particular cases."

I scratched my head. "Suitcase, computer case, CD case—it could mean anything! Case of beer for all I know."

"If this is something of value, I highly doubt it's a case of beer. I'm thinking maybe a briefcase or possibly case files."

"What are you, Sherlock Holmes?" Sophia said from behind.

Nate stood up from his squatted position. "Actually, I do like to think of myself as a type of Sherlock. He often had his nose in a book. Although, he probably put his knowledge to greater use than I did. Speaking of Holmes, hand me the other note you have."

I pulled out the crumbled note from my shorts pocket, recovered from the dumpster.

Nate put them side-by-side, sticking out his tongue and closing one eye as he held them up like he was taking a selfie. "Hmmm... the handwriting is similar, the bubbles in his letters are more of a stretched oval, and the letters are protracted and skinny. Yep, I bet the same guy wrote both notes."

I smacked my lips. "I could have concluded the same thing without the dramatics."

"Maybe *you* have a bad case of the Mondays," Nate mocked.

"Ha, ha, good one."

"Come on, back on track," Sophia said, snapping her fingers. "Check if anything is missing."

Nate and I examined the kitchen and living room before walking the small hallway toward my bedroom. I looked into the bathroom on the way. Everything from the cabinets lay on the floor.

"Might want a new toothbrush," Nate remarked.

I pushed open my bedroom door.

A tornado had passed through the room. My futon had a tear down the center with foam sticking out. My dresser drawers were empty. Clothing littered the floor. The honey-colored corner desk next to the window was on its side, crushing my laptop.

"Doesn't seem like they stole anything," I said as I retrieved the laptop from under the desk. The screen was cracked, but it still turned on.

"You said your door was locked?" Nate asked.

"Yeah, why?"

He walked across the room to the open window that led to the fire escape.

"Crap," I muttered. "I leave it unlocked to let Marrie in and out."

We went back to the kitchen to rejoin Sophia. To my surprise, she had already cleaned off most of the counter and swept the food on the floor into a pile.

"Well?" she asked as she tied off a third trash bag.

"Nothing seems to be missing," I said. "Just a bunch of damage."

Nate put a hand on my shoulder. "At least you're alive."

I pushed his hand away and sat at the kitchen table. "You guys keep saying that, but aren't you forgetting your lives might be in trouble now?"

Nate sat across from me with a faint smile. "We're in this together, CJ. I'm not going to leave you out to dry."

"I can't ask you to do that."

"You don't have to," he replied. "I'm going to help you figure this out."

"Me too," Sophia added.

My mind had come to a halt. I didn't know what to think. I didn't know what to do. The only thing that came to mind was my father's words.

Rule 15: Clean work makes for a clean escape.

Nate laid the notes on the small table in front of us. "Maybe there are some clues we can take from these? Can you think of anything?"

I skimmed over the notes with him, but my mind was an empty void.

"Maybe we clean the place," Sophia said. "And if you think of anything, you let us know."

Only one thought plagued my thoughts as we cleaned.

I have to tell them everything. I don't have a choice.

CHAPTER 17

A CONFESSION OF THE AGES

The sky had turned to dusk by the time we finished cleaning. This was partially due to Sophia being a clean freak. She had worked for a cleaning service before switching to office grunt at a magazine company. She wiped every baseboard, every fan blade, and every cabinet spotless. Not only did she clean, but she reorganized each room. It was like I moved into a new apartment.

Nate offered to buy dinner. We sat at the bar downstairs. Mr. Zhang was still annoyed, as I had been noisy *two* days in a row now, but he didn't turn down the large order.

I barely ate half a slice. I didn't even order a beer. Sophia took the opportunity to order Mr. Zhang's favorite cocktail, yuzu and gin (the only Asian thing on the menu, which he always clarified originated from China and not Japan), along with three appetizers.

After our meal, I decided to come clean.

"So... my mom's not actually dead."

Both pairs of eyes from either side of me shifted in my direction. A half-eaten onion ring hung from Sophia's mouth.

"Or... maybe she is. I actually don't know." I stared at my slice of pizza. Heat crept up my neck, turning my cheeks the color of pepperoni.

Well, that was a lousy way to start this conversation.

"What I'm trying to say is that I lied about my parents. My mom left when I was fifteen."

"And your dad?"

I faced Nate. "Shot at a gas station during an attempted robbery."

"Oh my gosh!" Sophia said, covering her mouthful of food.

"My dad was a businessman—well, more of a scam artist. He owned a store called Trade with Jiles. It was a warehouse full of junk, the kind of things you'd find at a garage sale. He had this notebook full of rules that he made up. Apparently, they made him successful."

I took a large gulp of water before continuing, my lips quivering with the words only Marrie had ever heard.

"Long story short, Mom was a drunk, and Dad was a thief. My parents started fighting a lot, and Dad was hitting her. One night, Dad caught her cheating. The next day, she was gone."

I bit the inside of my lip, staring at my plate of food.

"After Mom left, Dad picked up her drinking habit. He was more of an operating drunk than my mother, but he had a temper. One day, a woman called the police on my father after finding something in his shop that he stole from her.

"Adam and I were taken in for questioning. At the time, we knew nothing of his business practices. We had our assumptions, but we didn't spend a lot of time at the store. Adam and I were regular teenagers with friends and lives. We were the two kids in high school with trainwreck parents that no one knew about."

Sophia took my hand in hers. My body felt numb as I spoke.

"With little evidence, my father was never charged with anything. I kind of wish he was because it would have changed everything. But word travels fast in a small town. Everyone knew my father was guilty. Kids at school asked Adam and me about it. We were popular for a few days."

I stopped to clear my throat and take a deep breath. Nate leaned forward on the bar, fully invested. I continued, my voice cracking every few sentences.

"That summer, we ran out of money. My father didn't tell Adam and me, but we knew because the power was cut from the house. That's when he..." I paused, taking another sip of water, the glass shaking in my hand, "he asked for our help."

"You mean he asked you to steal?" Nate corrected.

I nodded. "He said he was hiring us to help with the business, that we'd take it over for him one day. He had a way of saying things, making it sound like he was teaching us a valuable trade."

I pulled off my hat, staring at the eight-bit rooster above the brim.

"We didn't go back to school that year, and sales at his store were at an all-time low. He first had us take odd jobs to help with money but saw the opportunity of stealing to be greater.

"After a few jobs, our father wanted to take the business on wheels. He had bikes in his warehouse we used, his with a cargo wagon on the back. We went from town to town, sometimes buying things but mostly stealing and selling. He always stressed how much he *needed* us, how much he *loved* us, that he would never leave like our mother."

"How long did this go on?" Sophia asked. A tear dropped from her violet eye, running down her freckled face.

"Too long," I answered. "He died when I was eighteen. Adam and I continued living out his legacy for the next few years."

"How did you end up here?" Nate asked.

"Adam and I were on the move a lot. It's what we knew, but it came to a point where I was tired of living that way. I didn't always want to feel—"

"Like a target was on your back?" Sophia said.

I nodded solemnly. "I got a job mowing lawns, which led to being able to afford an apartment and getting a car. Getting my license was a headache because I first had to get a copy of my social security card, but once I had identification, everything else became easy... normal."

"What about your brother?" Nate asked.

I shook my head. "I think he's still living the way we always did. Once we got that apartment in Murdell, he made friends with a local party crowd, which kind of ended our friendship. There were times he was gone for over a week. I don't know how he took care of himself. *He* doesn't even remember. "He got into drugs, which led to buying and selling his own. He tried to get me into doing it, too. He sounded so much like my father, talking about how much money we could make and how I could be so valuable to him." I grimaced at the thought, tossing my hat next to my plate. "My father never touched the stuff, saying it was too risky to sell, but Adam saw it as a chance to get rich. It's what moved us to Wilkes City. Adam said there were big opportunities here."

"George Morris?" Nate asked.

I shrugged my shoulders. "I didn't ask. I didn't want to go. I was happy mowing lawns, but," my voice dipped, "I couldn't let Adam go alone."

Sophia let go of my hand, rubbing her arms like she was cold. "I'm so sorry. I never knew your past was so broken."

I downed the last of my water.

"So that's how I got here," I said, confidence finally returning to my voice. "Adam, Maryann, and I made the cross-country trip."

"Wow!" Nate exclaimed. "That old rust bucket did a cross-country trip?"

I couldn't help but chuckle at Nate's remark.

"Yeah... Maryann surprised me more than once before breaking down."

"So is Adam like," Sophia lowered her voice before continuing, "a drug dealer?"

Nate laughed at her caution. "It's more common than you think, Soph."

"I don't know! I've never met a drug dealer before."

"Sure you have! Studies say one in every fifty people you pass every day is regularly buying or selling illegal substances."

Sophia rolled her eyes. "So, is your brother still doing this, CJ?"

"I mean, I haven't asked, but I would assume so. Before I moved out, he was raking in more money than I had ever seen my father have—more money than I've ever made myself."

"Sounds like the Jiles family is a bunch of ponzi-scheming entrepreneurs."

"Thanks, Rodman," I muttered.

He punched my arm softly. "I'm glad you've turned out to be a good egg. Well, other than the counterfeit jewelry gig you got going on, but I guess that's small in light of your family history."

I finished the last few bites of my pizza and slumped in my seat, sighing with relief.

"There you have it. That's my story."

"A confession of the ages," Nate remarked.

"And now it looks like it's not over with this stupid blackmailer who's peeved about something I did."

"So out of all the years you were doing this stuff, you don't have an idea who it could be?" Sophia asked.

I shrugged my shoulders. "I tried to make a list, but it fell short."

Nate rubbed his chin as he thought. "Any friends you would have told about what you did? Anyone else who can maybe help jog your memory?"

"My only friend was—"

I stopped short, my heart beginning to thump in my chest.

"Who?" he asked, but I barely heard his voice, silenced by my thoughts.

I scrambled alert, searching my pockets. "Did either of you find a picture frame when we were cleaning?"

"A picture frame?" Sophia asked.

"I don't think so," Nate replied.

I pulled the notes from my pocket, pointing at the most recent.

"Rodman, you were right! They're talking about a specific friend."

"What do you mean?"

"A picture of Adam and me was hanging where this note was!"

"You mean, you think..."

"I have to call Adam!"

CHAPTER 18

EARS AGAINST THE DOOR

"I'm sorry, but the person you are trying to reach does not have a voice mailbox set up yet. Goodbye."

"Answer your freaking phone, Adam."

I tossed my phone in the cup holder and sped down the highway, taking the third exit for North Fisher Ave.

"Ugh! Privileged Parkway. I guess your brother does make good money."

Nate wouldn't let me go alone, but he agreed that Sophia would stay behind this time. She protested, but we didn't give her a choice.

I ripped Cindy Lou around a tight turn, her high beams showering the dark streets with rays of light. Her engine purred as I slapped the shifter into third, passing two cars on the left side. One of them swerved. I reacted just in time, rearing further toward the curb. Leaving their blaring horn behind me, I ran a red light and powered onward.

Nate gripped the handle above the passenger door. "Man, I hope you don't drive Uber passengers like this."

I made another sharp turn onto the long one-way drive into the community of homes. Streetlights hung on either side of us every block. Well-trimmed bushes and gated driveways barricaded the homes. The upkeep around here was far beyond the tidiest corner of Southside.

I pulled up to the house with a screeching halt behind Adam's beat-up Corolla, bumping the curb as I threw Cindy Lou into park. I jumped out of my seat before Nate could get his seatbelt off. Lightning flashed, illuminating the sidewalk for a split second. A rumbling thunder from the distance shortly followed.

"CJ, wait!" Nate shouted in a hushed voice as he climbed out the passenger side.

I stopped on the front step.

"What if *he's* in there?"

I took a few steps back to join Nate on the sidewalk, looking up at the dark windows. A raindrop touched my face as I stared at the house.

"And what if Adam's in there too?" I replied. "We can't wait around."

Nate grabbed my arm before I ran back to the door. "Let's just be quiet about this, yeah?"

I nodded and continued forward.

We put our ears against the door, staring at one another as we listened. We stood there in the ominous darkness for a few long seconds. The street around us was quiet, with few lights seen from the windows. The only noise came from a neighbor's wind chimes singing in the wind.

Adam's house was quiet too; not a sound was heard (not that we expected to hear much through the front door).

I shook my head. Nate nodded toward the door handle. I gave it a turn, but no... my heart sprang into my throat.

To my surprise, it was locked.

CHAPTER 19
CLICK! CLICK! CLICK!

Panic flooded my veins. A bright flash of lightning lit up the sky; yellow caution lights blinked in my brain. Something was wrong. Like the storm ready to break around us, I could feel it!

"What is it?"

"It's locked," I whispered. "I-I-I was here the other day, and it wasn't locked."

I shivered as a rushing breeze whipped through the night.

Why is the door locked? Why is his door locked? He never locked the door! Why is the freaking door locked?

Nate tried the knob himself as if he didn't believe me. "Maybe he decided to lock it today."

I shook my head and paced in circles, staring up at the white siding. "It's not like Adam. It wasn't locked the other day. I don't know."

We both turned on our feet as someone across the street let their dog out. I stared up at the sky as another flash imprinted the outline of clouds.

"We can't keep standing around, CJ. Someone's going to call the police on us. Is there another way in?"

I looked to the side of the house, calling Adam for the millionth time.

Of course, he still doesn't answer.

I peered through the bars of the tall, black gate on the left side of the house, guarding a parking spot that led to the backyard.

"Give me a boost."

"I don't think we should—"

"Just give me a boost, Rodman. There's probably a back door."

He cupped his hands over his thigh, giving me a step just high enough to pull myself over the metal fence. I got down low to the ground as I landed on the other side, creeping my way along the sidewalk that edged the home. I carefully stepped over miscellaneous things Adam had left out—a dry-rotted garden hose, empty beer bottles, a disregarded vape pod. Around the corner, I found a back door.

I twisted the handle, but this one was locked as well.

I crept back the way I came. Nate held onto the gate waiting for me, peering between the bars like a prisoner in a jail cell, his hands wrapped by the long sleeves of his Father Christmas sweater.

"There's a leather pouch of tools in my glove compartment. Grab it for me."

Nate returned from the car with the small, black bag.

"What's this for?" he asked as he handed it through the bars.

I pulled out a tension wrench and lock pick gun.

"CJ, you can't be serious."

"I have to get in there!"

"Pick the front door then."

"I'm already over here. Besides, you said we can't draw attention. Just stand watch or something."

"Open the front door when you're in."

I ran to the back door, scraping my knee as I dropped in front of the entry.

Should've worn jeans, I thought as the heat of fresh blood warmed my kneecap.

With my tension wrench in the top of the keyhole and the pick gun in the bottom, I pulled the trigger a few times.

Click! Click! Click!

I turned the tension wrench, and the lock moved smoothly. I was in.

CHAPTER 20
POLAROID

The last time I used my father's pick gun was at a liquidation repository. Adam and I sneaked our way through the back, searching pallets with flashlights, hoping to find re-salable merchandise. We found refurbished and returned electronics but a security guard chased us out before we filled our bags.

I shut Adam's squeaky back door and locked it behind me. Staying low to the ground, I duck-walked through the mudroom, littered with unfolded clothes piled on the floor and laundry machines, reminding me of how I found my apartment (though I doubted this was due to the blackmailer).

Streetlights from the outside world barely peeked around shaded windows of the ground floor. When I reached the kitchen, I stood up to take in the surroundings, my eyes struggling to adjust to the darkness. From what I saw, the kitchen had no signs of being torn apart. A pot and an empty box of mac and cheese were left out. A few dishes were in the sink, one being a metal pan with rust forming from being submerged for too long. I looked through the frosted-glass cabinet windows, but things seemed in place, untouched.

I breathed a sigh of relief. *Maybe they haven't been here yet.*

I stepped into the front room (the only clean room of the house), forgetting about Nate for a moment, as the outside light hit a small metal picture frame and caused a glare that caught my eye. It was a picture of my brother and I with our father's arms wrapped around our necks. I touched the square photo with my thumb; the scent of my father's jacket and reeking beer-breath seeped from the image. It was taken after my mom left—I knew from our shaved heads and the bike tire in the background. It was shot with a Polaroid (probably something we had stolen), potentially the only picture in existence from that time of our lives.

An explosion of thunder brought me back to reality, and I went back to the task at hand. I unlocked the front door and opened it slowly, doing my best to stay silent, but to my surprise, no one waited on the other side. I peered out the doorway, craning my neck to the left and right, but

Nate was nowhere to be seen. The night had fallen silent.

"Nate," I whispered. "Psst, Nate!"

No one came, but something replied.

The creak of a floorboard came from behind.

CHAPTER 21
A GHOST

The chippy breeze from the night's cool air sent goosebumps crawling on my skin. A storm was brewing; clouds were ready to cry at any moment.

I turned around, half-expecting someone to be directly behind me, but there was no one. I was alone, watching the staircase a few steps before me.

Did the sound come from upstairs? Did it come from somewhere down here? Was it Adam? Is the blackmailer here? Maybe Nate hopped the fence?

Everything inside of me said to run out the door. Escape while you can! A flash of lightning blinked behind me, causing my shadow to cast before me, but it wasn't a shadow—I saw my father, dead, screaming up at me.

RULE 18: LEAVE WHILE YOU STILL CAN!

The nightmare disappeared as quickly as it presented itself. I took a few steps back, holding the front door's frame to support my shaking legs as I exited the house. Rain started crashing down, dampening my hair and silencing my senses. Frozen in time, I floated in another dimension. I looked at the dark staircase inside the doorway, but it appeared miles away, far from my reach. I had to go up there. I had to check on Adam. I saw him reaching out to me, his ghostly hand pleading to be grabbed, but something stopped me.

I wanted to run, but my muscles were tense, avoiding to budge. Like a locked seatbelt, the weight on my shoulder held me firm. My name echoed in the distance. It hurt my ears while simultaneously sounding no louder than a whisper.

"CJ!"

The name became loud and clear. Another flare of lightning revealed Nate standing next to me. He held my shoulder, keeping me upright.

"Rodman!"

The tension finally released from my body, and I threw my arms around him. I didn't know why I felt afraid, but he hugged me back all the same.

The pouring rain peeled the sticky dread from my skin as we released.

"You all right?" he shouted over the rain, angst shrouding his voice.

"Yeah." I nodded frantically. "You?"

"I'm fine. You look like you've seen a ghost."

I swallowed the lump in my throat. "I did."

"What?"

I swatted at the air. "Never mind. Were you inside?"

"What?" he said again. "No!"

"I heard someone inside," I said, lowering my voice.

We stared at the dark, open doorway ahead of us.

"Do you think—"

"I don't know."

Nate approached the door, stopping at the entrance to look back at me.

"Well, come on. We've blown our cover at this point."

CHAPTER 22

ACCIDENTAL OVERDOSE

The sound of rain evaporated to a subtle whoosh as the door shut behind us. Nate pulled out his phone and illuminated the room with the flashlight.

"Aren't we supposed to stay discreet?" I whispered.

"We were shouting outside the door. If someone is here, they already know we're coming."

He examined the living space to the left and right that wrapped the stairs and led to the kitchen.

"I already checked the area," I said. "But I haven't been upstairs."

Nate flicked a light switch at the base of the stairs; an orange glow scared away the shadows. We ascended, taking each step cautiously, our feet thudding against each wooden step.

"Ugh," Nate muttered, pulling his soaked sweater over his wide nose. "It smells worse than your apartment did."

Upon reaching the top, he hit the next light switch, illuminating the open room. To the right was the corner bar my brother had custom-installed, covered with used glasses. In front of us lay the crumb-embedded couch, but no Adam lay upon it. The room was as messy as I found it the week before. I was embarrassed with Nate seeing the honeycomb bong on the floor, a pipe on the coffee table, and empty takeout boxes piled next to it.

"He's not here," I said, my voice sounding hollow.

"He's not in there?" Nate asked, pointing to the small hallway to our left.

I opened the doors to the two bedrooms, knowing Adam wouldn't be inside. I only found a bed covered in clothes and a guest room full of boxes ingrained with dust.

Nate peaked into the bathroom but quickly regretted the decision and shut the door to trap the odor inside.

I checked behind the bar and under blankets on the couch, knowing full well that Adam wouldn't be there.

"You don't think he's in trouble, do you?" I asked.

"Let's not jump to conclusions," Nate replied. "I don't take your messenger as someone who's looking to abduct anyone."

"But I swear I heard something," I said.

"Maybe you didn't," Nate argued. "You were kind of out of it for a few seconds when I found you."

"Where were you, anyway?"

"A car passed in front of the house and then came back. I didn't know if they were watching me, so I went around to the side by the gate."

"Someone saw you?"

"I don't know. I didn't catch their face, but they passed by slowly three times."

"Great, the police could be on their way here right now."

I tried Adam's phone again.

"Wait... do you hear that?" Nate put his finger in the air, his voice falling to a whisper. "I hear something."

I pulled my phone away from my ear to listen. Rolling my eyes, I dug into the blue couch cushions, pulling out Adam's buzzing phone.

"Idiot. He could be trapped in some guy's trunk with no way to call me."

"What time is it?"

I checked my phone. "Almost midnight. Why?"

"You said your brother's a partier, right? You think he might be out?"

I shoved the coffee table away in defeat, knocking over Adam's bong as I sat on the couch. "I guess it is a Saturday night," I replied with a lack of emotion.

Nate wiped crumbs off the seat and sat beside me. "So we wait and stay optimistic. He can't be out that long. Most bars close around one or two."

"Yeah, maybe."

"Watch, he ends up staying at a buddy's place. How funny would that be?"

Nate elbowed me, but I didn't find it amusing.

An awkward silence fell between us. Nate turned to his phone to text Sophia. I turned to my thoughts of distress over Adam.

I hadn't worried about Adam like this in a long time. The last time I remembered feeling this way was shortly after our father's death. He locked himself in a bathroom stall and attempted to overdose on cough syrup. After sticking my fingers in his mouth and being covered in vomit, I had to drag him out of the store before someone called 911.

Since then, my concern had slowly dulled to the dangerous decisions he made. Maybe it was because he wasn't actively trying to kill himself anymore. Maybe it was because I pretended to stop blaming myself for not taking his hand that terrible night, leaving him to experience our father's death alone.

What if he's out there, alone in the rain, and it's all my fault? Or worse... maybe he's not alone. Maybe he's with some deranged killer.

Part of me believed Adam lived the way he did in hopes he would die, that it'd look like an accidental overdose. Perhaps he numbed the pain to escape but hoped that one night he would escape forever.

Or maybe he's getting back at me. Maybe he hopes to die so I have to live with both their deaths haunting me.

"I'm sure he's alright, CJ."

"Yeah," I answered. "I just... I really thought I heard something."

Nate pursed his lips to the side, unsure of what to say. "Well, I guess we can be thankful that you didn't. Nobody else is here."

CHAPTER 23
THE SCENT OF DEATH

The sound of the front door slamming woke me from my slumber. I found Nate unconscious next to me. I gave him a nudge to jostle him awake as my whistling brother climbed the stairs.

Drenched from the rain, his white (now transparent) boat-neck shirt clung to his skinny frame. He looked presentable (I guess he was partying). He must have applied pounds of pomade because his quiff hairstyle was still intact.

"CJ!" he rejoiced as he entered the room.

"Thank God you're alive."

I jumped from my seat and hugged my brother, the first embrace we've shared in years.

"Alive?" He gently pushed me away with a puzzled expression.

"I was worried about you."

I sat back down without another word, unsure of what to say or how to say it.

"I'm more than alive, my man! I'm livin' good! Man, is it Christmas?" he said, pointing at Nate's sweater. "It must be 'cause I never see you this often."

He squeezed between Nate and me on the futon, throwing his orangutan arms over our shoulders.

"And you brought a friend! Is this a special friend, or just a friend? I never took you for being gay, but I like his California-do."

"What?" I blurted.

He disregarded my outburst. "Did ya show 'im the crib? I hope CJ made ya feel comfortable, bro. Sorry 'bout the smell. I can set up the diffuser if you want. Lemongrass makes it a hundred times better. What's your name by the way? You hungry? We can order Chinese if ya hungry. I know a place that delivers twenty-four seven. The food's sub-par, but it's best you can get at this time of night. Hey, why you here at 4:00 AM anyway, CJ? You're not here to ask for cash, are ya? Hey, look! My phone! It was on the coffee table this whole time. Ha! And it's still holdin' a charge. Believe me when I say I can't rememba the last time I charged this thing. It's been weeks, and I mean WEEKS!"

"Does he always talk this fast?" Nate questioned, pushing away from Adam's rain-soaked body.

"*Always talk this fast,*" Adam mimicked in a sarcastic voice with a chuckle. "I like this guy."

He kicked off his high-top Nikes, freeing the scent of death hiding within.

"Oh, gosh, Adam!" I jumped from my seat, now fully awake. "Please, put your shoes back on!"

"Come on! It ain't that bad. Plug in the diffuser by the bar. Yo, one time, I was with this girl. Her name was Barb... or actually, maybe it was Bri. I forget. But man, I had her over after meeting her at the club, and things were smooth sailin' if ya feel me. That was until she kicked off her shoes. I sent her out the door faster than I dragged her in! And I'm not like that. I don't like to be that guy, but sheesh! Bro, her little piggies had been rilin' in the mud if you know what I'm sayin'."

I was embarrassed of my brother, but Nate smiled, seeming to enjoy the lively personality.

"I'm Nate by the way," he said. "Nate Rodman. It's nice to finally meet you, Adam."

"You guys wanna play somethin'? I've been playin' this car soccer game. I'm kind of dog, but you know I be ballin' sometimes. I got two controllers so we can take turns.

Or there's this new show that just came out. Bro, it's hilarious! The one guy on the show doesn't know he's on a show, and they pull the craziest stunts on him."

I sat on a barstool across the room. Nate joined me as Adam continued rattling on about something and stared at the TV screen.

"You're brother's... interesting."

"He wasn't always this way," I replied in a low voice. "He went quiet after Dad died. Then, he was different, almost overnight. I think the party scene changed him."

"He seems happy to see you."

I managed a smile. "Yeah, I guess he does."

Although Adam had become somewhat uncontainable, he was still my brother. I only understood half the things that came out of his mouth, but I was glad to see him alive and well.

"Think we should tell Eddie Murphy about the notes?" Rodman questioned.

"Eddie Murphy?"

"Your brother," he elaborated, "reminds me of that movie with Eddie Murphy where he talks a lot?"

Yeah, like that narrows the list down.

"I thought you read books."

"Sophia made me watch it," he shrugged. "Anyway, what do you think? Is it better if he doesn't know?"

Part of me wanted to leave him in the dark. Would he care anyway? He'd probably tell us we were overreacting, only leading to an argument.

Just then, Adam made the decision a whole lot easier. As he rattled on about a Youtube video that we *had to see*, he emptied his pockets. His wallet, keys, and vape fumbled onto the coffee table. Sitting amongst the keys was a crumpled yellow paper.

"Hey, what is that?" I pointed at the pile.

Adam stopped his rant and picked up the vape. "Raspberry lemonade. This flavor's da bomb! Want some?"

"Not that."

I walked across the room and picked up the note. My eyes became boulders as I gaped at the writing.

"Oh, that. Yeah, found it on the front door. Prolly the mailman tellin' me I wasn't home to sign for a package or somethin'."

"What's it say, CJ?"

Nate joined me and read over my shoulder.

That was a bit pedestrian,
Crispin Jiles.
You shouldn't come looking for
me empty-handed.
Return the cases before
someone gets hurt.

CHAPTER 24
SPITTING VENOM

The rain had ceased, and the morning sun rose as we arrived at Harper's Diner, a place Rodman said he'd been coming to since childhood.

We planned to meet Sophia for a much-needed coffee and even more needed fresh air. I grew accustomed to the scent of Adam's home, as the apartment I shared with him years prior smelled similarly, but Nate said he couldn't stand it any longer.

"My eyes actually burn," he said when we left.

My head was foggier than the misty morning, the lack of sleep catching up with me. I hadn't gone so long without a full night of rest since my early twenties. Would I dare to say I actually felt old?

Nate and I entered the diner, a bell ringing above our heads. Sophia waited in an emerald-colored booth to our right, pulling on the drawstrings of her hoodie nervously. She leaped from her seat when she saw us, hugging us both before we sat down. She wore her black square-frame glasses. She didn't wear them often, but I liked when she did.

"I haven't slept all night," she announced. "You guys had me worried sick."

"We barely slept either," Nate replied.

"Your brother didn't come?"

Duh, I thought, my tiredness making me irritable.

Instead, I replied kindly, "He fell asleep while I told him about the notes."

"At least he's okay. Had the blackmailer been in the house?" Sophia asked.

I slumped in my seat, sliding so low my eyes were nearly level with the table. "I was pretty sure I heard something last night, but maybe I was wrong. Maybe they left before we got there. What are the odds we would show up at the same time they were there anyway?"

"I don't know," Nate replied next to me. "I think they were there at the same time and sneaked out or arrived after us. They wouldn't have left a note if they didn't know we were there. Plus, if they were there before us, they would've torn the place to shreds. It doesn't match their M.O. to search without making it known."

"*M.O.?*" Sophia repeated.

"It's detective talk for someone's habits," I explained.

"Actually," Nate added, pointing his finger in the air, "*Modus Operandi* derives from Latin, literally meaning 'mode of operations'. The phrase is originally found in a lot of old commentaries on Aristotle. The philosopher Francisco de Toledo used the phrase a lot in his writings."

"Who?" Sophia and I said in unison.

"Oh, come on! First Jesuit to be made a cardinal in the Catholic church? He literally helped persuade the pope to forgive Henry IV of heresy before France crowned him. Don't you guys know anything about history?"

"And he tells me he's not religious," I whispered to Sophia.

"Can we stay focused here?" Sophia piped. "You guys nearly had a run-in with this psychopath and you're talking about something that happened a century ago."

"Four centuries ago," Nate muttered.

"Rodman!" Sophia slammed a fist on the table.

"Anyway," I said loudly to return order, sitting up in my seat, "what Nate's saying is that maybe they were searching when we arrived and didn't tear the house apart before leaving."

"Or arrived after us," he added. "But it's just a theory. For all we know, they planned for CJ to show up and were watching the house. Maybe they never went inside. I did see someone drive by a few times. This could all be a charade, a way to show dominance."

A woman older than the ripped, ancient booths we sat in made her way leisurely to our table, the only occupied table in the diner. She had fiery red-dyed hair, brighter than the apron and cursive on her nametag. She struggled with a fresh pot of black coffee in hand, spilling it along the way.

"Well, aren't you three up bright and chippy this morning?" she said in a feathery voice as she poured our coffee with tremorous hands. "Good to see you, Nathaniel. It must have been months since I last saw you, honey. How are your parents doing?"

"They're doing well, Zita. I'll let them know you asked."

The little woman took our orders, skipping Nate as she said she remembered what he always ordered, and bimbled back to the kitchen.

"I guess I'm not the only one hiding my full name," I mused.

"Actually, my name's Nathan, not Nathaniel. She almost had it."

"I thought your parents passed," Sophia said.

"They did. I've told her before, but she doesn't remember. Just like she doesn't remember I was here a few days ago."

"At least she remembers what you order," I said.

Nate laughed. "Actually, she doesn't remember that either, but I enjoy the element of surprise, so I let it be."

The coffee was dull, with a vegetable taste that didn't appeal to me, but it was better than nothing. I had developed an acquired taste for *good* coffee after meeting Rodman. His coffee was bolder than anything a diner could provide.

I sipped from the white mug, slowly warmed from the inside out, ensuring not to slurp to avoid Sophia's wrath.

Sophia ruined her coffee with five creamers and eight sugars. An embarrassed smile emerged between her freckled cheeks when she noticed my stare. Even with bags under her tired eyes (maybe that's what the glasses were supposed to hide), I found her face enchanting.

Part of me wanted to say something.
So that's what makes you so sweet.
No, that's stupid.
I've been thinking about you a latte.

Ugh, I sound like a Hallmark movie.

Before I could say something, Rodman beat me to it. "A healthy daily sugar intake is around thirty grams. You've just about reached your limit."

"Oh, shush! I'll have all the sugar in my coffee I want."

She added more sugar and stuck out her tongue despite what Rodman said.

The jesting was short-lived. Nothing was the same anymore. I wanted to enjoy the downtime with my friends, but crippling fear would remind me that this was no time for snarky comments and chortles. Like laughing at a funeral or crying at a birthday party, it was out of place, unwelcome, sinfully inappropriate.

I tried to live life in the fast lane, forgetting my tank was on empty, running on fumes when time was fleeting.

Sophia must have read my thoughts as she turned the conversation back to its original seriousness. "So does the third note have any clues?"

I pulled the Post-it notes from my pocket and laid them on the table in chronological order. Wrinkled waves passed through the yellow paper.

"*A bit pedestrian,*" Sophia read.

Nate nodded. "Like I said, I think they're trying to show dominance. They're mocking us."

"Not us. Me," I corrected.

"What do we do now?" Sophia asked.

I ran a hand through my short, brown hair, realizing I had forgotten my hat at the bar. It felt both greasy and stiff, like my aching body. I needed a shower. I needed sleep. I needed to get out of this mess.

"I don't know," I said after an exaggerated pause. "But I have to figure this out before something else happens."

Sophia continued to examine the newest sticky note. "Do you think they'll actually hurt someone?"

"It's tough to say," Nate answered. "They haven't yet, but they also haven't led us to believe they're bluffing."

"I mean, we can't sit around and wait then, right? We have to do something."

"I agree, but what, Soph?" I said. "We don't know who this person is, and we don't know why they're after me. We literally have nothing to go on. What can we do?"

"I don't know. I'm just trying to think positive. You're the smart one, Nate. What do you think?"

"I think we should start with what we do know."

Sophia pulled a notepad from her purse. "Let's just write it down."

We listed everything we knew, starting with the dates I received each note and the actions taken by the blackmailer.

The bell above the diner door jingled. A man seated himself at the bar to eat an early breakfast. We kept our voices low as we continued.

"They're keeping you alive," Sophia suggested.

"Yeah, good point," Nate said. "You're still alive for a reason."

"Meaning what?" I asked.

"Either they don't plan to take you out, or whatever you have is valuable enough that they won't kill you until it's returned."

"Well, gee, that's reassuring," I muttered.

"Also, there was a week stretch between notes one and two," Nate commented. "Only one day passed between note two and three."

"What's your point?" I asked.

"If my theory about this person being at your brother's when we showed up is true, they're getting impatient. They're raising the stakes, giving you less time to return whatever it is you've stolen—or whatever they *think* you've stolen, I should say."

"Meaning," I mumbled.

"I don't like this," Sophia gasped.

Nate shook his head. "If this isn't a bluff, my guess would be that his next stunt is coming fast."

My father's words tickled my thoughts.

Rule 11: A bluff is just as terrifying as a bullet.

I returned to my slumped position, wishing to sink through the ripped vinyl seat and drop into oblivion, leaving all thought and worry behind. This person knew my name, my address, and my past. I felt naked, ashamed, and, most of all, afraid.

"There has to be something," Sophia pleaded. "This is getting too big for us. I think we should consider going to the police."

"You know I can't go to the police," I answered. "I've never done a background check on myself, but I'm sure if they ran my file, it wouldn't be clean. If I show cops a note that says I stole something, I'd probably be found guilty on over a dozen accounts."

"Have you ever been caught?" she asked.

"No, but it doesn't mean they don't have anything."

"They probably have pictures from robberies at the very minimum," Nate added. "Do you look different?"

"My dad shaved our heads after leaving home, thinking it'd hide our identities or something, but I'm sure my face would still match if they had pictures. Besides, I've sold counterfeit jewelry in my car. They'd probably nail me for that."

"Maybe they wouldn't though," Sophia insisted, keeping her voice low. "You don't know if they have your name on file. And you said it was over four years ago and not in the city. You might be clean."

I slid my coffee back and forth between my hands.

"I can't risk it, not with Adam now being involved too. The blackmailer might go after him if they can't get to me."

"But CJ—"

"No." I cut her short. She dropped her head, and I immediately felt sorry for the harshness that entered my voice. "I'm sorry, Sophia," I continued softly, sitting up straight, "but going to the cops is out of the question."

Silence fell over the table, the only sound coming from a buzzy tube light that needed to be changed.

Across the table, Sophia sat uncomfortably. She rubbed her mouth with both hands as if to cover what she said.

"I," she started, then took a breath, rubbing her mouth again before continuing. "I looked you up."

Rage sparked within as the words caught me off guard. Even Nate dropped his jaw.

"What?" I shouted, suddenly on edge, forgetting to be courteous to the other guest in the diner.

"I'm sorry! I know I shouldn't have gone behind your back, but it was obvious you were hiding something from us, and it was eating me alive."

"How could you?" I shouted again, now having no care for the sharpness in my voice. "I begged you not to! How could you break my trust like that?"

"*Your trust?*" she squeaked, her voice cracking under the impending flood of emotion. "How dare you say that? *You're* the one that broke *our* trust! You lied about everything for the last three years, and you want to talk about *me* going behind *your* back?"

"For Pete's sake! I'm sorry I didn't grow up in the perfect, cookie-cutter home like you and have a dark past I don't want to share. I don't need my so-called friends to be snooping through my files, files *I* haven't even read before."

"All right, can we take a breather, guys?"

Sophia showed no acknowledgment of Nate's protest.

"How full of yourself are you, CJ?" she cried, crossing her arms over her chest, tears like razor blades freely cutting down her face. "And I actually believed you were innocent, but from how you're reacting, I don't know anymore. God knows what else you're hiding."

"*What else I'm hiding*," I mocked, putting my hands behind my head as I let out a haughty laugh. "I guess you can't believe a freaking word that leaves my mouth anymore, can you?"

"What option do I have when you act like a child?"

Sarcasm and hatred intertwined. My words came from the lips of a viper, spitting venom with every emphatic syllable. "Oh, I act like a child now? So sorry I have a deadbeat mom I can barely remember. I'm so sorry my only role model was a loose cannon control freak who took a bullet to the chest, a bullet that should have hit me. I'm so sorry my brother's a drug addict digging his own grave. And I'm so *terribly* sorry that my *childish* actions have been such a burden for you! If you can't handle the weight, then get out of here. It's not like any of your input has been meaningful anyway."

"CJ!"

"What, Rodman?" I barked, but I knew exactly why he yelled.

Ashamed, I turned back to Sophia, only to see it was too late. The words cut deep; the venom seeped deeper.

Half hidden by her dark hair falling over one side, a pale look of confusion shadowed Sophia's presence. Her soul left her body.

She didn't say another word; she didn't have to. It was written all over her face.

Suffocating guilt pressed against my throat. My words came out in an airy, desperate attempt to breathe. "Sophia... I'm... I didn't mean... I shouldn't have..."

She stood up before I worked out a single sentence, wiping her tears as she escaped the diner, muffling her cries in the sleeve of her hoodie.

"Nice going, idiot," Nate mumbled.

I held my head to cradle a throbbing headache.

There goes any shot with Sophia.

Zita returned to the table a few moments later.

"Pork roll egg and cheese on a Kaiser for you, and your favorite, Nathaniel, a mushroom-spinach omelet. Should I leave your friend's scrambled eggs here, or—"

"She had to leave, but you can put them in a to-go box and I'll take them," Nate said flatly.

I pushed my sandwich away, no longer hungry. How could I eat after a miserable performance like that?

"I hate mushrooms," Nate sighed.

"You can have mine," I said. "Not hungry anymore."

When Zita returned, Nate generously tipped her and packed up the food.

"You're not eating here?"

"Nope," he replied in a dull voice. "And don't worry about driving me either. I think I'll call an Uber."

"Rodman, I—"

"I don't want to hear it, CJ. We're all stressed and need sleep. Call me when you have your head on straight."

Before Nate left, he patted the man at the bar on the shoulder, apologizing for the scene—the scene *I* created.

The man continued to pick at his lip as he nodded in reply.

Nate proceeded toward the exit, stopping to send one final glance in my direction. With disappointment in his expression, he shook his head and walked out the door.

What have I done? I should just let the blackmailer come kill me now and put me out of my misery.

I need Nate and Sophia, I thought, but part of me said I didn't. *They're better off, safer not hanging out with me. Who knows what will happen next?*

I wallowed in sorrow. It was ice cold, a lonely island freezing in the Arctic. Even the vegetable coffee could not warm the chill of isolation.

But then, something else did.

A spike of adrenaline ignited my veins as my wandering eyes fell onto the man at the bar. My heart pounded as I stared at the back of his head. A hot panic slipped over my skin; goosebumps scaled my back. Something about this man made my nervous system go haywire. Was he a passenger before? Did he give me a hard time? My subconscious attempted to warn me of imminent danger.

Suddenly, as if knowing my thoughts, he turned in my direction, his red lips glinting in the light.

Muscles tensing, heat rising to my head, we locked eyes for only a split second, but a split second was all I needed to connect the dots.

I recognized this man, but not from my car.

Is this guy... following me?

CHAPTER 25
CAT AND MOUSE

The bell above the door clanged as the mysterious stalker darted outside.

I first thought, *Chase him!* but my body said, *Freeze!*

Glued to my seat, I couldn't move. I pressed my hands against the table, fingers spread like spiderwebs, ready to spring myself forward like a lion after its prey, but I didn't push up and rise to the occasion.

Why? Why couldn't I move?

The unanswered questions laughed in the dark corner of my skull, holding me back. Nate once told me, "There is nothing man fears more than truth. Man is a slave to deceit by choice, but it is the very truth they fear that will ultimately set them free."

The blackmailer has been this close the entire time, listening in on our conversations, always one step ahead—but then why not speak to me? Why the games?

There was only one way to find out.

A few seconds behind, I bolted from my seat and out the door. It wasn't difficult to spot what he drove. A black Volkswagen

Beetle was the only vehicle peeling out of the diner parking lot.

I jumped into Cindy Lou the Malibu and tore up the road after him.

We were on the west side of the city, where wide, multi-lane roads ruled the strip-mall area. It didn't take long for me to catch up to the blackmailer with morning traffic just beginning, making the high-speed chase become a dangerous altercation.

I felt guilty for driving this fast on a Sunday morning. Most of these people weren't the angry morning drivers on the way to work; these were good people, *godly* people, grinning and blaring worship music on their way to sanctuaries. They didn't deserve this maniacal exchange. I could only imagine what the church-goer gossip would be when they arrived.

Did you see those two drivers flying down the Salem Strip? God help their souls! Even Pastor Bill doesn't drive that fast.

Going fifty on a thirty-five, I tailed the turbo Beetle, weaving through the other vehicles. Brake lights and rays of morning sunshine blurred on either side. The sound of horns whined in the background as we cut past other drivers.

I'm driving like a lunatic, worse than last night. Even on my most inconsiderate days, I never drive like this!

The blackmailer took a tight turn unexpectedly, causing me to clip the curb in my attempt to follow. Cindy Lou showed no concern as she billowed over the sidewalk, her right mirror grazing a traffic pole.

We continued the zig-zagging chase for another few miles, wildly changing lanes and taking turns. The game of cat and mouse quickly became an annoyance, as his little Volkswagen had an easier time squeezing and shimmying through traffic versus my boat-sized sedan.

We're lucky the police don't start shifts until they finish their coffee and donuts.

The entire time, a mixture of paranoia and pessimism fueled my driving. I was angry; I was confused; I was nervous; but I demanded answers. This guy drove me mad for the past week. I was willing to risk an accident if it meant speaking to him.

We were bumper-to-bumper for most of the frenzy until the mysterious driver made an unsuspected move, whipping to the left, barely missing oncoming traffic before entering a Wendy's drive-thru.

I slammed my brakes, Cindy Lou's tires screeching in shock, slowing down just enough to cut through the median. I barreled around the food joint to find the Beetle pulling out onto an adjacent road.

I had to wait for two cars to pass before I cut in. I feared he might escape, but an eighteen-wheeler came to my aid, halting the Beetle in its tracks. Cars packed the three-lane road, making any thought of passing nearly impossible.

We stopped in line at the Milford Street light, one of the longest lights in Wilkes City. Trapped in the middle lane, the black turbo Beetle had cars surrounding it on every side. I didn't know where he was going or when he would stop. Ahead was the on-ramp to the interstate. He was leaving the city, and he'd definitely outrun Cindy Lou.

This might be my only opportunity.

I had to act now.

"Keep it running, Cindy."

I pulled the e-brake and ran up to the Beetle's window. Anger overtook me. There wasn't a single thought of how dangerous this was or how delusional I appeared. Perhaps my lack of sleep led to such irrational confidence.

A shadowy face in the side mirror stared back at me as I approached. I pulled the handle, but the door was locked.

"Open the door," I shouted, banging on his tinted window. "Open the freaking door!"

He kept his head low, unwilling to look back at me, only staring ahead, waiting for the light. Even with the tint, I saw a sly grin emanating from his raw lips at the scene I created.

When banging on his window resulted in nothing, I proceeded to shout at him.

"You've got the wrong guy! Okay? Stop following me! Stop sending me these stupid notes." I shoveled the sticky notes from my pocket and stuck them against his window. I pressed my forehead against the glass to see him more clearly. "I didn't steal anything. You're after the wrong person!"

There was no reply; there was only a smile.

I went berserk, flailing my arms in a desperate attempt to get him to look at me as the light turned green. He followed the truck in front of him, casually driving away. I chased after him a few steps, smacking the side of his car until it was out of reach, but it was no use. He put down his window and waved goodbye as he left.

I screamed as the Beetle disappeared out of sight onto the interstate, ripping at my tousled hair and pacing the center lane, cars passing on either side. The horns behind Cindy Lou were barely audible.

"Get out of the road," one man cried.

"I'm late for church," a woman shouted.

I was too busy seething in frustration to care for the saints.

Why wouldn't he talk to me? Why wouldn't he talk to me?!

I felt defeated; I felt deceived; I felt nothing but utter disappointment.

CHAPTER 26
PUNCHING BAG

The drive home was a walk of shame. Miserably tired, I found every little thing to be a nuisance. The sun was too bright, the temperature was too hot, and the traffic was too slow. Nothing about the city brought me joy when my vision was clouded by the image of his smile.

That evil, red grin plastered on his face evaded every inch of my brain, a ruthless reminder that he had the upper hand. He had me right where he wanted me—confused and out of control.

I stopped for gas and inspected Cindy Lou's body as she guzzled the fuel. There was paint scraped from the passenger side mirror. I looked in the reflection and saw the blackmailer—scruffy chin; choppy, black hair; chapped, thin lips; caucasian skin. I punched the glass as if physical pain would release the emotional tension within me. The glass cracked as the mirror sprang back like a punching bag. The mirage of his face disappeared.

Great... Two bloody knuckles and a broken mirror—just what I needed.

A middle-aged man with a blond mustache gassing up next to me showed startled bewilderment.

"Are you okay?" he called from his pump.

"What do you think?" I snapped.

Hanging his thumbs on the belt loops of khaki pants, the plump man strolled over. I avoided eye contact and stared at the rising numbers on the machine, cursing under my breath at the price of gas.

"Hey, everyone has bad days, but there's always something to be thankful for. I'd like to—"

"I swear, if you're about to invite me to church, I'm going to lose it."

The man frowned widely, flexing the muscles in his neck. He gave a slight nod before turning around.

The pump clicked, and I put the nozzle back in the stand.

"Why the heck are you asking if I want a receipt if I have to go get it from the cashier?" I yelled, kicking the machine that refused to print.

Stares from the other occupied pumps groped my skin. The man with the khaki pants showed a compassionate expression.

What's wrong with me?

Ashamed of my outbursts, I muttered a sorry to the man and sped away.

When I reached Bentley Street, I pulled into my usual parking spot next to The Pizza Bar. I stepped onto the gravel, staring at the back entrance to go inside. All I wanted was a hot shower and to climb into bed, to confide in Marrie about my difficult day, but I couldn't find myself moving in that direction.

Something about the place felt unwelcoming, insecure. A home was supposed to be warm, inviting, and above all, safe. Nothing about my apartment felt that way anymore.

I couldn't go to Rodman's. He wouldn't want to hear from me. And Sophia was definitely out of the question. Lost and uncertain, I found myself wandering toward Bentley Rink and sitting on the curb.

My heartstrings were severed. My thoughts were disconnected. My body was fatigued. Everything was wrong, and it all stemmed back to my own doing.

With my elbows on my knees, I cupped my face and cried.

CHAPTER 27
TRASH PANDA

I must have dozed off, but not for long. My eyes were wet with tears, my hands slimy with snot and drool. I woke to the sound of Jamal clanking a shot off a metal garbage can a few feet away from me.

"Hey, sleepy head," he said. "Wanna play?"

I quickly wiped my hands on my shorts and my eyes on my sleeve to hide my present state.

Clearing my throat, I answered, "Thanks, but not today, bud."

"You look like a raccoon," he giggled as he took another shot.

"A what?"

"That's what Mama calls me when I stay up too late."

I did my best to smile. "Yeah, I guess I stayed up past my bedtime."

"Why?"

He guided the flattened cola-can around with his copper-handled hockey stick.

"I've been a little stressed lately. A lot has been going on in my life."

He took another shot that flew through the air right between the trash cans into the brick wall behind me.

"Nice shot," I said. Writhing at my deadpan voice, I added, "You're getting better."

He came and sat next to me, putting his jury-rigged hockey stick on his lap, wiping the dust off his Wilkes Elementary gym shorts and bony knees. "Not as good as Marcus, though."

"One day you will be." I took a deep breath, starting to relax. "What are you doing here anyway?"

"Sometimes I go to church with Ronny. They go to the 10:00 service because they don't get up early."

"Slackers," I teased.

He giggled, wiggling his knees in and out, back and forth as we sat together. "Then we're going to the park."

I did my best to keep enthusiasm in my voice. "Man, I'm jealous. Sounds like a fun day."

"You should come!" he chimed.

"Maybe next time."

"What happened to your hand?" he asked.

I looked down, forgetting about the bloody knuckles I hadn't cleaned.

"Oh, this? I don't know. I woke up like that," I joked.

"Why were you sleeping here?" he asked.

Kids ask a lot of questions.

"Well..." I paused, wondering what to say. "Sometimes you need to be by yourself and think. You know what I mean?"

"Yeah," he replied. "I do that too sometimes. When Marcus picks on me, I like to be alone."

"I'm sorry he does that."

Jamal shrugged his shoulders. "It's okay. He's my brother. He's supposed to do that. But I don't stay by myself too long. It's not good for you."

I examined the little boy closely. "What do you mean, Jamal?"

He stared at the road below his feet, making circles in the dust with his sneakers. "It's like you get sick. You can't stay sick. You have to get better. Ronny makes me feel better. You too."

His childlike innocence mixed with moral enlightenment was touching. "Thanks, bud. You make me feel better, too."

"So you'll come?" he asked, his rust-colored eyes looking up at me.

I laughed and I stood up from my seat, groaning like an old man as I did so.

"I look like a trash panda, remember? I need to go to bed."

He jumped from the curb and grabbed the puck to keep playing. "Hope you fix your stress," he called as I walked away.

"I hope so, too," I said to myself.

My tired limbs struggled back to The Pizza Bar, my body leaning against the railing as I ascended the stairs. My hat was upside down on the landing. I guess Mr. Zhang had tossed it up for me.

Nerves wriggled up my back as I unlocked the door. Though I knew there wouldn't be a note, I felt watched in my own home.

I opened my door, thankful that the apartment was as we left it the night before.

Seeing the clean home made me think of Sophia. Even worse, she had left her hair tie on the wooden frame of the coffee table (which needed a new glass top). Holding the little band in my hand made me miss her more, feeling guilty all over again.

I put the band on my wrist and headed for my room.

Jamal's right. I need my friends back.

While grabbing clothes for a much-needed shower, I noticed the dish of cat food on the floor, still full.

"Marrie?" I called. "You home, girl?"

I searched the four rooms, but she was nowhere to be seen. I went back to my bedroom to see if she was sunbathing on the fire escape, and there it was—a fresh note waiting to be found. I dropped my clothes and rushed to the window at the end of my bed, staring out at the area below. Cindy Lou sat alone in the parking lot; Jamal still played street hockey.

He couldn't have placed this while I was out there! I would have seen him, right? I wasn't asleep that long! How is this possible?

I reached out the open window, peeling the note from its glass on the other side. The words caused more confusion than before.

Where were you going,
Crispin Jiles?
Return the cases, and you'll
never hear from me again.
Leave the city, and you'll end up
like your old man.

CHAPTER 28
LOST HIS FIDDLE

I only slept a few hours. It was surprising I slept at all with the words of the fourth note lingering in my thoughts. They gnawed at me, claws ripping at every fiber and cell of my being.

I stood at the entrance of the Wilkes City Park and Trails, waiting next to the ice cream stand. I didn't know why I chose to meet here; perhaps because Jamal had mentioned it.

For a Sunday evening, the park was more populated than suspected. I thought I'd feel safer in public, but it had the opposite effect on me. I was a dog that heard thunder, skittish and nervous as everyone passed me by.

I paced back and forth, slinging my hood over my head, bending the brim of my hat in my hand. I shivered from the cold despite the sun not setting yet. Even with jeans and a black zip-up, cold sweat painted my back and chest. Nobody else seemed bundled up. Was I getting sick?

I turned my attention to the nearby playground. Children went down slides, pumped on swings, and hung from monkey bars. Teenagers warred on the basketball courts, playing a back-and-forth pickup game. Couples laughed as they played ping pong. A bearded man taught a boy how to play chess. It was a scene of individuals, all living lives of their own, lives full of worry, hurt, and pain, yet none of their burdens were great enough to ruin the moment they were experiencing. Warmed by heartfelt moments, they were able to stop, put down their heavy loads, and enjoy a Sunday evening in the park.

But not me—I was cold, chilled to the bone, alone to deal with the isolation, caving under the weight of each passing second. Dying became a more suitable option to ease the pain if I didn't find someone to carry it with me.

"CJ!" called a voice from the parking lot.

Adam came jogging up from behind, his pomade-combed hair looking shinier than tin foil.

"Dude, I can't remember the last time I was here wit'-you," he said, throwing an arm over my shoulders, his breath tinged with liquor, his polo tainted with sweat. "Man, look at those guys out there. Remember when we used to play? I'll never forget that time in middle school I hit that game-winning three. That was so long ago. I betcha I still got it though. If I could just get a few warm up shots, I'd smoke every last one of 'em on that court."

I pushed his arm off me. "Adam, you're twice their size. Obviously, you could beat them," I said in a dull voice.

Ironic that I would be saying that.

I walked to the furthest picnic bench and sat down. Adam plopped onto the bench across from me.

"So what we doing, bro? Wanna take the trail to the soccer field? Does the shack over there sell hot dogs still? I haven't eaten since yesterday. Is your boyfriend Nate coming?"

"Slow down, Adam!" I rubbed my temple and attempted to relax my breathing. "I called you because I need some help. I got a fourth note."

"Oh, snap, man! Did he ruin your house again? If you brought me here to ask me to clean, you know I'm prolly not the guy for the job. I barely keep my own place tidy. In fact, the other day, I thought I heard somethin' in the house, and I grabbed a bat, you know, to protect myself, and then I searched the place, but I couldn't find nothin', but I kept hearing this noise, and I knew it had to be somethin'. Turns out, I've got a mouse! I tried to smash that sucker, but the lil rodent crawled right between my legs and I slammed my foot. I got a bum toe now and it's drivin' me nuts because the nail is cracked and I think it might fall off, which would really suck because I know that they can take ages to grow back."

"ADAM!"

His rampaging voice came to a sudden halt.

"Can you shut up for a second? I don't need you for cleaning, I don't care about your stupid pest problems, and I'm sorry about the toe, okay? Can you try to focus and help me figure out what's going on? I'm freaking out here, and I don't know who else to talk to right now."

His coy expression slowly turned to quizzically wrinkled brows. "So... I take it your boyfriend is a no-show then?"

"Rodman's not my boyfriend. Why do you keep saying that?"

"Hey, man. I don't know your tendencies. I just thought 'cause you never had any females growin' up. But now that we on the subject, you gotta girl in the picture?"

"What? No! Well... sort of. Never mind that."

"Oh, you have a girlfriend? This is new! Tell me about her. Blonde? Brunette? Or are you into redheads? I've been with a few gingers myself. Tall or short? Petite or Plump? Outgoing or lazy?"

I dropped my head face-down into my arms. "Ugh! You are literally impossible to communicate with," I said into the table.

"Aw, come on, CJ. I'm just excited to see you, man. Really, I want to catch up. It's been so long. I miss hangin', and all you seem to want to talk about are these stupid pieces of paper."

"My freaking life is at stake, Adam," I shouted, nearly jumping from my seat. "Yours too, maybe. Of course this is all I want to talk about!"

Adam laughed. "Dang, CJ, you're madda' than a fiddler that lost his fiddle."

"What does that mean?"

He shrugged his shoulders. "Hey, I know what will cheer you up! Drumroll, please!" He rhythmically slapped the table. "Ice cream! That always works with the ladies. They get cranky, take 'em out for ice cream."

I threw a leg over the park bench to stand up. "Forget it. I don't know why I bothered."

Adam put a hand on my arm. "Can we just take a break from the note stuffs, CJ? It's been too long since I've last seen ya.

Now I see you three times in a row, and I barely get a 'hello' outta ya."

Nothing came to mind as a justifiable reply. I was a jerk to Adam, and I knew it. I had the opportunity to reignite the inseparable friendship we once had, and I wasn't even giving it a chance.

I stared out at the friendly faces on the park grounds. I missed feeling that way, especially with Adam. Why was I so quick to push him away?

"I'll cut ya a deal," Adam said when I didn't reply. "We buy ice cream, my treat. Then, if you still wanna talk about the notes afterward, I'll give you all the focus I got. Ya feel me? No mystery mail stuffs until then."

Straddling my seat, I considered the proposal.

"Fine," I said, pulling my hat on my head. "But I'm getting a large."

CHAPTER 29

A JACKET FROM THE FIVE-O

"So who's this girl?"

We stood in line at the park's Twist 'N Shake when Adam asked the question, his tall, skinny frame shadowing me from the neon bulbs around the sign.

My phone chimed in my pocket. Nate had texted me a few times, but I decided not to read them. For all I knew, he was sending me scripture to convict me even more.

"Do we have to talk about this?" I asked.

"Have you talked to anyone else 'bout it?"

My voice fell to a mutter. "No."

"Get it off your chest then, bro."

I wished the line would pick up the pace so I could dodge the topic by placing my order. Instead, an older gentleman ran the shack alone, moving slower than a Prius. I shivered watching him hand ice cream to a young boy.

I'm freezing. Why did I agree to this?

"You gonna tell me or what, CJ?"

I hugged my arms and spit out the words. "Her name's Sophia. You would have met her if you came to the diner."

"Oh yeah, sorry 'bout that. I was beat! How long you known each other? Few weeks? Months? Years? Before Wilkes City? I lost contact with everyone before the city. I have Gibbs's number—you remember Slick Gibbs, the guy that knew ev'rybody and could get anythin' and ev'rythin' done— but he didn't respond last time I reached out. That was a few years ago. I'm guessing he got new digits or somethin' like that. Hope he's not in any trouble or some sh—"

"Are you going to let me talk?" I interrupted.

"Oh, yeah. My bad, my bad."

We moved up in line. A woman in a lime green tracksuit walked away with a twist, complaining she asked for sprinkles. Adam winked as she passed, disregarding her boyfriend's death stare.

"I drove Sophia in my Uber a few months after I moved out of our first place in Wilkes. She was a nervous wreck, trying to prepare for a job interview."

"Damsel in distress, huh?" Adam elbowed me with an amused simper. "How'd you hook, line, and sinker?"

I chuckled as I thought back to the anxious, deep-breathing, freckled girl trying to stay calm, batting her hand in the air as a fan, whispering affirmations every few blocks, reading over note cards as her dark chocolate hair dangled before her.

"I gave her some advice."

"What'd you say?"

"Rule 2."

Adam said the rest with me in unison. "Force them to feel personally connected." He then added, "Didn't know you still rememba Pop's rules."

"How could I forget? I told her to tell a story that makes her personable."

"She get the job?"

"Yeah," I smiled. "I waited outside for her. She ran back to the car all excited, telling me how she did it."

"Then you asked her out?"

I laughed and shook my head. "No, I don't move that fast. Actually, she got back in the car and called up Rodman."

"They were dating?"

"No. I thought so at the time, but learned they never dated—just childhood friends. Anyway, they wanted to celebrate. She asked if I knew any good pizza spots, and I told her about a place I liked in Southside. I picked up Nate on the way, and when I dropped them off, she offered to buy me pizza."

"Wait a minute," Adam stepped back and crinkled his nose. "Wait just one minute. You tellin' me *she* asked *you* out?"

"It wasn't like that, Adam. I mean, I guess she did. But it was more of a way to say 'thanks' for helping her out." I shrugged my shoulders. "That's how I met them both, and we've been hanging out ever since at the same spot."

"Dang, bro." Adam slapped my shoulder. "I haven't stuck with a chick more than a few weeks, one month tops! You been dating this long? Props!"

My smile faded. "Not exactly. I never ended up asking her out."

"Bruh, you have to be joshing. You had eyes for a girl this long and *still* haven't made a move?"

My face turned pink; my gaze fell to the patchy grass-beaten path. "I don't know. I've waited too long at this point. I wouldn't want to ruin the friendship we have by dating, you know? Or... at least I *didn't* want to ruin it."

"What you mean?"

I shook my head in defeat, the argument replaying in my brain. "I royally screwed up, man—big time. I said things I didn't mean, and... well... she's pissed. Rodman's pissed too. I don't know if they'll ever forgive me."

We were next in line before Adam responded. He ordered us both a twist, and we walked to the now vacant swings, cones in hand.

The sky's burning ember fell behind the trees that guarded the trail ahead of us. The park, once filled with happy faces, was left nearly empty. Twist N' Shake was closing up for the night. The automatic lamplights flicked on behind us, casting our silhouettes over the woodchip playground.

I licked my ice cream slowly but found it difficult to enjoy. My mind and my stomach weren't on the same page. Adam finished his before I even got to the cone.

"CJ?"

"Yeah, Adam?"

"You ever wonder where Mom is?"

A long pause passed before I answered. "I try not to think about it."

He leisurely walked his feet back and forth under the swing, taking a long draw from his vape.

"Yeah, I don't think much 'bout her either," he answered, his voice muffled in the clouds. "Screw her for all I care."

It was an awful reality to speak about our mother that way, like she was as worthless as a few dropped coins on the street. I could pick them up, or I could care less. Nobody would bat an eye at my decision (unless it was a quarter; someone might think I'm crazy for leaving a quarter behind).

It was odd that Adam brought up Mom. I couldn't remember the last time we spoke about her or talked about anything of importance for that matter.

The mixed feelings hadn't changed, making it difficult to truly care. She played a role in fifteen years of my life, but that role wasn't of a mother. It was more of a housemate, someone I lived with and saw in passing but rarely actually spoke to since we were no more than acquaintances residing under the same roof. She rarely made us dinner. Being two years older than me, Adam had more time with her, but it didn't seem to pay off.

"How 'bout Pops?"

My throat tightened. "Yeah, I think about him."

"Me too," he replied.

"Why do you ask?"

He spun in his seat, causing the chains above to criss-cross. His voice came out soft, broken, uneasy. "I don't know, I just—"

His words fell short.

"I miss him too."

He nodded, looking away to hide his eyes.

"I saw the picture at your house," I said. "The one downstairs—I didn't know we had a picture with him."

He turned back toward me, one side of his mouth slightly rising, still speaking in a melancholy tone. "Yeah. Legendary photo, him and that bomber jacket."

"Dad never took that thing off. Remember when he got it?"

Ebullience returned to his voice. "I'd neva forget! We were being chased through that outlet place, right?"

The memory enveloped reality, my melting ice cream no longer seen with thoughts overtaking my vision. "Steamtown Outlets," I said. "They had that big mural of a train on the side of the one building."

"Oh yeah," Adam dipped his head, "and they had that gazebo in the center with all the stores around it."

"Where all the cops were smoking," I replied.

"And Dad grabbed one of their jackets hanging over the railing."

"And then we hid in portapotties for hours."

"Dude! Mine smelled rank!" Adam laughed. "I tell you, the marbles on Pops to steal a jacket from the five-o. Thank goodness that place was a maze."

"Worked in our favor," I agreed.

"Isn't that when he decided to shave our heads?" Adam laughed again. "You still have that scar from when Pops nipped your ear?"

I felt the back of my ear's helix. "Probably," I chuckled.

We reminisced about other adventures, recalling the ridiculous moments we shared.

"Rememba the time your bike tire popped, sendin' you over the handlebars?"

"Remember when that slushy machine wouldn't stop and blue raspberry went all over the floor?"

"How 'bout that time we got locked in that convenience store ova-night?"

"I'll never forget that thunderstorm we rode through. Lightning literally struck within a few feet of us."

I had forgotten about my ice cream at this point. The melting mountain skydived from the cone into the wood chips below. We locked eyes for a second before bursting into another rage of laughter. My stomach hurt by the end of it.

"Re-re-remember that time," Adam started between breaths and chortles. "Remember that time Pops..." His voice became jittery. Mixed with humor and sadness, his emotions tried to stop the words from escaping his lips. "Remember the time Pops got shot?"

My laughter ceased. Adam's breathing became stifled. Tears pierced from the corner of his eyes, hysteria and shaking overtaking him.

I shuddered from the words. I remembered, but not like Adam did. He was there; I wasn't.

"Yeah," I barely managed to answer. "I remember."

The chains no longer creaked from Adam swaying back and forth. He was a corpse leaning against one side. Attempting to hold back his sentiment, his armor had fallen.

Adam licked his quivering lips. "I thought... like Dad, I thought I was gonna... and you were..."

I stared at the mushy pile of melted ice cream, my mind's eye flashing back and forth between the ice cream and the puddle on that dirty convenience store floor.

I tried to bring it up before. Adam never wanted to talk about it.

Why now? I wondered. *Why do I have to face this when everything around me is crashing down?*

I couldn't speak. My broken voice cracked under the pressure. I didn't know how to fix this. I didn't know what to say.

All my life, I ran from consequences, ran from authority, ran from heartache. I was running out of road, and there was nowhere else to go.

Nate was right. I can't run forever.

"Adam," I breathed, holding back the sobs. "I'm sorry I—"

Tears glossed his eyes. His face was thin. His flushed skin clashed with his oil-shined hair. He managed a smile and shook his head.

I barely made out the words through his cracked whisper. "It's okay."

I wanted to continue, to fix things, to make things right—but before I said anything, my phone rang.

I wiped my eyes before shuffling into my hoodie pocket. The name on the screen caught me by surprise.

"Who is it?" Adam asked.

I looked his way in confusion, then back at the phone, then back at Adam.

"It's Sophia."

He frantically wiped his face with both hands as if he just realized he was crying, ripping away any emotion he used to have, doing his best to bounce back to his cheery self.

"Well, look at that," he said, his lips turning upward slightly. "Maybe things aren't over yet."

We had a moment, and it was gone as if it didn't matter, as if it never happened.

"Well, go on," Adam beckoned. "Don't leave her hangin'."

I answered the phone on the sixth ring. "Hey, Sophia."

"Oh, thank God you're alright!" Her voice became distant from pulling away from the phone. "He answered. He's okay."

"Ask him where he's at," said Nate in the background.

"I'm with my brother," I said before she could pass on the message. "What's going on?"

"CJ, you have to get here now!"

"Where?"

Her voice hitched before she answered. "There was a fire at The Pizza Bar."

CHAPTER 30
CARCINOGENIC POLYCYCLIC AROMATIC HYDROCARBONS

Even with the windows up, I smelled the burnt scent from a few blocks away. Guided by street lamps with hazy clouds of smoke floating before them, I pushed Cindy Lou to the max and raced down the dusky streets.

Adam sat in the passenger seat. Unlike Nate, he didn't hold onto the handle above his head (which Adam called the "Oh, Shoot!" handle). He casually reclined into the pleather, undisturbed by the sharp turns and hasty accelerations. This wasn't our first time racing through the dark together.

"You thinkin' this was done by the nut sendin' you notes?" he asked.

I didn't reply. I didn't want to think about the cause. I didn't want to consider the reality of the situation.

Arriving at the scene, I dropped Cindy Lou into park next to the curb on Bentley Street. Police cruisers, fire trucks, and an ambulance crowded around Nate's yellow Mustang. The white decal of a horse on the back windshield reflected red and blue patriotically.

"Dang! Check out that Mustang! Dad would love that thing," Adam remarked. "Though, he was always sayin' someday he'd buy an F-150."

I ignored his comment, searching for flames. Thankfully, the flashing blue and red, along with Bentley Street's single flickering yellow lamp post, were the only form of light in the area.

"Ah, crap," Adam sighed. "The po-po's here."

"You can stay in the car if you want."

"Nah, it's fine. I just gotta keep my distance."

"Why?"

I hadn't asked Adam about what he's been up to these days, unsure if I wanted to know or if he'd tell me. It was one thing to think about what he was probably up to; it was another to hear him say it.

"Let's just say a job went sideways for a coworker recently, and I been layin' low the past few weeks." He gave me a sheepish grin, showing his stained teeth.

"Maybe stay in the car," I replied.

"But I wanna see your place," he pleaded.

"I don't know if we can go inside."

He crossed his arms. "Whateva."

Leaving Adam behind, I jogged across the street to Nate and Sophia standing on the corner. Down the street, a few families stood outside, Ronny and his mother included. They waved when they saw me.

From the road, the building appeared undamaged, but even in the dim light, I saw smoke rising from the back doorway.

Sophia hugged me when I approached, her mascara-smeared eyes pressed into my shoulder.

"I'm so glad you're okay," she whispered.

"What happened?" I asked.

"We came to see you," Nate replied.

He wore a collared button-down that showed off his brawny chest, unfittingly matched with baggy sweats. I assumed he was coming from one of his video meetings (he only had to dress the part waist-up).

"Came to see me?"

"We were worried," Sophia scoffed. "You haven't talked to either of us since yesterday morning. And then we were here and thought you got kidnapped or something!"

"Actually, *she* thought you were kidnapped," Rodman corrected. "I said you were probably fine."

"Sorry, I was busy."

"Busy with what?" Sophia pushed away and folded her arms. "Stealing? Avoiding us?"

I guess she's still mad at me.

"You must be CJ," said a blonde firefighter walking over from The Pizza Bar. I shook her hand as she continued. "You live upstairs, right? You can count your lucky stars that the fire didn't spread."

"What happened?" I asked again.

"Sophia and I were sitting at the bar," Nate answered. "We were waiting for you to come home when we smelled smoke coming from the kitchen. I was able to put the fire out before they arrived."

"The fire started from unattended food," the firewoman added, her hands on her hips. "The stove, backsplash, and overhead cabinets will need to be replaced, but there's no structural damage to the building. It'd be best to let the building air out for at least forty-eight hours before sleeping here again, and I suggest having the place cleaned as there may be a health risk. I recommend this local cleaner."

She handed me a business card.

"Health risk?" I asked.

"Smoke lingers," Nate replied. "Carbon monoxide, sulfur, dioxin, and other chemical particles are likely present from the smoke, and soot contains carcinogenic polycyclic aromatic hydrocarbons."

"Genetic poly what?" Sophia said.

"Ever heard of PAH exposure?"

The firefighter, Sophia, and I stared in confusion.

"They literally talked about it in the newspaper last month. The Wilkes City Museum had an article titled *Canary in the Coal Mine*. Don't you guys read?" He clicked his tongue. "Soot can lead to things like cancer and respiratory issues. Studies say it can lead to mental illnesses."

The firewoman tipped her helmet toward Nate. "Smart guy."

"Where's Mr. Zhang? Is he okay?"

Sophia pointed to a gurney in the parking lot. "He was unconscious at the bottom of the staircase leading to your apartment. He took our order and then—"

I rushed past her before she could continue.

"Mr. Zhang," I shouted. "Mr. Zhang! Is he okay? Mr. Zhang, can you hear me?"

One EMT stopped me as two others carted him into the ambulance.

"He's going to be okay," he said, arms wrapped around me from behind. "He needs to rest."

"CJ?" came his little voice from the back of the ambulance.

I pushed away his arms and leaped inside, taking hold of Mr. Zhang's wrinkly hand. One arm was in a sling. Blood-stained gauze wrapped his head, his right eye swollen shut. He looked foreign to me without his oval glasses.

"Mr. Zhang, what happened?" I asked.

"No go inside."

His voice was barely audible. I put my ear close to his dry lips as he spoke.

"Man upstairs."

I kept my voice low. "Who's inside, Mr. Zhang? Did they do this to you? Did they start the fire? What happened? What do they look like?"

"Blood mouth," he managed, but before he continued, his left eye shut.

CHAPTER 31
TULIP LIKE THE FLOWER

Nate and I went up together, escorted by the red-headed firefighter for safety reasons. There was no sign of anyone in the apartment, and thankfully, other than the rolling scent of smoke, no sign of fire damage either.

Marrie's food bowl was still full. I worried where she had been, but I had other things on my mind. I placed her food out on the fire escape and closed the window before following Nate to his place (making sure to lock it this time).

"You guys want coffee?" Nate asked when we arrived.

"Strongest thing you got?" Adam jested.

No one laughed.

"Coffee sounds good," I answered in a deadpan voice to save him.

Nate pulled me aside, allowing Sophia and Adam to enter first.

"You sure we can trust your brother?" he whispered.

"Adam?" I watched him walk through the living room, following Sophia to the kitchen table. "Yeah, I mean, he's a little delirious, but he's not harming anything. You don't trust him?"

"I don't know," Nate replied. "You both seem buddy-buddy all of a sudden. You never spoke highly of him before, and now, when everything starts happening, he's back by your side."

I tried to follow his thought process, but I found it difficult to care, drained from exhaustion and anxiety with my focus on Mr. Zhang. "I don't think he's smart enough to play us if that's what you're implying."

Nate patted my shoulder. "I trust your judgment," he said as he stepped inside. "Just be watchful."

I joined Adam and Sophia at the circular marble table in Nate's kitchen. After a few minutes, he placed a silver-bodied French press between us next to the four Post-it notes. Steam slowly rose toward the dank lighting of the Edison bulb hanging from a white pole. The dark orange loom made my tired eyes heavier by the minute.

Rodman left the room in search of mugs. Sticky silence scaled the walls of the kitchen. The low hum of the refrigerator behind me was the only sign of life.

I bent the brim of my hat back and forth in my hands. It lost its flat-brimmed look and became more of an awkwardly wide *U* shape every time I wore it.

Sitting across from me, Sophia wouldn't look up from her phone, let alone say anything. Maybe she was waiting for me to speak first, but my lips twisted in knots, and the words couldn't find a way out.

Adam sat on my right, drawing his vape every few moments, sipping from a flask every other moment, clawing his ribcage each moment in between. Fidgety as a hamster, he waited for something to fill the void.

Inhale. Exhale. Scratch. Swish. Scratch. Inhale. Scratch. Exhale.

"So!" he said too loudly with outstretched hands. "You must be Sophia. CJ can't shut up 'bout you."

I kicked his shin under the table.

"Nice to meet you," she replied, not a single ounce of enthusiasm in her voice.

"Sorry, I couldn't join ya for breakfast the other day."

"You didn't miss much," she said coldly, still staring at her phone screen.

Adam leaned toward me, covering his mouth with his hands. "Yo! Ask her on a date," he whispered.

"You're such a child."

"Trust me, man. I broke the ice for you! Say somethin'."

Sophie shot daggers at me. Adam was an awful wingman and even worse at keeping his voice low (probably due to whatever he was drinking).

I cleared my throat. "I... uh... wanted to—"

Rodman came up from the basement with a mug in hand. "I knew I had a box of dishes somewhere," he announced, shutting the door behind him.

Well, there goes my opportunity.

"I don't understand why you don't keep them in the cabinets," Sophia said, returning her phone to her purse.

"Waste of space," Rodman replied as he washed the mug. "Why keep more than three up here? It's not often I have an extra guest."

"The cabinets are a waste of space if they aren't used."

"Yeah, I guess you've got a point, Soph," Nate chuckled. "Any news about Mr. Zhang?"

I shook my head. "Called the hospital on the way here. He's got a concussion, but no further updates."

He joined us at the table, placing a black ceramic mug in front of each of us before taking his seat by the sliding glass door to the backyard. Sophia pushed the mug away after Nate told her he didn't have cream or sugar. Adam filled his mug halfway, adding a few dribbles from his flask.

"A fourth note, huh?" Rodman held the note, analyzing the writing as he loudly slurped his coffee.

"Could you please not make that sound?" Sophia asked with a face of disgust. Her fingers flexed and tensed around her ears.

Rodman took a final slurp, long and exaggerated, grinning at her before continuing. "So, where were you headed, CJ?"

I caught everyone up on the events of that morning.

Surprisingly, Sophia was the first to comment on my monologue. "But wait, that doesn't make any sense. Why would he ask where you were going if you were chasing him?"

"Exactly!" I replied. "It doesn't make *any* sense."

"No stoppin'? Went straight home after?" Adam asked.

"I mean, I stopped for gas, but that was it."

Nate squinted his eyes. "I don't think that's enough time for him to beat you home. Where did you find it?"

"The fire escape window."

"Did you take a shower? Maybe he left it while you were doing something," Sophia said.

"Well, I did fall asleep for a few minutes. And then I was talking to Jamal. But I was right there! I think I would have seen him."

"Not seein' much with your eyes closed," Adam said.

"It was only a few minutes. Ten minutes tops. And why would the guy risk leaving the note with me right in front of him?"

"The answer is obvious then."

Adam, Sophia, and I shared glances before Rodman continued.

"The guy you chased was not the same person that left the note."

"You sayin' two peeps are leavin' notes now?"

Nate shook his head. "I don't think so."

"Then what, Rodman?" I poured myself the remainder of the coffee.

"I think you've got the wrong guy."

"How do you figure that?" Sophia asked.

"Well, CJ's definitely being watched. I, too, thought the guy at the diner looked familiar."

"I know I've seen him around," I agreed.

"Ya never thought that was *sus*?" Adam asked.

"I see so many people from Uber driving. Everywhere I go, faces blend together, and I feel like I recognize half the people I see. It didn't faze me until this morning."

"That guy that drove by Adam's the other night..." Nate paused, drumming his fingers on his mug. "I didn't see his face, but I'm pretty sure he was driving a Beetle."

"Why didn't you say something?"

"I didn't think it was a meaningful detail at the time." He tucked his hair behind his ear. "Did you get a good look at him?"

"Black hair, white skin, about my height, maybe in his thirties or something."

"That's not much to go on." Sophia frowned. "Anything specific?"

"Well, he has really red lips, like he's always chewing them or something. The bottom lip was scabbed."

"Didn't you say Mr. Zhang mentioned the guy had a bloody mouth?" Rodman said. "That must be who he saw in your apartment."

"So then it *is* the same guy leaving notes," Sophia said.

He shook his head. "No, I still think this guy is someone else."

"But wait," Adam said. "How we know lip guy and note guy aren't the same? What if note guy is a lip guy? Then we got two lip guys. Or maybe lip guy is also a note guy. Then we have two note guys and two lip guys. Bruh! That makes like four guys now."

"Tulip like the flower?" Sophia raised her eyebrows.

"No, like the guys we speakin' 'bout."

I joined Sophia in bewilderment. "I don't think a single thing you said makes sense."

"Ha!" Adam slung back the last of his concoction. "That makes two of us!"

"Back to what I was saying," Nate started, "I don't believe the person from the diner left the notes. The timeline doesn't add up."

"What do you mean it doesn't add up?" Sophia argued. "It sounds like he's been around at the same time notes have appeared."

"Except for this time," Nate said. "The note was *obviously* written after CJ chased him to the highway. The next exit after the on-ramp from Milford isn't for ten miles. There's no way he could've beat CJ home."

"So maybe two people have left notes," Sophia suggested.

"Doubtful," I replied. "They have the same handwriting." I sipped my coffee before continuing. "But Mr. Zhang saw the same guy from the diner. Either this guy pulled a fast one on us, or two different people have been in my house."

"Maybe start locking that fire escape window," Rodman suggested.

"I did before we left," I mumbled

"Surprised it took two break-ins for you to learn your lesson," Sophia remarked.

I let out an agitated groan. "Okay, so let's run with this for a minute. If Chapped Lips isn't the same person writing the notes, then how is he connected?"

"Maybe he works with the blackmailer?" Sophia suggested. "Maybe he's dropping off the notes?"

"But this note makes it seem as if the writer didn't realize I was chasing anyone."

"All the more reason to believe there's two stalkers," Nate said. "Unless he's toying with you. Like I've already said, the guy could be leading you astray. For all we know, it was the same guy, somehow he left the note without you knowing, and this is just some twisted game."

"Which means I can't believe a word this blackmailer even says to me."

"He coulda even left it early," Adam said. "If this blackmaila got the smarts, maybe he planned the goose chase all along."

"Side note, but are we still going with 'blackmailer'?" Nate asked. "I'm beginning to lean more toward 'extortionist'."

Sophia rolled her eyes. "What difference does it make?"

"Well, technically speaking, a blackmailer *is* an extortionist. Extortionists force through threats, while blackmail specifically refers to threats through leaking information."

"Does it really matter?" Sophia asked.

"Yes, actually," he replied. "Do we think this person is threatening to reveal CJ's past? Or do we think this person is threatening to ruin CJ's life in another way, like tearing his house apart? Knowing his motive might help us figure out who he is."

"But have you forgotten?" I tapped the speckled marble table with my pointer finger. "I don't think this has anything to do with me. *He's* the one that's got the wrong guy!"

"Or so you say," Sophia scoffed.

"I'm innocent! I swear!"

"Bro, we both be guilty of thievin' and you know it!"

"Shut up, Adam!"

"Whether you're innocent or not," Nate began, "someone believes you stole something. Typically, blackmail is personal. But if this isn't blackmail and it's not personal, then maybe it doesn't have to do with your past like you thought."

Great! So I told my friends my deepest, darkest secrets for nothing.

"So, how can we know?" Sophia asked.

"We need to consider what he knows about CJ."

"He's got my address," I said. "And Adam's."

"He knows what you drive," Sophia added.

"He mentions your father in this note," Nate said. "Anything else?"

I searched my thoughts for answers, sipping my black coffee quietly so as to not disturb the peace, but nothing else came to mind.

"Prob not much," Adam interrupted the silence and folded his arms, a haughty grin sliding across his lips. "I had our records wiped years ago."

"What?!" I spewed coffee across the table, nearly reaching Sophia.

All eyes fell on Adam.

CHAPTER 32
BACK FROM THE DEAD

Adam grinned ear-to-ear like he'd won the lottery.

"Why didn't you ever tell me?" I asked.

"Musta slipped my mind."

"But how?"

"I don't know. Lots of stuffs slips my mind."

I rubbed my eyes, pinching the bridge of my nose. "No, Adam; I mean, how did you wipe our records?"

"Oh, right! Remember earlier I mentioned Slick Gibbs? I was his rock dealer. I don't touch the stuffs. One time was 'nough for me. But Gibbs hit the pipe hard! Normies hit that stuffs two times a day, three times tops. But not Gibbs. Gibbs had it breakfast, lunch, and dinner with a few side dishes between if you know what I'm sayin'. One time, I found him dead in his apartment. Well, he wasn't dead. But he looked dead! Like really dead—dead as dead can look. And I had to pump his chest. I didn't know if I was doin' it right, but I musta, 'cause he came to. That was scary!

You never expect a giant like Slick Gibbs to be flat on his back like that."

Sophia covered her mouth in shock; Rodman was cool as a cucumber.

"Get to the point, Adam." I rolled my hands in the air.

"Right! So after bringin' Gibbs back from the dead, he said he owed me. He tol' me he could get me anythin' I wanted, 'cause, as you know, Gibbs had a pocket of dough bigga than the Grand Canyon."

"And you asked him to expunge our records?"

"He rattled off a list of stuffs, and when I heard he could wipe slates clean, I said to myself, 'That might come in handy someday for CJ,' since you were tryin' to get on the straight and narrow, so I went with that."

"And he actually did it?"

Astonished by the question, Adam replied, "I ain't never doubt Slick Gibbs in the past. Why doubt 'im now?"

"There's one way to know if he did it," Rodman mumbled into his mug.

I met Sophia's eyes. She dropped her jaw in surprise, her freckled cheeks burning red. "Don't even ask!"

"Sophia, please, I'm sorry I freaked out."

She ran her nails through the roots of her hair. "Freaked out is an understatement."

"I was stressed out and hadn't slept."

"No excuse."

"I was afraid of what you would find. I didn't mean what I said. I swear!"

She slapped a hand on the table. "You're only saying that because you need me *now*."

I reached across, taking her hand. "Please, Sophia! You're one of the most important people in my life."

"Behind me," Rodman muttered.

"And me," Adam chimed.

"I'd do anything to fix the mess I made."

A long pause fell between us. I kept my hand stretched across the little table. She hadn't pulled away. Instead, she examined the hair tie on my wrist. I felt childish for wearing it, ashamed that she saw it.

Adam tipped his chair toward me. "Maybe offer takin' her for ice cream."

"Can it!" I growled.

Sophia took a deep breath and pulled away from my hand. I thought she was letting go of my apology, letting go of our friendship, letting go of any chance I thought I may have had with her, but no, she reached into her purse hanging on the side of her chair and pulled out a folded piece of paper.

She pushed aside the empty French press and unfolded it in the center. "This is everything the internet has on you."

Rodman, Adam, and I stood from our seats and hovered over the paper, the lonely bulb hanging between our heads.

"It's so empty," Rodman said. "You disappeared."

It had my home address in Gainesville, with the middle school I attended, and then another in Murdell, the small city Adam and I lived in before moving east. A Wilkes City address was on file, but it was old—the first apartment Adam and I had before I moved into The Pizza Bar. There was little-to-no information on relatives, occupations, social media, or even phone numbers. The only other information was that I got my license in Murdell and worked for Uber.

"No crimes," Sophia said.

"And no up-to-date home address," Nate added.

"Slick Gibbs pulled through," Adam said excitedly. "Prolly how you even able to get a license."

I slumped back in my chair and stared at the popcorn ceiling. "This just makes things more confusing."

"How so?" Rodman asked.

I went to take a comforting sip of coffee, but the mug was empty. I slid it away in defeat.

Reality sunk into the pit of my stomach. It seemed obvious to search my past, but according to this, the past was erased from existence.

"If my current address isn't on file, how did he find me? How did *they* find me?"

CHAPTER 33
MAZE OF UNCERTAINTY

My eyes were ready to fall out of their sockets as I struggled to study the whiteboard in Rodman's office.

Sleep became a foreign concept. It was 2:00 AM; everyone else had called it a night.

Adam was first. He crashed on the couch before I could offer to take him home. Sophia was next. She said she had work in the morning (I forgot it was Monday already), and cozied up in the recliner.

Rodman didn't have a guest room ("waste of space," he said), but he put a blanket and pillow on the floor for me. Though tiredness filled every ounce of my being, sleep wasn't an option. My mind ran rampant, cycling through every possibility, every explanation that might shed light on my sticky situation.

Is it personal? Could he be from my past? How did he find me? What does he think I have? Are there two of them? Is Chapped Lips the blackmailer or not?

I searched Rodman's office as if answers would reveal themselves in a secret compartment or book on the shelf. Maybe if

I searched every nook and cranny, a magical new note with all my answers would make itself known. If only it were that easy.

The room was small and minimalist. His tidy desk sat against the adjacent wall with a large computer monitor and tower. Next to the tower was the voice recorder Nate used for notetaking. A calendar mat lay in front of the keyboard with *X*'s crossed over previous days of the month except for Sunday, which had *QUARTERLY MEETING* circled twice and *WHITEBOARD PRESENTATION* underlined in red.

I'd hate working on a Sunday, but Rodman said he didn't mind. It was one of the only scheduled days of the year. The rest of his work week was as flexible as Uber driving.

A skinny shelf pillared the one corner, full of books older than Mr. Zhang. I passed my fingers over the titles and authors, feeling their fabric bindings, a light residue of dust clouding the air. Most of the books were classics with familiar names—O. Henry, Spyri, Burroughs, Dickens, Poe. The top shelf had a complete collection of Sherlock Holmes, along with a book called *The Lost World* with a dinosaur under the horizontal title.

I never read any of these books myself. Rodman stressed the importance of reading multiple times, but my reading comprehension was worse than half the boys from street hockey. The only book I remembered opening as a child was a Berenstain Bears picture book, and even that I never actually read.

The books reminded me that Adam used to read. What started as a book report for school became a hobby. I listened to him read before bed some nights. It helped drown out the shouting from down the hall.

I had forgotten about the old Adam. I struggled to believe the Adam of today was the same person. He was a hotshot for all the right reasons, the type of teenager that was good at everything.

Like the time someone came into school and solved a Rubik's cube—a week later, Adam solved it thirty seconds faster.

Or in eighth grade, when he tried out for basketball. He was the lead-scorer before the end of the season.

During his freshman year, he subbed in for the statewide math meet. He helped secure the team a second-place finish.

He was that guy—the guy everyone expected to have a successful life one day, probably in real estate or computer science, something that paid the big bucks.

Too bad Mom was too selfish to notice. Too bad Dad couldn't pay the bills. Too bad I wasn't there for him when he needed me most.

He deserved better—a better home, better parents, a better brother, too. It's our fault he turned out the way he did, throwing away knowledge for substance.

I went back to the whiteboard that had the sticky notes on top (two of them being held in place by magnets). I also had Sophia's note with bullet points from the diner.

- *First note found on the car Friday night, August 11*
- *Second note found at CJ's house Friday night, August 18*
  - ➢ *Apartment vandalized*
- *Third note found at Adam's Middle of Night Saturday, August 19*
  - ➢ *Was he there?*
  - ➢ *Next note coming soon...?*

Her last line stunned me.

  - ➢ ~~*Is CJ guilty?*~~

Even with the words crossed out, her disbelief was apparent.

Do Rodman and Adam doubt me, too?

I wrote a few things on the whiteboard but ended up erasing most of it. I guess I joined the club of doubters. I couldn't trust my own conclusions. A dense fog engulfed my mind, making my thoughts a maze of uncertainty.

I tried again, but my brain turned to mush with every passing minute. The laced cocktail of tiredness and alertness made it too difficult to concentrate on any single hypothesis. One thought came, followed by a question; then came an idea, but another thought pushed it away before I recorded it. Like the faded words on the whiteboard, the presuppositions became translucent as another idea erased them from memory. It was right there, on the tip of my tongue, but just out of reach that I no longer remembered.

I threw the Expo marker at the board in defeat. A plastic chip from the cap hit my chest.

As I left the room, only one line remained unerased with a big arrow pointing at it.

→ *He knows about my father.*

CHAPTER 34
CELESTIALS

I sat at the nonexistent campfire in Rodman's backyard. I shivered from solitude, reclining my seat to stare into the sky, hoping the celestials would provide a shining star.

Images appeared in the speckled night like a dot-to-dot coloring book—my brother and I with our father; the grim, red smile of my stalker; Sophia's crying eyes behind her square-framed glasses. None of them gave me the answers I needed.

Sophia's face became a reality when she emerged from the sliding door to my left.

"Have that hair tie?" she asked as she sat next to me.

I pulled it from my wrist. She tied her thin hair into a messy bun, joining me in searching the moonless void.

"Can't sleep?"

"Yeah," I said. "You?"

"Same."

The small talk ended as soon as it began, the only sound being the distant noise of the city (which wasn't much on a night before the work week started) and the lonely, rasping croak of a katydid.

"Can I ask you a question?" I said.

"Sure."

"Do you think I'm innocent?"

Sophia squirmed in her seat, tucking her legs into an oversized sweater she must have found inside. Her entire body disappeared under its diamond pattern.

"I think so... yes," she whispered. "But I don't know what to think, CJ."

I nodded, turning back to the sky.

"Do *you* think you're innocent?"

I spent a long time contemplating her question. I wanted to say yes; every fiber of my being wanted to believe the answer was yes.

My father's words were louder than any belief I mustered.

Rule 9: One man's lie is another man's truth.

"I don't know anymore," I admitted.

"Why?" she asked, leaning closer.

I looked back at her face, which was more of a shadow, with its features shrouded by the night. Only the freckled bridge of her nose was visible, her eyes and perfect lips unseen.

"I feel there's no other answer," I replied, "like I'm guilty for something I'm not sure I've even done."

She reached out her hand. Her tender touch warmed my cheek.

"Then I believe you're innocent."

"But why?" I asked, putting my hand to hers, cupping the side of my face.

I waited for her answer, the heat of her breath on my skin, smelling the familiar bergamot perfume she always wore. We were close, so close we could almost—

"Instinct."

She pulled away and stared up at the stars.

I lay back in my seat, my tired eyes beginning to take over.

I regained her faith, but fear still tingled in the corner of my thoughts, warning me not to let her down.

You better be innocent. You better remember what you did if you're not.

I reached over to her armrest, finding her hand and sliding it into mine. She invitingly accepted, taking hold of my own.

"But where do I look if I'm innocent? The past seems empty, and I can't think of enemies I've made since moving here."

There was no reply. She had fallen asleep.

Questions rolled and looped around the stars, shooting off in different directions and disappearing into the night. I tried to consider each question before it was gone. One question seemed important— something Nate said earlier, something Nate had warned me about—but it shot through the galaxy and out of mind before I could mull it over.

A final question came flashing through the stars; like on the whiteboard, this one stayed. It was the only question remaining as reality bled into dreams.

How does the blackmailer know about Pops?

CHAPTER 35
NUGGETS OF GOLD

I didn't know why everyone hated hospital food; the chicken breast and mashed potatoes I received were better than anything I'd made myself.

I sat in a wooden chair with a cheap, plushy cushion that provided little-to-no lumbar support, stationed at Mr. Zhang's side as I ate my dinner. The news played on the TV strapped to the ceiling. A man with wood-framed glasses talked about a murder investigation from a week ago.

Mr. Zhang's circular face looked deflated, his wrinkles more pronounced. He had aged at least five years in the past few days. Squeezed closed with stitches, dry blood and purple blemishes scribbled the scar above his ear. Nuggets of gold hid in the tiny corners of his eyes. His drooping left eyelid showed signs of a blow, but the swelling had dwindled since the night of the incident.

It was my third night at the hospital. Mr. Zhang got in touch with Wilkes City Fire & Smoke Restoration from the card the firewoman handed me (although I did most of the talking). When I unlocked the doors for the cleaners, they said to wait another twenty-four hours before returning.

I didn't think that'd be a problem for Mr. Zhang. The nurse said he couldn't be discharged until Friday anyway. It didn't matter personally, either. I felt safer sleeping at a hospital than at home.

Nate, Sophia, and Adam offered to let me stay with them. I didn't stay with Adam for obvious reasons, but I told Nate and Sophia it was best we kept our distance. They kept close tabs on me through texts nonetheless.

I checked the apartment each day for new notes, but I found nothing. I spent a lot of time reading and rereading the four notes I had, trying to decipher the words. My confusion only grew. Everything became complicated after Nate said there was potentially a second guy stalking me. I found that hard to believe, but I didn't know what to think anymore.

After finishing my dinner, I stood by the hospital window and counted every Chevy I spotted in the evening light of the parking lot to pass the time (saving Cindy Lou for last). It was a game my father used to play with my brother and me while we rode our bikes from town to town.

"Whoever sees the most cars before the next stop wins," he would say.

My father always chose Ford. I would choose the far-superior make, Chevrolet. Adam was a wildcard. Sometimes, he chose Mazda; sometimes, he chose Dodge; other times, he chose Honda. Once, he chose Buick as a joke and somehow managed to win.

After counting the Chevys, I counted the Fords.

"I guess you still win these days, Pops," I whispered.

I didn't know why I liked Chevrolet more than Ford. I couldn't differentiate between the makes other than their emblems. Perhaps it was a subtle way to butt heads with my father. Even beyond the grave, he had a hand in my rationalities (and he was still winning). Maybe that's why I became an Uber driver, doing two things he never could—maintaining a job and freely driving a vehicle.

"CJ?" came an airy voice from behind.

I took off my hat and returned to my seat, nudging it forward to be by Mr. Zhang's side.

"You're awake," I said. "You've been out for nearly twelve hours this time."

His eyes opened and closed as he wrestled against his sleepy body. He searched the room in confusion.

"We're at the hospital," I reminded him.

He nodded slowly. "What day today?"

"Wednesday," I replied, holding up a plastic cup of water for him.

"When I go home?" he asked, each word taking a great amount of effort.

"Friday."

"No," he replied. "I go home tomorrow. Tell them I go home tomorrow."

He said the same thing the previous night before falling back asleep, but the nurse advised against it.

"I think you should stay until Friday, Mr. Zhang."

"They want money," he scowled. "They want me stay for more money."

I didn't argue with him. Whether he was right or wrong, I wasn't taking any risks of asking to have him discharged early.

He closed his eyes, muttering something in his native tongue.

Every time he woke, he fell back to sleep in a matter of a few minutes. I turned back to the window to let him rest.

"CJ," came his voice when I left his side. His eyes were still closed, but his voice was clearer than before. "Know who did this?" he asked slowly.

I tried to discuss the event with Mr. Zhang before, but he wouldn't comment, only wishing to go home. I had assumed he had forgotten what he saw or didn't want to talk about it.

Gazing at the floor, I bent my hat back and forth. "I don't know, Mr. Zhang."

"Bad man upstairs."

"Did he push you?" I asked, sitting back down and taking hold of his hand.

"Hit me," he answered, struggling to point at his eye. "I hear him go upstairs. He go up quiet. I knew it not you."

The third note said someone would get hurt.

"You said he had red lips?"

"Blood on lips," he answered. "Need Rùn chúngāo."

I couldn't understand the words, but I knew it had to be the stalker from the diner.

"Why he here?" he asked, anger filling his voice. "Why he hurt me?" He gripped my hand tighter.

My eyes welled with tears. "I don't know, Mr. Zhang." I choked on my words. "I'm sorry this happened to you."

"You know," Mr. Zhang demanded, his words coming out crisp but slow. "Why he hurt me? Tell me why he upstairs."

I viewed my reflection in Mr. Zhang's glasses on the table next to me.

"Someone..." I started, "someone thinks I stole something."

"Ah." Mr. Zhang opened his eyes. "Guǒbào."

"I'm trying to figure this out, Mr. Zhang, but I don't know what to do."

He took a steady breath. "Find man. Fix problem," he said. "He find you. You find him too."

"I don't know how he found me."

Mr. Zhang then said something that sparked an idea.

"Find man where he work."

I shot up from my seat. "That's it," I answered, looking up at the TV screen hanging in the corner, "I might know where to look."

CHAPTER 36
AN OVERLOOKED CLUE

I couldn't believe it—Adam actually answered his phone.

"CJ, my man, how we doin'?" His voice was cloudy from taking a puff of his vape.

"I'm on my way to pick you up," I shouted as I steered Cindy Lou into the left lane.

"Pick me up? I thought you's with the landlord?"

I spoke almost as fast as he did. "I'll explain when I get there. I think I know something. Be ready in five minutes."

"You got it, bro. Hey, where we headin'? You eat today? I'm starving, dude! You wanna pick up some grub on the way? Or maybe we can stop somewhere? Hey, did I ever tell-ya 'bout the hoagie place my buddy owns down on—"

I tossed my phone to the passenger seat without hanging up. I dropped Cindy Lou into second, speeding by the other vehicles, Adam's faraway voice drowned out by the accelerating engine and swooshing air from the open windows.

Wednesday night traffic was always hit-or-miss. Sometimes, it was worse than Friday rush-hour. Other times, it was quieter than the rural streets back in Gainesville. On this occasion, it was somewhere in between—some roads backed up for two blocks, others without a single car parked on them. I turned left and right, down one avenue and up another, doing my best to find the fastest route to Adam's.

Excitement forced my weary eyes to stay vigilant as I cruised my way toward Privileged Parkway. I focused on one thing, and one thing only: an overlooked clue.

I can't believe it. How did I miss it?

City lights reflected on Cindy's silver hood, sliding by as I drove toward the north side of the city. Most of the drivers around here drove like a grandma (or how I assumed a grandmother would drive since I never met mine), but one car behind me stuck out, zipping along as fast as myself.

I took a sharp turn off of Edgeworth, noticing the speed demon behind me doing the same. I glanced in the rearview, and to my surprise, the headlights of a black Beetle stared back at me.

CHAPTER 37
T-BONE

"ADAM, are you still there?"

I searched the passenger seat, my eyes jumping between the road and the rearview mirror.

"Adam, he's following me!" I screamed, hoping he heard me. "Chapped Lips is following me!"

I doubled the speed limit, pushing Cindy Lou to the max, flashing past every grandma-driver in my way.

I considered pulling over and questioning the mysterious man, but instead, I put up the windows in defense.

"Adam!" I shouted again, whipping a right turn as a light turned yellow. "If you can hear me, the blackmailer's chasing me!"

I checked the rearview again as the interior of my car lit up from the Beetle's nearing high beams. He was nearly bumper-to-bumper with me.

I brake-checked the stalker to build a gap between us.

In retaliation, a handgun emerged from his open driver-side window. I swerved to the right lane as the crack of his pistol came from behind. My left side mirror exploded into a million pieces.

"ADAM!"

I took the next turn and pressed the pedal to the floor, shifting into fourth.

He fired again, but the bullet went wayward as I didn't hear it make impact with Cindy Lou.

One hand on the steering wheel, the other patting down the passenger seat, I felt everywhere in hopes of finding my phone, keeping my head as low as possible.

My phone wasn't on the seat. I leaned further, fishing for it on the floor. I felt a pen, used napkins, and a deodorant stick. Finally, I found my phone.

I slammed it to my ear. Adam's voice rambled on the other end, still going on about the sandwich toppings he wanted.

I only took my eyes off the road for a millisecond, but at sixty miles an hour, that fraction of time was enough to be deadly.

By the time my focus was back on the road, there was no hope of stopping. A hundred feet ahead was a red light, the final light before Privileged Parkway. The only lane open was the center. Stopped vehicles occupied the left and right turning lanes.

Time froze as I considered my options.

I could swerve to the far left, but I'd risk a head-on collision.

I could hop the curb onto the sidewalk, but I might kill someone!

I could take my chances and shoot through the middle lane, but oncoming traffic could T-bone me.

"Adam, I love you."

I went with my final option and held my breath. I flew between the two stopped sedans, their horns blaring on either side. I floored the gas pedal as I passed under the red lights.

Tires screeched as drivers slammed their brakes. An orchestra of honks crescendoed from both sides of the four-lane intersection. A firework display of lights spun in my peripherals.

Then, a more pronounced, deep-toned horn roared from my left; white headlights illuminated my driver-side window.

The last thing I saw before closing my eyes was the blue Ford emblem on the grill of an F-150.

CHAPTER 38
FATHER TIME'S HOURGLASS

When one meets death and stares into its ugly eyes, they are often reminded of the most beautiful things.

This was not the case for me. I didn't go back to the old days with Adam, nor did I see a snapshot of good deeds. I did not think of Nate and Sophia, of street hockey, or of Mr. Zhang.

There was no thought—only guilt swaddled with fear.

In the bright glow of the headlights that peeled through my eyelids, I saw the dirty tile floor of the convenience store. It wasn't my father lying dead in his brown bomber jacket; it was me.

With an aerial view, I looked down upon myself, my body surrounded by yellow Post-it notes scribbled with my father's handwriting, braided with his terrifying anger.

That bullet was meant for you.
Why couldn't you just listen?
You're guilty! You're guilty! You're guilty!

Teenage Adam, with a buzz cut and carrot nose, stood over me and reached out his hand. With glazed eyes and a distraught expression, I lay still. My desire to reach his hand was as dead as my carcass on the floor.

"Leave him," my father shouted from outside the stickered glass door.

Adam held out his hand for another second, but when I didn't accept, he left me.

He was gone. I was alone.

Like a whirlwind, the yellow notes flew into the air around me. My limp arm was tugged by the unseen hands of reality, sliding me across the floor and out the convenience store door. I fell into a black abyss, the deepest cavern of the mind, lifelessly skydiving to no end. What felt like an eternity was merely a single grain of sand dropping through the neck of Father Time's hourglass.

Crashing through the midnight black deep, lights flooded my senses. I was back in the driver's seat of Cindy Lou.

I was alive.

CHAPTER 39
MANICURED LAWN

After flashing through the intersection, blinded by headlights, I hurtled into darkness. Cindy Lou bashed into garbage cans on the side of the street. I slammed the brakes and whipped her sideways to avoid wrecking into someone's beautiful Mercedes. Instead, I took out their mailbox, trampled their hedges, and tore up their perfectly manicured lawn.

My ears rang. I heaved for air. My heart was ready to rip a hole through my gray v-neck. My muscles tensed, and both feet pressed hard against the brake and clutch.

Not realizing I was still gripping the phone to my ear, Adam's voice came into focus.

"CJ? Hello?" he drew out the *o* as he waited for my reply. "CJ? You there, my man? Bruh, what the heck is goin' on? Soundin' like there's a lotta traffic. Ya hearin' me?"

Struggling to process the events, I put my free hand to my chest and took a deep breath.

"I'm... I'm here. I almost got in an accident."

The blackmailer!

I looked out the driver-side window toward the intersection I had penetrated. The black Beetle was nowhere to be seen. Traffic had returned to its usual movement as if the near-miss had never happened. One vehicle stopped on the corner (the F-150 that nearly punted me). The driver rushed in my direction waving his hands in the air, shouting, "Hey, are you alright?"

I then saw the porch lights flick on from behind me.

"Aw, shoot!"

I stepped on the gas and ripped up the yard more than before. Dirt rained through the air as I peeled back onto the street and headed for Adam's. The mailbox latched to the bumper, hanging on for dear life, dragging behind me along the street.

"Adam, I need you to do me a favor."

"Anything, bro. Say the word."

"Open the gate to your backyard. I need to hide Cindy Lou."

"Uh... I'll see if I can find the key."

"This is serious, Adam! The blackmailer shot at me, and I ripped up one of your rich neighbor's lawns!"

"Say no more, brotha. I gotch-you."

CHAPTER 40
CRUMPLED MAILBOX

I fell out of the driver's side into the dirt, every limb jittering. Adam closed the black gate and ran to my side, sniffing and rubbing his nose.

"You'll never guess where I found it!" Adam announced, extracting the key from the pocket of his glittering fleur-de-lis hoodie. "I searched everywhere, bro. I checked the drawers in the kitchen. I checked the bathroom cabinet. I checked my dresser. Heck, I even went through pants pockets. Couldn't find the darn key nowhere. But then I thought 'bout where I'm always findin' stuffs. Guess where? The couch, bro. It was hidin' in the cushions!"

I struggled to my feet, holding Adam's shoulder for support.

"Y-aight, bro?"

"No, I'm not *aight*." I slammed the car door, nearly falling again. "I was nearly killed! Chapped Lips shot at me, and all you care about is your stupid sandwich and where you found this key."

I threw my hat on the ground and braced myself on my knees, a wave of nausea overtaking me.

"Hey, sorry, CJ. I'm glad you ain't dead."

Not that I deserve to be alive.

"Didn't the last yella note say he'd kill ya?"

I didn't answer, too focused on processing what happened. It wasn't the chase that turned my stomach; I had never teased death with such serendipity.

After regaining my composure, we rounded the car to examine the damage in the dim backyard lighting. Both side mirrors (at least what was left of them), were hanging by wires at this point. Cindy Lou's smile was full of branches and spiked leaves, some of her teeth from the grill completely gone. Her left eye was punctured. Her Chevrolet nose was missing. The front bumper and right side trim were ready to fall off, crinkled and dented every few inches.

"I was nearly T-boned," I said. "This was the aftermath."

I considered telling him more about my near-death experience, but I decided against it.

"Went off-roadin', huh? You know whose house?"

"No idea." The words came out fragile, more damaged than Cindy Lou.

We walked over to the back bumper, staring down at the crumpled mailbox. Claw-like scrapes from road burn lined its black aluminum body. The red flag was gone, but the door was still intact.

Unable to open it by hand, Adam kicked off the bent door. Inside, he found a few envelopes and held them up in the light.

"No way," Adam said. "You messin' with the wrong guy, CJ."

"Who is it?"

He handed me a bill.

"George Morris?"

"Yeah," Adam gulped. "My old boss."

CHAPTER 41
WAREHOUSE JOCKEY

Pushing the dark blanket to the side, I peeked out the window of the second floor, watching patrol cars speed down the street. It was obvious they were looking for me. I only hoped that George Morris didn't catch my plate on camera.

Adam poured us both a shot of amber bourbon from his home bar. I joined him on the couch and, this time, drained the shot to calm my nerves, not giving the frosted, dirty glass a second thought. My upper lip wriggled as heat passed from my mouth, down my throat, and into my lower abdomen.

"George Morris runs the underground of Wilkes City," Adam said as he poured me another. "Fish scale, Molly, kitties, blues— you name it! He's got 'em all, bro."

I decided not to ask what any of his slang meant. "And you moved here to work for him?"

"I heard Wilkes City was a hub for hustlers. Morris delivers all over— distribution centers on his payroll. They're not just deliverin' the stuffs you see on shelves at Walmart. Remember when we moved here, and I worked in the McMurray warehouse? That's one of the regional dispatchers Morris got around his finger. Then he's got OTR drivers with Triathlon Truckers."

I put my glass on the table, disregarding the second shot. "So, how'd you find out about this?"

"Back in Murdell, my dealer was Redneck Ricky. I don't think that was his real name, but that's what he told e'rybody. Ricky was a sneaky little snake, but I followed him one night and saw him talkin' to some trucker. I waited 'til Ricky left and asked truck-guy what was up. You know, 'cause Rule 12: Information is power."

My father's words echoed in unison with Adam's in my head.

"And he told you he was delivering from Wilkes?"

"Yup."

"Don't truckers log their stops? How would they get away with it?"

Adam downed the last of his alcohol. "Beats me. George Morris owns the paper mill. He prolly knows a thing or two about paper trails."

"I don't think owning a paper mill teaches you anything about smuggling drugs," I replied.

"Either way, the guy's like super protected. I've neva met 'em. He's a ghost. And the guys that have met George Morris, they don't come back."

I leaned back into the couch, its navy blue cushions hissing with dust.

"So George Morris is your boss?"

"*Was* my boss," he corrected. "But if you wanna get specific, LaNysha was the boss I actually spoke to. But that's not her real name. I'm not sure what her real name is. E'rybody got cover names. Mine was Skinny."

Wonder why.

"But I thought you got fired from McMurray?"

"Nah, LaNysha transferred me. I went from warehouse jockey to salesman. I got all the locals signed up."

"Signed up?"

"Yeah, bro, like a Netflix subscription service. You pay monthly, and your fix is delivered right to your door. The drug I got people signed up for is fish scale. Morris has the purest and finest on the market. It's da safest way to deal if ya ask me. And it's all kept hush-hush. You don't meet your delivery man. Don't even see 'em, or so I'm told. I was just a salesman, though. I was never deliverin'."

"What about the other drugs?—Molly and blues or whatever you called it."

"I think they're only sold in bulk. I was on packrat duty at the warehouse and saw 'em there. But I'm not too sure 'bout that. Maybe otha boys selling otha stuffs. All I know is I got sign-ups for coke."

"How do you know Morris is connected?"

"Come on, bruh, everyone knows he's dirty. No one mentions Morris, but we all know he's the real boss."

He sounds like Rodman.

I went back to the window to watch the road below.

"So you don't work for LaNysha anymore?"

"Nah, business gettin' too risky."

"You just said it was safe."

"Not anymore. I'm tryna lay low for a while 'til things simmer down. Not sure I'll go back." Adam scratched at his side, grabbing my shot I left on the table. "Someone stirred up trouble. I dunno who, but don't wanna find out. LaNysha and I are tight, so she tol' me to stay off the streets until this is settled. Everyone's a suspect.

She said I don't wanna be questioned by the big man."

I took the shot from his hand and gave him a knowing look. "I need you sober tonight. That's why I called you, remember?"

"Where we headin'?"

"The same place that might have record of my name. Can we take your car? I'll drive."

"What about Morris?"

I ran down the steps as I replied. "Let's hope I don't have to worry about him. I've got enough on my plate."

Waiting at the landing, I gripped the doorknob. Adam appeared at the top of the steps a moment later. He wiped his nose before throwing his glittering hoodie back on.

"This place gotta name?"

We locked eyes as I opened the door.

"Ever hear of a company called Private Rides?"

CHAPTER 42
FALSE EXPECTATIONS

The luxury homes appeared dismal as a fog settled upon the street, cloaking them in its shadow. I drove Adam's black Corolla slowly, scanning the blanketed shroud.

Adam kicked the radio a third time as I drove.

"Dang! Sometimes, if I hit it right, it comes to life."

It took every ounce of self-control within me not to reveal his boisterous composure got under my skin. A police cruiser or black Beetle could be lurking on any of these misty corners. Paranoia told me they'd hear Adam's banging and tail us under suspicion.

I took the long way around to avoid passing the wreck site, crawling my way out of Privileged Parkway. My knuckles were white from clenching the steering wheel. Every part of me wanted to speed away, but I knew unwanted attention would follow.

My nerves relieved me of their death grip as we exited the foggy road undisturbed. I flicked the blinker, looking both ways twice as I approached a stop sign.

I let out a sigh of relief, leaving my anxiety behind us, but the nerves were back as quick as they left me when a ringing noise came from my right. We rolled a few feet past the stop sign before I slammed the brakes. We both lurched forward. A jolt of panic shot through my legs. Adam hit his head on the visor. The Corolla stalled from neglecting the clutch.

"Relax, bro," Adam laughed, fixing his quiffed hair. "It's just my phone."

Forgetting to breathe, I gasped for air.

He showed me the screen as he answered, putting it on speaker.

"You're awake!" I said between ragged breaths.

"I am now," came Rodman's voice from the other end. He yawned as he continued. "So you're heading to Private Rides, huh?"

"They're the only place I can think of that might have The Pizza Bar address on file."

"Sophia know?"

"No, I haven't—"

"I'll tell her. Be there in twenty."

"No, you don't—"

He hung up.

Having Adam with me was enough of a liability; I didn't want to have to worry about Rodman, too.

"Why do you still drive this piece of junk?" I asked, taking out my annoyance on the steering wheel.

I turned over the ignition and resumed our drive.

"Corollas ain't junk!" Adam argued. "I'll keep this beauty anotha five years if I'm lucky." He patted the duct-taped dashboard fondly. "It's a '98, and sure, the bumpers held on by zip ties, and the air conditionin' don't work, and my radio a lil' jank, but what I need a nice car for? This thing runs smooth as butter."

His attachment to the car reminded me of my father. Before moving out of Gainesville on bikes, he always bought beaters, never able to afford anything else. He had a "new" car every year (mostly Fords, of course). My father taught us both how to drive stick before we were old enough to get permits.

Right on cue, the transmission's gears made a grinding gurgle as I went to shift.

"Oh, forgot to tell ya. No shiftin' into third. Won't work sometimes. Gotta hop from second to fourth. That almost got me in a car accident more than once. I took it to some dude downtown last year, but he made it worse."

"Yup, Corollas last forever," I said.

"Why you so uptight? You actin' like your boxers in a bunch."

I scanned the area, studying every parked car we passed.

"I feel watched."

The dark streets were quieter than the hour prior. The Corolla's halogens barely lit more than fifteen feet of road ahead of us, unlike Cindy Lou's LED lights. The Westside's traffic lights assisted our vision, providing a green loom every few hundred feet.

"Really thinkin' Private Rides got your name and address?" Adam asked.

"It's the only confident hunch I've had," I replied. "I can't think of anything else."

"Have you considered the notes comin' from someone that rode in your Uber?"

"It's an endless list. It'd be impossible to narrow it down or find the person." I tapped the steering wheel as I thought. "Still don't understand how they know about Dad."

My own words made me consider Adam. Maybe he ran his mouth to the wrong person, saying things that the blackmailer used against me.

"Just be watchful," Nate had said.

I pushed the thought aside. I didn't like thinking he was involved.

Adam reclined his seat, putting both arms behind his head. "Guess we'll ask 'em how they know when we meet 'em. How is Uber drivin' anyway? Get any good tips? I might give it a shot if it's a good hustle, you know, since things are a little hectic." His voice raced on faster than his beater could ever go. "May not return to the way things been before. Might be best if I find a new gig. I'd have to go through the hassle of gettin' a license though. Test can't be that hard; I could prolly swing it. Hey, where do you go to get a license anyway? I'll Google it—anyway, once I do get a license, cruisin' 'round town sounds fun! Bet I could pick up a few chicks here and there. You ever pick up any girls? Oh, forgot. You said you met Sophia Uber drivin', right? Last time I had a lady in this car, we parked up on Summerset Hill and—"

"They wouldn't accept your car," I said as we stopped at a light. "It can't be older than fifteen years."

"Dang! Dumb rule. Whateva though. Like I said, I don't drive much these days anyhow."

I bit my lip, considering my words. "You don't drive because you're always intoxicated."

He shrugged his shoulders in the corner of my eye. "Heh, partly true," he admitted.

"And I don't mean alcohol."

He hesitated before answering. "How'd you know?"

"Come on, Adam, it wasn't a secret when I lived with you." I looked his way as I made a right turn; he dodged eye contact and stared out the window. "I see you wiping your nose before coming out of a room like you used to. You have a bong on your living room floor, and you made a joke at Rodman's the other night."

"It was a joke."

"I'm not dumb, Adam."

He shifted in his seat. "At least I don't do the hard stuff anymore."

"Doesn't make what you're doing now any better. What if *your* third gear starts slipping?"

Adam didn't answer. His racing voice had stalled out.

We had these conversations years ago, but anger laced our words. This was the first controlled conversation about his addiction I ever had—the first time my voice truly matched my feelings.

There was another difference—Adam didn't typically get defensive. He'd usually brush it off or say a joke, his way of evading reality and coping with fear.

"Listen, Adam," I continued softly, "I didn't agree with Pops on much, but one thing he never did was get involved with drugs."

He still didn't reply.

As if my father were sitting in the back row, his haunting voice came to my ear in a whisper.

Rule 8: Keep them talking; stop their thinking.

Coincidentally, the radio started working, cutting the conversation short.

The last five minutes of driving passed without conversation, the only voice being a country singer accompanied by an acoustic, sharing his sob story full of heartache and false expectations.

CHAPTER 43
AN UNLIKELY TRIO

Adam munched on chips, and I sipped from a bottle of water he bought inside a gas station—anything to avoid conversation.

Across the street, tall hedges and security fencing guarded the perimeter of the Private Rides parking lot. A security booth was stationed by the entrance.

Shortly after our arrival, a yellow Mustang pulled up the street, backing in next to us.

"Nice ride!" Adam shouted as he spun the window handle.

"You too," Nate replied, his window sliding down at the push of a button faster than Adam could crank. "So what's the plan?"

"Not sure yet," I replied.

"Are we about to do something illegal?"

"No," I said quickly. "Well, maybe."

"Why are we here when it's nearly midnight? Why not come back in the morning?"

"What if I don't have until morning?"

"You think you're running out of time?" Nate asked.

"I think I'm running out of options."

"Chapped Lips shot at 'em earlier," Adam added.

"You were shot at? I guess maybe he is your extortionist. You alright?"

"I'm fine. Tell you later. Point is, I need to know if they have the application I filled out. This has to be where he got my info."

Nate stepped out of his car. "Alright, well, let's go."

Adam poured the last of the crumbs from the chip bag into his mouth, tossing it in the back before we jumped out to follow Nate's lead.

"Wait, where are you going?" I asked.

He glanced back at me while in stride. "The guard shack." He nodded toward the entrance. "Why not ask?"

I jumped in front of him. "We can't just ask."

"Why not?"

"What if they know the blackmailer?"

Nate grinned and patted me on the shoulder. "Even better. We can finally meet him and let him know you're innocent."

Adam oohed at the idea. "Now that would be interestin'."

I pulled Nate back before he proceeded.

"Come on, man. It doesn't work that way. What, are we gonna schedule a trip to the driving range where we can have a few beers, share a few laughs, and hit a few golf balls? More likely, he'll bash my head in with a driver, demanding I tell him where these mysterious cases are!"

"Personally, I'd use an iron," he said matter-of-factly. "Their heads are typically solid, whereas drivers are hollow."

I shook my head. "Aren't you always saying we should think about things before taking action?"

"Listen, CJ, you're innocent, right?"

"Yeah, but—"

"Then it's time to stop living on the run like you're guilty."

I considered his words.

"I promise," Rodman continued. "What's the worst that can happen?"

Adam nodded in agreement. "And if things get hairy, we can go back to lookin' guilty and just run."

Two against one, I agreed and followed their lead.

We waited for a car to pass before crossing the street. I imagined the bewildered expression of the security guard behind the dark glass when he saw three guys walking toward him—me, an average Joe, with my hat, plain shirt, old slacks, and dirty sneakers; Adam, a light-skinned string bean in his designer hoodie and black jeans riding halfway down his cheeks; and Rodman, taller than me but shorter than Adam (and stalkier than both of us), with yarny hair tied in a top knot, a brown geo-patterned sweater, and flip flops. We were an unlikely trio, less intimidating than the three blind mice.

We stood at the gate, viewing our dark reflections in the glass window of the security booth, a single light bulb buzzing above us. When no one slid the glass window open, I tapped it with my water bottle, but there was still no answer.

Adam put his face to the glass, cupping his hands around his eyes. "Nobody home."

"I thought they were a 24/7 service," I said.

"We hoppin' the fence then?"

Nate sliced his hands through the air like scissors. "I'm not hopping anything."

As fate would have it, headlights made their way toward the other side of the iron gate.

"Looks like we won't have to," I said.

A Hummer Limousine stopped at the barrier. The driver put his arm out the window, scanning a card. We stepped aside as the gate opened for the stretch to proceed onto the road. They didn't stop, and neither did we. Taking the opportunity, we ran through before the gate closed.

"I don't like this," Rodman said between steps. "We should turn back."

Nervousness emanated from his oversized sweater. Outside his natural habitat, Rodman seemed skittish as a cat.

I looked behind us at the closing iron bars. "Too late."

CHAPTER 44
EASY PICKIN'S

Black and white vehicles, ranging from limousines to Tahoes, were parked on either side of us—one of them was even a Malibu Executive Limousine.

Man, I'd love driving one of those.

Three buildings lay ahead, two being garages to the right, one being a cement-bodied service center directly ahead, where I had filled out an application a few years before. Yellow light fell from the glass door on the blacktop.

Upon entering, the wood-paneled room was empty.

"Huh," Rodman muttered, "No one's here."

A sigh of relief escaped his lips.

Hooks of keys and fobs lined a wall next to a door behind the front counter. Next to a laptop was a clipboard of time cards, one column on the top page labeled *IN*, the other labeled *OUT*.

Adam jabbed me with his elbow. "This place would make easy pickin's back in the day, am I right?"

"Except we're on camera," Nate said, pointing to the black sphere in the corner. "Think this is a good idea, CJ?"

"Most places don't check their cameras unless they have a reason." I then used his own words against him. "Just be watchful."

I put my bottle of water in my back pants pocket and walked behind the desk, first checking the laptop, but the user was signed out. I then crouched down to search through the drawers.

"How sure are you they still got your application?" Adam ran his fingers along the keys hanging by their rings.

"I'm not, but I don't have any other ideas." I flipped through yellow folders filled with files, some a few weeks old, others years old. Bills, applications, invoices—the folders were mixed, and none had labels. *Whoever manages the paperwork here is doing an awful job.*

"Hey, CJ, look what I found."

I stood from my squatted position. Rodman pulled out a time card from a few weeks prior, buried beneath more recent pages. Rodman spun the paper to face me; his finger hovered over a familiar name.

Crispin Jiles.

Before I could react, someone opened the door behind me.

CHAPTER 45
LOLLIPOP

A woman, more intimidating than the three of us combined, sidestepped her way through the back door.

"Who're you?" She boomed, her voice heated by temper and wet with saliva as she sucked on a lollipop. She flipped her long, purple faux locs over her shoulder. "And what're you doing behind my desk?"

I looked between Nate and Adam; they stared back at me expectantly.

My father's words lingered in my mind.

Rule 7: Sweet talk the simpleton; silence the sage.

I took a sip of my water to stay casual before facing the woman. She leaned against the doorway with her arms crossed, waiting for an answer. Dressed in ripped jeans and a black t-shirt with the name of a rock band I'd never listened to, she studied me with a cocked eyebrow.

"Sorry." I searched her shirt for a name tag.

She pointed her green lollipop at me. "Eyes up here, perv."

"No! I didn't mean—" I cleared my throat. "I just can't remember your name."

"Like every other person that comes in here." She stuck the lollipop back in her mouth. "Name's Ronda."

"Ah, yes, Ronda. How could I forget?"

"Don't be acting like you know me. I smell liars from a mile away."

"Right." I scratched the back of my head. "Well, it's a nice name. Maybe you can help me out, Ronda."

"Don't go sweet-talking me, boy." Her voice was louder than any volume I've ever reached on my radio. "Answer my question. Who are you?"

"I'm C-," I stopped, looking back at the time card. "I'm Crispin Jiles."

She scrunched her nose, a mix of mockery and disarray. "No, you ain't."

Confused by her reaction, my face matched hers. "Yes, I am!"

"Boy, you don't even work here." She directed her lollipop at each of us. "None of you do."

"How do you know?" I replied, raising my nose at her.

"Look at the way you're dressed," she laughed. "Where're your suits?"

"Left 'em at home," Adam chimed.

"I ain't talking to you, Slim Jim." She turned back to me. "And I know everybody that comes through those doors. Don't be playing games with me." She stepped closer, her eyes traveling up and down my figure. She wasn't taller than me, but the boldness that seeped from her presence made me melt. "Stop messing, and tell me who you are."

"Look for yourself. I'm not lying."

Finding no other choice, I cautiously slipped my hand into my jean's pocket and pulled out the sticky notes.

"Someone's been blackmailing me. I'm trying to figure out how they found me."

She scrutinized the notes.

"Outta my way."

Putting a hand on my chest, she pushed me against the paneled wall with ease, the keys next to me jingling from the thud. She flopped into her wheeled office chair and scooted toward her laptop.

"Look," she said as she clacked on her keyboard.

She opened a program that showed the active Private Rides employees, scrolling down to the *J*'s. She clicked on *Jiles, Crispin*, pulling up a picture.

Her voice dropped a few decibels. "Well, isn't that strange?"

I looked at the screen; my license headshot stared back!

"What?" I gasped. "No, this can't be right."

"You sound surprised," Ronda said quietly with her back to me. "As if you expected to see someone else. As if that's not your real name." She scanned Adam and Nate, then spun in her chair to face me, her voice returning to its boiling point. "You lying to me, boy?"

"No."

"I've never seen you before." She pointed her lollipop at me again. "You're not the Cris Jiles I know."

"Cris Jiles?" Nate asked.

"There's anotha CJ?" Adam said.

She ignored their comments, keeping her full attention on me, her death stare pinning me to the wall. "You wanna tell me what's going on here, Mr. Jiles?"

I bit the inside of my lip, doing my best to hide the timidness she brought upon me. "Why am I in your database if I don't work here?"

She squinted, returning the lolly to her lips. We locked eyes as if in a staring contest.

"Get out from behind my desk!" She flailed her arms, causing me to blink. "I can't think with you breathing down my neck."

I slinked back to the other side next to Adam. "Tell me why it says I work here."

She swiveled back to face us. "I should be asking you the same question. Why don't you tell me why *you're* here?!"

"I was looking for the application I filled out when applying." I took a sip from my water. "I... I thought there was a mistake on it."

She studied me before scanning the computer screen. "Says here you've been an active driver for nearly five years."

"Does it say my address?"

"442 Bentley, Apt A."

"Guess it's right," I gave a sheepish grin, wringing the water bottle between my hands. "Thanks for the help, Ronda. We'll be going now."

We turned to leave but halted at the sound of her voice.

"Not-uh." She shook her head. "You think I believe you'd be snooping behind my desk to check if your address was correct?"

No one replied.

"And why am I seeing you where Cris should be?"

When I didn't answer, Adam said, "Looks like someone messin' with the info."

"Yeah, it does." Ronda slammed both hands on her desk as she stood, glaring at us like a bulldog ready to pounce. "You wanna explain what's going on here?"

I put up my hands. "Your guess is as good as ours."

Nate stepped forward. "Anyone else come in here inquiring about a Crispin Jiles?"

Ronda crunched her lollipop between her teeth, chewing the hard candy before tossing the crystal-layered stick into a nearby bin and receding to her seat. She held her head high with a smug expression. "I don't gotta tell you nothing."

"Listen, lady," Adam started, "my brotha here been havin' some issues lately. We're just tryin' to get to the bottom of this, ya feel me?"

She licked her front teeth before continuing to search the screen. "I haven't seen Cris in over a week."

"You never thought to check his info?" I asked.

She stopped typing. "That ain't in my job description." She clicked her mouse a few times before shaking her head. "I can't find a picture of him. I only see a picture of YOU."

"It wasn't me. I swear!"

Nate put a finger to his chin. "Does Cris Jiles happen to have chapped lips?"

"They ain't chapped." Ronda corrected, rolling her eyes. "He's always picking at his lips."

Adam gaped at me. "Chapped Lips got the same name?"

"So you DO know Cris?"

"No!" I answered. "Well, sort of. Do you know where we can find him?"

"You think I've gotta leash on the man?" she boomed.

"It didn't cause any red flags that he's been skipping work?"

"Tooly had half the fleet laid off with the heat of the press."

"The shooting," Rodman said. "Do you know who was involved?"

Ronda crossed her arms, smirking as she looked out the glass door behind us. "Our little chit-chat here is over."

We followed her gaze to find two cars pulling up the drive.

CHAPTER 46

THE ONLY CASUALTY

We rushed out the front door, shielding the headlights with our arms.

"Come on!" I yelled, pulling Adam and Rodman to the side of the building, finding shelter in the darkness.

"We can't run from the police," Rodman said. "We'd be lucky to just get a misdemeanor for trespassing. If we get caught running, they might tag on a felony."

"How sure are you that they're police?" I asked.

"Who else would she call?"

"Well, I didn't see any flashing lights."

"They don't always use lights," Nate said.

"The Five-O announces 'emselves," Adam said. "If they don't say nothin', we can know for sure."

Both cars came to a stop. A car door closed around the corner, followed by another. The engines purred. Boots thumped on the pavement. They didn't speak, nor did they enter the building.

Rodman swallowed a steady breath. "If they're not police, who are they?"

The three of us slid our way toward the back.

Rodman jumped when his sweater snagged against the cement siding. "I can't do this," he said in a shaky voice just below a whisper. "I'm not running."

"Good as dead if you don't," Adam breathed, scanning our surroundings in search of a way out.

Nate wiped his forehead with his ripped sleeve. "Maybe we can talk to them. Maybe they'll let us leave."

We rounded the back corner. The boots thumped closer. Iron rods and hedges were before us, the back of the service building behind us. Footsteps made their way on either side.

"CJ!" Nate hissed hastily, "Now would be a good time for a plan."

Suddenly, a car alarm went off somewhere in the parking lot.

The boots came to a stop. The glow of the hazards blinked around the side of the building.

The alarm went silent, followed by the starting of the engine.

The two pursuers rushed toward the sound.

I looked at Nate. He shrugged his shoulders. We turned to Adam, who was holding a key fob.

"Quick!" I said. "Now's our chance."

We ran to the opposite side of the parking area, following the hedges to the back of the garages. Incoherent voices came from somewhere to our right.

Adam hit the key fob again, sounding the panic alarm. "They won't hear us. We gotta hop the fence."

"No way!" Nate replied.

"Come on, Rodman," I groaned. "You can't be serious right now."

"First, I help you break into your brother's house. Now this? I'm on camera; I've trespassed. You're turning me into a criminal!"

"We don't have time for this!"

Bushes ruffled next to us. Before we knew it, Adam had already landed on the other side.

"It's easy, my man," he said through the bars, unseen from the hedges.

A flashlight loomed around the corner of the garage.

"We're running out of time!" I said through gritted teeth.

Tugging on Rodman's sleeve, we booked it across the parking lot, ducking beside a white Tahoe Limousine.

"CJ, this is insane." Panic glazed his voice. "I can't do this."

"We don't have a choice, Rodman. You have to trust me."

He wasn't convinced.

I'd never seen Nate so afraid. His confidence when it came to conversation and studies was a mirage, seemingly stifled by real-life action.

I put a hand on his shoulder as we squatted. "My father's rules grounded me in situations like this. His golden rule was Rule 18." My father's voice echoed with mine. "Leave while you still can."

Whether the words held any meaning to Nate, or perhaps he saw no other choice, he gave a trembling nod in reply.

Our pursuers were inaudible due to the car alarm percussioning throughout the parking lot, but I knew time thinned with every passing second.

Overhead lights suddenly came to life. There were no shadows to hide among any longer.

"I'm going to cause a distraction. Climb the fence when the coast is clear."

Darting to the other side of the lot in the open, I surveyed the perimeter. It didn't take long for me to find the two predators—one searching around the blaring car, the other charging from my right. They both wore suits and ties, the same attire of a Private Rides chauffeur.

"Over here," the man chasing me shouted.

I sprinted through the open lane, diving in between two limos. Both pursuers attempted to corner me, one in the rear, one blocking my escape. From years of experience, my preemptive knowledge came to life. I popped the top off my water bottle, spraying the remainder in the face of the man blocking my exit. Instinctively, he jumped back against the trunk of the car as the splash soaked his face and suit, allowing me to pass through unscathed.

The other pushed past him, continuing to chase, but I had built up space between the two of us. I ducked and weaved between vehicles, hoping he wouldn't shoot. When I was confident he was far enough away, I made a beeline for my escape and jumped at the iron bars. Like a squirrel on the trunk of a tree, I scaled the fencing.

Reaching the top, a hand clutched my pant leg. I dropped a few inches, my grip slipping from the iron. My torso slapped against the bars, but I managed to hold on. I kicked back, managing to strike him in the teeth. The grimy fingers of my pursuer slid down my shin, only taking a shoe for his prize.

From the buzz of adrenaline, the thought of how I'd land was not at the forefront. I rolled onto the hedges on the other side and plummeted to the earth. While I did not find comfort in the stabbing branches, the hedges cushioned my descent.

Scratches covered my arms and neck. A trickle of blood crawled down my cheek.

Should've worn long sleeves.

There was no time to itch at the burning scrapes; I got to my feet and continued around the perimeter to the front.

Reaching the corner of the fencing, Nate and Adam were both in their cars on the side of the road.

I jumped in with Adam, who kicked it into high gear (skipping third, of course).

He gave me a grin. "Been years since we've done that together."

Victory dwarfed the panic within me. I couldn't help but laugh as I looked down at my muddy sock, the only casualty being my shoe.

CHAPTER 47
HOLES IN A SWEATER

We pulled into the gravel lot behind The Pizza Bar, Nate directly on our tail. Adam yipped as he exited the car and plopped onto the trunk, his nonexistent shocks becoming known with the Corolla's excessive bounce.

"Man, I haven't felt so alive in ages."

I slapped Adam on the arm, a smug smile forming on one side of my lips.

Nate stepped out of his Mustang and stood across from me. The flickering Bentley corner lamp loomed from behind, his distraught expression barely visible amidst the shadows.

I guess my shoe wasn't the only casualty.

"You alright, Nate?"

His eyes stayed fixed on his sleeve as he passed his fingers through the holes. "This was my father's sweater, one of his favorites, actually."

I dug a small divot into the gravel with my shoe. "Sorry about that...," I managed. "I—"

"It's not your fault. Not like any of us expected to be jumped." He raised his gaze to match mine. "Although, I wish I never found myself in that position. If we didn't trespass—"

"If we didn't trespass, we woulda neva known 'bout this other CJ," Adam snapped. "Don't be makin' my lil' bro guilty for that. We didn't sign up for this."

Rodman turned to him, a gleam of hostility sliding through his teeth. "But it is something you signed up for—both of you. Not me! I've lived a clean life. No cop chases, no trespassing, no stealing—actions will follow you to the grave. You should know that first-hand."

I took a step forward. "What did you say?"

Tension filled the air like humidity.

Rodman scratched at his bristled chin. "Listen, CJ, you're my best friend. I'm always here for you. But I can't be breaking the law for you. It's not in me to do this type of stuff. I mean, look at this." He grabbed the sleeve of his sweater, stretching it toward me. "We're lucky they were holes in a sweater and not holes in one of our chests."

"They had no Glocks," Adam butted in. "If they did, they woulda shot."

"Or they wanted us alive," I suggested.

"Do you hear what you two are saying? You think if they had guns or not makes a difference here?"

I swallowed the growing lump in my throat. "You said you believed me. You said you'd always be there for me."

"And I am."

"Then what are you saying?"

He rolled up his geo-patterned sleeves to hide the imperfections. "Decisions in life are binary; you either do it or you don't. And I can't be doing this! It's not in my DNA."

"Then what is?" My shaky voice rose. "What role do you play if you're not willing to stand on the front lines?"

"That's the problem, CJ." He shook his head, a frown beginning to arch across his face. "This survival mindset you have is like fight or flight, and it's going to get someone killed. I can't blame you for thinking this way. The things you've been through—I can't imagine! But it's molded you into this persona of perceiving life like you must always take action. From the very beginning I told you not to be hasty with your decisions, to be watchful. I mean, you said you were shot at for crying out loud! We're lucky they didn't decide to shoot us at Private Rides. Can't you see that what you're doing will only lead to your demise?"

"For Pete's sake! Listen to yourself," I exploded, waving my hands. "Look at you, all high and mighty, too perfect to see beyond your own pride. *You're* the detective, Rodman. *You're* the one that's been helping me put these pieces together. What? Did you think you could sit back with your spiels of advice and hope that things worked out?"

He lowered his voice, the anger dismissing from his tone. "No, I'm saying I think we're taking this too far. How low are you willing to stoop to access the truth? Is it worth breaking the law? Is it worth dying for?"

I folded my arms. "Unlike you, I'm not afraid to die."

"You're missing the point, CJ. I'm not worried about how I die; I'm worried about how I live."

"Well, I won't have a life to live if I sit around speculating the best course of action."

A sigh, long and exaggerated, produced from his lips. Nate looked drained, hunched over, and tired, only a shell of his former self.

"I don't want to argue, CJ. I just don't want you to forget what you have, only to be reminded once it's gone."

Nate returned to his car and drove away.

I stared at the ground, at my muddy sock, thinking of the shoe I lost—something replaceable.

Adam hopped off his car and put a hand on my shoulder. "Don't let 'em getcha down, man. I'll fight or flee with you any day."

I gave him a lousy smirk. "No, Rodman's right. It was careless to chase after a clue like this. I nearly died three times in a matter of a few hours." My smile fell as the thoughts struck deeper. "I was so worried about you guys being involved at first; I don't know what I'd do if something happened or if it was my fault someone died... again."

Adam grabbed my other shoulder. Insistence poured from his hazel eyes. "Now you listen, CJ. Pop's blood is not on your hands. You betta get that straight and outta your head. I hated Pops, and I think you did too." His voice hitched as tears pricked the corners of his eyes. "But I couldn't stop lovin' him anyhow, 'cause in his own twisted way, I know he loved us. There's no doubtin' that fact! If it weren't for you, I prolly would've joined him."

Tears freely wet my face.

"And your gang, Sophia and Rodman? They solid. I can feel it, man. They ain't in this just for the ride; they really care about you. He's only mad 'cause of that."

"But what if—"

"Nah, man. No *but*s. Stop thinkin' that way. You can't let fear stop someone's sacrifice. It didn't stop me from takin' your hand."

He was right, and I knew it, but acknowledging the truth didn't make it any easier to swallow.

CHAPTER 48
THE DRAFTING TABLE

I knocked on the door labeled with a copper *E* in a defeated manner, bobbing my change of sneakers from home against each other. I shouldn't have come here. I looked over my shoulder, feeling watched, alone in the solitary hallway.

This was a mistake.

Starting back the way I came, the door opened.

"CJ?" Sophia peeked out the door, dressed in an oatmeal-colored robe. "What are you doing here? What happened to your face?"

I had forgotten about the scratch on my cheek, reaching up and touching the dry blood with my hand.

Before I answered, she turned to the side and held the door open to me. "Come in, come in."

I hesitated, looking behind me again. Seeing no one, I took the risk.

This was my fourth time at Sophia's apartment, but it felt new every time I came. The curtains, which were previously blue, were sage green; an old painting (new to me) of a hand holding up the iconic Time magazine cover "Is God Dead?" replaced the Eiffel Tower painting from last time; she moved the couch from the corner to the center of the room; animal knickknacks lined the mantle above the TV. The last time I was here, Nate teased that she redecorates more frequently than Nepal celebrates holidays.

I wouldn't usually take notice of small changes (I didn't even notice when Mr. Zhang had new flooring installed in the barroom), but with Sophia, it was the little details I appreciated most.

"Did you paint this?" I asked, walking toward the picture above her workspace.

The drafting table was tiled with cropped photos and cut-out blocks of texts. Sophia had told me she now worked on the layout design team for the magazine company. I had never seen her work in action before. I assumed most people did this electronically.

"No," she called from the kitchen. "Nate bought it awhile back from some nearby shop. I didn't know the dusty thing was anything special until he explained. Although, I don't really remember the significance."

And he says he's not religious.

I sat on the couch and helped myself to an unopened water on a corner table, then hung my hat on the lamp shade.

She appeared from the kitchen with a wet paper towel and a bottle of peroxide, tightly wrapping herself in her fuzzy robe as she sat next to me. Typical, over-exaggerating Sophia probably thought I was in a knife fight.

If only she knew I was shot at.

"Sorry if I woke you," I said, staring at the blank TV screen ahead of us.

"You didn't," she replied, dabbing my cheek with the paper towel.

I winced at the sting of peroxide. While the medical assistance was completely redundant, I desired her comforting touch.

After a long pause, I asked, "Can you do me a favor and pick up Mr. Zhang from the hospital?"

"When?"

"Friday."

"Why can't you?"

"Cindy Lou's in the shop," I lied.

"Sure."

"Thanks."

And the silence returned.

Traffic from fifty feet below came to life when a light turned green. The walls rumbled as a large truck passed. Sophia always complained that silence never lasted more than sixty seconds since moving to Center Street Lofts, but living a block from the office was a virtue she wasn't willing to pass up.

"Is anyone else coming?" she asked, tending to the wounds, now turning to the scratches on my neck and arms.

I shook my head, avoiding her gaze.

"Nate told me you guys were going to Private Rides."

I nodded.

She stopped dabbing my neck, cupping my chin between her thumb and index finger. "Talk to me, CJ."

I sighed, finally looking into her violet eyes, galaxies glittering ever so softly in the dim lamp lighting, contrasting with her pale skin.

"Rodman thinks being a criminal is in my," I used air quotes as I finished, "DNA."

Sophia pursed her lips to one side, grief reverberating from each crease above her eyebrows. "He said that?"

I faced the TV. "Something like that. I don't know. We almost got caught trespassing, and—" I crossed my arms, unsure of what to say. "I didn't want him to be there."

Sophia moved closer, putting a hand on my arm. "I'm sure he was there because he's concerned about you."

"But being there made him upset with me. If he wasn't there, then—"

"Then he would have worried from home, like me." She tilted her head to the side, her dark brown hair falling from her shoulder. "Whether Nate was there or not wouldn't change his concern. It doesn't change mine."

I dropped my head, looking down at my empty hands, wondering what I had left to offer toward finding my blackmailer if I couldn't use experience to my advantage.

"You know Nate; he won't hold it against you," she encouraged, beginning to dab my scrapes again. "Did you at least learn anything useful?"

I sat back, half my body disappearing into the fluffy cushions. "Actually, it was Rodman that got the information."

I guess it was good he was there after all.

"There's another person with the same name as me."

Sophia's hand paused in mid-air. "You mean there's another CJ?"

"He goes by Cris, according to who we talked to. But yeah, there's another Crispin Jiles."

"That's crazy. What are the odds?"

She placed the paper towel and peroxide on the opposite corner table, sitting against the arm of the couch and putting her feet up between us. Part of me wished she didn't create the distance, but I kept the thought to myself.

"Do you have a picture of him?" Sophia asked.

"No, but we know what he looks like. It's the guy from the diner."

"Wait, is this guy who they're actually after, or do we still think he's the blackmailer?"

I stared up at the ceiling. "Still trying to figure that part out."

She squinted, deep in thought. "It seems weird that you'd have the same name. Do you think it's fake?"

"I don't think so. The woman we spoke to made it sound like she's known Cris for a while."

"That can't be a coincidence, right?"

I tapped my thumb against the water bottle in hand. "Problem is that even if he is the real target, that doesn't get me any closer to who the blackmailer is, and it doesn't answer why this Cris guy's been following me."

"Leading us back to believing Cris *is* the one sending notes?" she said more like a question than a statement.

"I know Rodman thinks there has to be two guys, but wouldn't I have seen this other guy?"

"Unless Cris has someone working with him. Maybe someone that knows about your past."

"Or this is all some twisted game to him. I just don't know why. There has to be a reason he actually thinks I stole from him in the first place."

"What if this other CJ thinks you stole his name or something?"

I considered this, nodding my head. "Now that I think about it, that could be plausible." I sat up in my seat. "He's a driver for Private Rides, and where his information was supposed to be, mine was! It had my address and picture!"

"Holy crap! So someone else *is* involved!"

"I don't know. Either Cris swapped it himself for some reason, or someone else did," I replied. "Maybe the blackmailer, but I don't know if that even makes sense."

"Extortionist," she corrected.

"Whatever." I stood from my seat and paced the floor. "But you've got me thinking—let's say Cris *does* think I stole his identity."

"Okay," Sophia said, drawing out the last syllable. "But then why the notes?"

"From his perspective, if he thinks I stole his name, maybe he thinks I stole more than just his name. Maybe he was supposed to receive these cases or something."

"That still doesn't answer why he'd go through all this trouble in the first place," Sophia said. "And it means that someone else is making you out to look like someone you're not."

I stopped to think about this, but no answer came to mind.

"I don't know, CJ. Now that you've said your information was swapped at Private Rides, it doesn't add up to me. Doesn't it seem more realistic that the other Crispin is supposed to be receiving these notes?"

"But that doesn't make sense either. All these phrases in the notes point at *my* past. And Cris has been following me. None of it adds up. He must know something." I walked a circle around the couch, tapping the water bottle against my thigh. "It's too much of a coincidence for him to start coming around at the same time I'm receiving the notes. He must be the blackmailer. I'm convinced of it. I just don't know why! I feel like I'm starting to make things up at this point. If only I could talk to him."

After another lap, I sat back down, thwarted again. Every new idea, every new clue, only seemed to lead to another obstacle.

"What if there is a way?" Sophia asked.

"What do you mean?"

"You know he's stalking you, right? Maybe you can talk to him."

"I don't follow."

"Plant a note, CJ."

Electron and neutron fireworks collided in my brain as the idea became clear.

I shot back up from my seat in excitement. "I could leave him a message!"

Sophia stood next to me, joining in the excitement. "Where will you do it?"

"I'm not sure yet, but I'll figure that out." I pulled Sophia into a hug. "You're a genius, Sophia! I could ki—"

I stopped myself, frozen in our embrace, before pulling away. I caught her gaze in mine, lost in her brilliant, amethyst eyes.

"I, uh..." Clearing my throat, I looked back to the blank screen, wishing to hide beyond the black glass. "I should go."

I slung my hat off the lampshade and rushed past her. She grabbed my hand before I made it to the door. Her touch sent ebbing heatwaves up my arm. I kept my head low, too afraid to know her expression, to know her thoughts on what almost left my lips.

"Be careful," she whispered. "And don't you dare do this alone."

I gave a single nod before leaving.

Closing the door behind me, I stopped. Before taking another step, something small caught my eye, something yellow.

A fifth sticky note was placed over the peephole of Sophia's apartment door.

My watch is ticking,
Crispin Jiles.
You have 48 hours.
I hope you still have your bike.
It's a long walk to the Eastside.

CHAPTER 49
NOT YOUR MINX

The elevator came and went. I didn't get in; I didn't know where to go. Instead, I sat against the wall, only five doors down from the apartment with the copper *E*.

Bringing danger closer to Sophia was the last thing I wanted to do. I didn't know if she was safer with me keeping watch or hiding out somewhere else.

Sleeping at The Pizza Bar went against the cleaners' policy (my excuse so I didn't have to be there alone). I didn't fancy my chances of waking Nate for a second time that night. Ironically, when I went to call Adam, this time *my* phone was dead. Taxis were far and in between at this hour, so going to the hospital was out of the equation, too.

And there was no way I would go back to Sophia's door, not after how I left things.

I pulled out the sticky notes, the first now a scrunched wad of paper that attempted to roll away as I emptied my pocket. I flattened them on the brown carpeted floor in a column, reading each slowly in the dingy lighting, trying to do as

Rodman had told me and consider if any had personal connections.

The first note hinted at my past of larceny.

The second one mentioned visiting a friend, who turned out to be Adam.

But did strike one allude to anything? I never played Little League.

The third note said someone would get hurt.

Mr. Zhang must have been targeted. But 'pedestrian'... 'empty-handed'... why use those words?

Notes four and five were the most confusing. How could someone know about the bikes, about my father, about any of this?

Cris tried to kill me. But how does he know me?

Perhaps Cris overheard conversations, but I found it hard to believe he would climb the fire escape without being noticed.

I fell asleep, but I wasn't out that long. And wouldn't Jamal have seen him?

Everything pointed to the past, but the past was seemingly an exhausted dead end. I couldn't think of anyone from my childhood who'd know these things, let alone share the same name as me.

Cases, my father, my bike, the strikes—what did it all mean?

Thinking about how the past and present connected turned only toward one person—Adam.

Nate warned me the night of the fire. I considered his involvement, but never in that way.

The more I thought about it, the more I hated it. It seemed obvious. Adam would know every detail, mess with my emotions, and use it all against me.

But he wouldn't; we just started getting closer, right?

I thought back to the night I broke into his house.

Was he home? Was he watching, waiting for the right moment to appear, planting a note, and acting ignorant the entire time?

I couldn't decide if it made sense or answered every question. My thoughts were a tangle of wires, too jumbled to find each end.

Maybe Adam told Cris... or maybe Adam and Cris are working together... or maybe Adam is—

The elevator next to me dinged. Like a bowling ball, the sound crashed into every thought and scattered the pins.

I pulled in the notes and forced them back into my pocket before a heavyset guard exited the elevator, his sagging stomach keeking below his shirt. He didn't turn down the hallway; he turned directly toward me and sighed as if he were disappointed to find me there but expected me nonetheless.

"Let's go, bub. Time to leave," he said, pointing over his shoulder. "No loitering." His lower lip overlapped the upper as he spoke.

"I live here," I lied hesitantly. "Forgot my key."

"No, you don't," he responded hoarsely, pulling at the front of his security vest with both hands. "I saw you on the cams."

I looked up to find the all-seeing-eye hanging from the ceiling.

"Let's go!" he demanded.

It was obvious this wasn't the first time he had to kick someone out.

Standing to my feet, I stooped into the elevator. The husky man followed behind me, his boots clapping on the elevator's vinyl, keys chattering on his belt.

He fat-fingered the buttons for floors three and two accidentally. The bald reflection in the elevator mirror shook its head in disdain.

"They should really make these bigger," he muttered, thumbing the correct button.

We waited awkwardly as the elevator whined, making pit stops at floors three and two.

"You said you saw me on the camera?" I asked as the doors shut the third time.

"Yup," he answered, his bottom lip making a popping sound as it enveloped the top.

"Did you see anyone else?"

"Nope," he popped again.

The doors opened, and he waited for me to go.

"Maybe you saw someone within the last hour or so?"

He didn't answer.

"I'm just worried about my friend. I thought someone came to her door."

"Did they break in?"

I sheepishly scratched the back of my head. "No."

Irritation seeped from his eyes. "Then I don't care."

"I could pay—" I reached into my pocket, only to realize I left my wallet with Cindy Lou.

"I'm not your minx," he growled, taking a step toward me.

His hand shot up from his side. I jumped back, cowering with my arms raised, expecting a blow to the face. With a loud slap, he stopped the elevator doors from closing.

"Now beat it!"

Shoulders hunched, I scurried out of the elevator toward the exit. Before leaving, I noticed a pad of Post-it notes and CSL-branded pens on the front counter. I scribbled *Meet Me!* on the top note, peeling it from the pile as I left.

I scanned the street in front of Center Street Lofts. The sidewalk was empty, but I didn't have to see to know he—or they—or *someone*—was watching me.

The very city I once called home had become the present nightmare, a sinister snare intertwined with my dark past. At the nearest corner, I slapped my note to the traffic pole, leaving it in the hands of fate.

Goosebumps prickled my exposed arms, tingling the scratches from earlier. I tightly pressed them to my sides, hands shielded from the night's chill in my pocket, the five yellow messages clenched in my trembling, bloody-knuckled fist.

My feet led an aimless wander, but my thoughts pointed to one specific name. The poignant theory was crippling. After our last conversation, I didn't want to think this way, but the plausible consideration answered most of my questions.

Who else but Adam knows these things?

CHAPTER 50

AUDITORY HALLUCINATIONS

A hand slithered up my leg, touched my thigh, and fell into my pocket. It was not my own.

Auditory hallucinations of ambulance sirens blared in my ears. My eyes shot open, and I rocketed upright from the park bench I slept upon.

An old man with a braided beard that swept the ground jumped back, looking more like his ancestral primate from the way he stood. One dirt-smeared fist pressed against the ground; his other hand shielded his face, ready to defend himself. In his grasp was a yellow note.

I put up my own hands, stumbling off the bench as my limbs came to their senses. Like a bobblehead, I sized up the hermit.

Post-it notes scattered along the ground. I picked them up one at a time, not daring to peel my eyes from the man, snatching the one from his hand last before backing away.

I didn't remember coming to the bus stop. I planned to walk until the sunrise, feeling safest on the move. I tried to recall the last thing I did, but the entire night after leaving Center Street Lofts was a blur.

I made my way to the nearby Wendy's, knowing they had a free charging station inside. I must have looked like a mess (or smelled like one), because everyone in line gawked at me smugly. I pushed through the morning breakfast rush toward the jumbled wires hanging above a counter.

I reached into my right pocket to find it empty.

"You've got to be freaking kidding me," I grumbled. "No car, no wallet, no phone. Just great."

The hermit would be gone by the time I went back. I dropped onto the stool, throwing my rooster-embroidered hat at the spaghetti of wires coming from the wall. Running my hands through my hair, I contemplated what left I could do.

Back when my father was alive, we would sometimes go days with little to nothing to eat, biking for miles, only resting for a few hours at a time. How did I do it back then? How did my father, who was nearly fifty? Any youthful vigor or fortune on our side back then had seemed to be long gone. Even my adrenaline only ran on fumes.

I sat in the red-and-white fast-food chain, watching with glazed eyes as customers came and went. I noticed the sideways glances from workers fulfilling orders, probably waiting for me to leave.

Watch me get kicked for loitering again.

Nodding in and out of reality, my sleepless body rocked back and forth as a woman walked by and dropped a breakfast sandwich on the table. Her stride never wavered; her eyes never met mine. I didn't catch her face. I wasn't quick enough to realize what happened, too busy staring down at the friendly gesture. Before I could thank her, she was out the door.

Maybe Rodman's God does exist.

But if He did, His satire was cynical.

I unwrapped the breakfast sandwich and found a yellow note attached to the bottom of the wax paper. It was the very sticky note I had stuck to the traffic pole the night before.

Meet Me! was scribbled in my own writing; *FIND ME!* was written beneath it.

Flipping the note over, I read:

BLUE RIDGE LODGE
TODAY NOON
ALONE

BRING BRIEFCASE
ROOM 312

"Briefcase?" I whispered.

I turned around in my seat to find a small, silver briefcase left by my chair.

CHAPTER 51
A FLIGHT ATTENDANT

I crossed to Mulberry Street with a crowd of suits and ties, skirts and blouses. The sun scorched the morning.

Sophia's words thundered with each step of men and women on the crosswalk. "Don't you dare do this alone."

I hadn't given much thought to what I wrote, nor was I giving the response from my blackmailer the amount of consideration it deserved. Calling Rodman was the obvious thing to do, but I didn't have spare change (I'm not sure I even know how to use a payphone), and I wasn't going to ask to borrow someone's cell.

The note was clear—I was to go alone. I thought it'd be better to keep my friends out of it anyway. If anyone got hurt, better me than them.

The briefcase was the most confusing part of it all. I assumed this was a case referred to in the notes, but why give it to me? I tried opening it, but there was a combination lock.

The metal case was about the size of one of Mr. Zhang's twelve-inch pies and maybe the weight of a half-gallon of milk. I tried to guess what it carried, but it could literally be anything (and shaking it didn't give any clues).

I considered taking it, but that only painted a larger target on my back. I was innocent! I didn't need to give a reason that *actually* made me guilty.

I also thought a bomb could be inside. Likely or not, it scared me enough to follow instructions. Getting rid of it as soon as possible was in my best interest, only adding more to the reason why I shouldn't tell anyone I had it.

A clock tower rang from above, notifying the city it was eleven o'clock. I was early, but it was better than being late. There was no time to waste. Caution to the wind, I marched onward.

As I reached Blue Ridge Lodge, I thought back to the last time I was there. I picked up a woman.

A flight attendant, I think.

I remembered where she stood near the blue awning at the front door, pressing the wrinkles from her skirt before approaching with a nervous smile.

Wonder if she'd still get in with me looking like this.

I hadn't realized how ridiculous I appeared until I used the bathroom at Wendy's. My hair was a grease-fest hiding beneath my hat; my plain, gray shirt had stains of dirt and sweat; my arms and neck had cat-like scratches that had turned bright pink since the night before; and the cut under my eye looked worse than it felt.

I looked like an addict with a habit of itching, worse than Adam.

Adam...

My violent thoughts siphoned through my brain as his name came to mind.

Would it be Adam that I find on the other side of the hotel door? Was he truly a mastermind, manipulatively using the notes and my emotions to get close to me, to get back at me, to seek revenge on me? Did he really forgive me for abandoning him that night and for the last three years?

Part of me wanted to turn back, unsure if I could handle finding my brother waiting for me, but I couldn't live without knowing the truth.

The other thought was that the woman who left the sandwich was the blackmailer. She seemed to be a messenger, paid to make the dropoff, but how could I be sure? For all I knew, a messenger left every note.

Each probable scenario twisted through my mind, more confusing than a traffic circle with a dozen entries and exit points. With an oncoming headache from the strenuous theories, I pushed them away and proceeded toward the building.

The lodge was more of an old-fashioned hotel, not the rural cabin-stay in the mountains some may expect from the name. The outside was ordinary, a basic small-scale hotel, but I crossed into a new world as I pushed through the revolving doors.

Entering the lobby, the smell of chicory and cinnamon filled my nose. A bellman and receptionist, both dressed in royal blue with gold cufflinks and tie bars, greeted me. I nodded, avoiding eye contact as I headed directly for the steps.

A well-polished gold plaque on the wall proudly announced its 100th year in business. The antique floorboards and cabin-like fireplace seating area gave the illusion that it was cold outside. Hot chocolate and coffee stations welcomed travelers by the front desk. I wouldn't think a place like this was fitting for Wilkes City, especially when temperatures rarely dipped below forty, even during the coldest months, but if they're still in business, what did I know?

With the briefcase in hand, I climbed the old stairs two at a time, making my way to the second floor, then the third. Rustic barnwood doors and bright blue runners lined the hallways. I kept the brim of my hat pulled low with every person I passed, not wanting to attract attention. I cursed under my breath after doing this. I had nothing to hide. Looking guilty only worked against me.

I reached the end of the left hallway, standing before the last room next to the fire exit. I held out the sticky note, looking back and forth between the note and the numbers branded into the wood: *312*.

Pocketing the note, I took a deep breath. The moment had finally arrived. Every question's answer was on the other side of this door.

Please, I thought, *please, don't be Adam.*

I gave the door a knock; it clicked as it opened.

A familiar face sneered back at me. "Hello, CJ."

CHAPTER 52
DISGUSTING HABIT

He flicked a piece of skin torn from his lips, a hideous, red simper beginning to form.

He held no gun; he held no knife. I could run if I wanted.

As if someone flashed their high beams at me, warnings of danger coruscated in my mind.

"Don't you dare do this alone," she had said.

Sorry, Soph.

I accepted his gesture and entered the room.

A six-point buck mounted the wall above a mantle and fake fireplace display. Every fabric was beige—the carpet, bedspread, lampshade, and blinds. Everything else was a hunter's fantasy. Criss-crossed revolvers hung next to the window; antlers made up the bedside lamp; a portrait of cowboys and Indians hung above the bed frame.

On the bed lay an identical briefcase to the one in my hand.

"Please, take a seat," Cris said as he shut the door. "I'm glad you received my message."

I stood in the center of the room, malfunctioning, debating, wondering if I was in danger or if I was safe. The man who shot at me the night before had welcomed me into a room alone with him. I was thankful not to see Adam, not that this completely precluded him from the equation, but I couldn't decide if this was any better.

Why did I come here? Why didn't I turn around?

I considered clocking him with the briefcase. He wouldn't expect it, and it'd give me time to tie him up. But what good would that do?

Do I just figure it out from there?

Father's words begged to differ.

Rule 10: Dialogue is the predecessor to violence.

"No need for alarm," Cris said, reading my mind. He licked his bloody lower lip before continuing. "I'm not going to hurt you."

Everything wanted to come out at once. I was the opposite of my brother. Adam seemed to vomit every word that came to mind. For me, I wanted to ask so many questions that they clogged in the back of my throat.

Is he the blackmailer? Does he think I stole his name? Is he in kahoots with Adam?

He sat in a chair next to the bathroom. "Well? Are you going to sit?"

I turned to the bed.

He wouldn't have me sit next to the briefcase if he really wanted to hurt me, right?

I slowly sat on the edge, doing my best to hold my composure.

I studied him, trying to consider my words. Tufts of black hair fell from his head like the leaves of a tomato, some longer than others, revealing portions of his eyebrows and forehead. His face was clean-shaven except for his chin, which had scraggly bits of fuzz. His nose was long and skinny, like my father's. He was young—no older than thirty-five, I guessed.

We played chicken, neither of us breaking the silence, seeing who would be the first to bite.

His eyes were dark brown, inkier than the common color most have, reminding me of old oil, the same shade as his shoes. His pants were too short, revealing his white socks, one pulled high, the other riding low.

He wore a belt with a large buckle that screamed, "I mean business." His tucked-in button-down was white with thin blue lines, making him appear leaner when he stood, but it did little to hide the beer gut when he sat.

"Well?" he said, being the first to break.

"Why am I here?" I replied, holding my fortitude.

"Ha!" he spat (literally). "What kind of question is that?"

I raised an eyebrow.

"You reached out first, did you not?" He crossed his legs, placing his hands over his knee as if this were a formal gathering.

I bit the inside of my cheek, evaluating every option, proceeding with caution. I couldn't reveal too much; I couldn't provide too little.

Rule 4: Bring value to the light; keep knowledge in the dark.

"When did you begin following me?"

Cris smiled, squinting his eyes, taking his time before answering.

"From the time the incident occurred."

It's a trap.

Of course, he wanted to see if I'd ask what he referred to, but revealing my ignorance would be my downfall.

"Why me?"

"Well, because we have the same name, of course! Who better to choose than an identical twin? Seeing your name in the log made it a simple copy and paste. I wasn't sure you'd find the clue or not."

So, he swapped the names.

"And the briefcases," I began, glancing at the one behind me, "you've had them this whole time?"

"Oh! Have you been looking for them?" he laughed.

My head pounded. None of this made sense.

"But why give one to me?"

He picked at the corner of his lip as he spoke, never forgetting to smile. "The final test to see if I could trust you."

A quiet tick filled the void. I noticed a gold watch glimmering under his cuffed sleeve.

The last note mentioned a watch.

"Why do you need my trust?"

He pricked another shred of skin from his lip. He pulled a tube of lip balm from his breast pocket and applied it generously.

Disgusting habit, I thought.

Nate once ranted about a book he had read. "Kinesics is the study of nonverbal communication." If only I remembered the cues and their meaning.

"Because I've decided to show grace." He dropped the lip balm back into his pocket and wiped the corners of his lips with his index finger and thumb. "You've proven to be of more value than I originally deduced. I've been watching you for weeks, slowly making myself known, testing your resilience."

"You call shooting at me a test?"

"And you passed."

I couldn't trust him; I wouldn't trust him.

"Did you really think I was trying to kill you, that I couldn't have killed you in an easier way by now?" he continued. "It wouldn't be the first time I've taken a life."

I tightened my grip around the briefcase hanging before me.

A murderer and a thief; subtle threat— am I supposed to be afraid?

"I could have killed you when I first tracked you down. You've done well to disguise your identity."

He paused to gloat in his research. A devilish smirk slid across his face.

"I could have killed you when you became aware of my presence. I had the chance to kill your friend, your brother, the old man, and your pretty little girlfriend. I had plenty of chances to do as I pleased but decided to spare you the heartache."

I grimaced at the mention of my friends. "What's your point?"

"I'm giving you a chance, Crispin. Or should I call you CJ? I never used the nickname myself. I always thought it sounded childish, but I think I heard your albino girlfriend call you that. Remind me, what was her name?" He paused to wait for a reaction. "Sophia?"

I stood from my seat, raising the briefcase to slug him. "Don't you dare let her name leave your bloody lips!"

In an instant, Cris pulled a silver pistol from his back, nonchalantly tipping back in his chair.

"Hey, calm down, CJ," he laughed. "No need to escalate things. We were just beginning to bond."

Huffs of hot air left my mouth.

He motioned toward the bed and I sat back down, dropping the briefcase between my feet.

"What do you want from me?" I said, trying to hide the whiny desperation in my voice.

"Ah, finally, a question of significance. *Why?* Isn't that what we all want to know?" He stood from his seat, flapping his arms with every question, swinging the silver gun above his head before slapping it back down against his leg. "Why is there illness? Why do we die? Why do bad things happen to good people? Why do the rich get richer and the poor continue to suffer? Why! Why! Why!"

He stepped toward me, the gun pointed only an inch from my chest, enunciating every word slowly. "Why not kill you now and be done with it all? Or maybe this is another test."

My heart rampaged in my chest. The gun moved closer, now pressed firmly against my sternum, the only divide being the thin cotton of my v-neck. I clenched at my pants, balling my hands into fists. My eyes nearly crossed as I stared at the silver barrel. I forced them shut, swallowing the saliva forming in my mouth.

That bullet was meant for you, said the demonic voice of my father from the depths of my mind.

One second passed, then two, then three. I counted them each from the ticks on his wrist.

Cris laughed with mockery, pulling the gun away. "But that's no fun! I won't kill you, CJ. As long as you behave, of course."

My breathing became sporadic as life was spared. Part of me wished he had done it, wished he ended it now. But no, I couldn't die without understanding his ways.

His snake-like tongue passed across his lower lip.

"I've waited a long time for this moment. Whether you were dead or alive, I couldn't say, but I knew the day would come when we'd be face-to-face."

He leaned past me, keeping the pistol pointed in my direction as he grabbed the briefcase from the bed.

"Look at that," he mused. "Two Crispin Jileses, both with a silver briefcase in hand. Don't you want to know what they hold?"

"I don't care what they hold," I replied, kicking over the briefcase between my feet. "I want my life back."

"Oh, is that true?" he asked, returning the gun to his back. "Are you sure you couldn't be tempted with a life anew?"

I studied him, trying to look past the bloody delusion spewed from his lips.

"What do you mean?"

"Each case holds fifty thousand dollars."

"Prove it."

He put in the combination on his own and held it open to me. The old presidents gave me a wink, held in place by their own, individual sleeves.

"I know where we can get more," he said as he closed the lid.

"I don't get it." I shook my head. "After everything I've been through, why give me one? Why make an empty promise?"

"I've been watching you, CJ. Have you forgotten? I know you are no ordinary man. The stripped records, breaking laws unscathed, not turning to the police—you have experience that can come in handy."

So he is my blackmailer.

My mouth twitched. "Get to the point."

"The briefcases are dropped off at a warehouse in town, but it's a two-man operation. I can get us in; you can get us out."

"Why would I help you?"

Cris let out a sadistic laugh. "Did you not hear me, CJ? If I wanted you dead, you would be. Don't make me change my mind."

We locked eyes again before he headed for the door.

"You have a choice. Leave, try to make a run for it, let this escapade continue, or you can wait here and have a better chance of survival with me. But know that if you leave, I won't hesitate to end our little game the next time we meet."

"Where are you going?"

"To settle my bill at the front desk, of course," he said with a barbarous grin. "Your decision will be made known when I return."

Before he exited, I stood from the edge of the bed. "Wait!"

He stopped halfway into the hall.

"Why should I believe you?"

"Consider me leaving you with one of the briefcases as a token of my trust." Cris turned, giving me a final bloody smirk. "Think about it. We can be thick as thieves."

CHAPTER 53
SIREN'S MELODY

I ran to the door as soon as it shut, putting an eye to the peephole. He was gone.

I took off my hat and paced the floor, bending the brim between my hands. The clock was against me; each second that passed was another second closer to Cris Jiles's return.

Would I be here when he came back? Would I hide in the bathroom and mug him when he came? Would I cower in the coat closet and wait for his reaction when he believed me to be gone?

I stared down at the briefcase on the floor; it glared back at me, its intentions as insidious as a siren's melody.

I put it on the bed, fiddling with the combination to no avail. Whispering curses under my breath, I continued my pacing.

I should leave. He's lying to me. There's no warehouse. I should run while I have a fighting chance.

But looking back at the briefcase, my thoughts changed. It was sad I even considered partnering with a murderer, but maybe that was a lie, too. For all I knew, it was all a facade.

I replayed the conversation in my head, trying to remember his exact words.

He confessed to swapping our names. He made it sound like he planned for me to figure that out. Was the blackmailing a test of wits? But how did he know about my past?

It didn't make sense.

But what if he is telling the truth? One last hit, one last job. What if he'd spare me?

I thought back to my days of larceny. Pops was the mentor; Adam and I were his grunts. I always saw myself as the more tactical of the group. After my father died, I orchestrated each run, and Adam followed my lead. But how much of that did Cris know, and how much of his spiel was lying through his teeth?

Unless he is working with Adam. Maybe Adam met him through work. Maybe the warehouse is real.

Depending on the job, it might be easy. I've had plenty of close calls, none of which resulted in being caught. One could chalk it up as dumb luck, but I believed I had a knack for outwitting my enemies (ironic under the circumstances). Even the jobs where we went in blind ended with success, or at the very least, a clean escape.

All except for one.

I picked up the briefcase and headed for the door. I stopped at the door handle and went back to the bed. I turned for the door but found myself unmoving, only to return to the bed all over again.

It was a constant cycle, both physically and mentally. I was drained of certainty, running on empty.

I tried to consider what my friends would say or what they would do in such a situation.

Sophia would never find herself here. She would have never entered in the first place, and if she did, she'd run at the first opportunity.

Nate was tricky. He was smarter than me and would find the positives in both options, considering how to outplay each. But then again, he was a Nervous Nellie in the face of danger and made it pretty clear he never wanted to break the law. Ultimately, he'd choose to leave as well.

Adam would obviously take the bait, but was that because he was involved or simply because of his love for the chase and greed for the green?

But what do I do? What do I, CJ, think is the right option?

I looked down at the briefcase in hand.

Fifty thousand Gs. More than I've ever seen all at once.

I thought of Mr. Zhang. He could have died because of me.

I thought of my father. He *did* die because of me.

Giving it one final thought, I knew where I stood.

"Leave while you still can," I whispered.

Tossing the briefcase onto the bed, I fastened my hat to my head and turned my back. I was no longer a thief.

I'll deal with this blackmailer another way.

Proud of my decision, I went to leave.

But I was too late.

The moment I twisted the handle, the door shoved open from the other side. Thrown off-kilter, I had no time to react. Before I knew what was happening, someone tackled me to the floor.

CHAPTER 54

WRITHED AND WRIGGLED

My feet left the ground. My body slammed the floor. My neck snapped back, and my head hit hard.

A forearm pressed against my face, the black coat sleeve blocking my field of view. The sweet scent of leather hit my nostrils. With a kick from my attacker, the door slammed shut.

The room spun, the ceiling and floor swapping places. I tried to look beyond the sleeve but could only see to my left with my face forced into the carpet. The weight of the intruder's chest was against my own. I attempted to speak, but oxygen was limited. All that came out was a few gasping breaths.

"I warned what would happen if you tried to run, Crispin Jiles."

The words came in an echo. The baritone voice was familiar, but it wasn't Cris. I felt like I was under water, pressure building on all sides, black splotches crowding my vision.

I writhed and wriggled, my hat rolling off in the process, but the attacker held me down expertly—boots locked around my legs, one arm across my face, a hand braced for balance.

Hot air spilled across my temple. "Where were you going?"

"I... can't... bre—"

Pushing off the floor, the death grip loosened just enough to let me speak.

I turned to meet the intruder's eyes. As the blots of ink faded, he came into view. I couldn't believe who I saw.

I've had thousands of Uber passengers, only recalling a few if they were repeats or made an outstanding impression. I rarely remembered them outside the environment of my back seats. But this face was unforgettable. The grizzled beard, the baseball cap, the shades—it was the bouncer from The Jigger.

No emotion eclipsed his face. He was stoic in composure, even under the circumstances—almost calm, as if in his comfort zone.

"Remember me?"

CHAPTER 55
POWDER

Pinned to the floor, I stared up in confusion.

"Joe?"

It was the only thing I managed to say.

Is he in on this too?!

He stood to his feet, adjusting his leather jacket. Like the last time we met, he wore all black.

"Get up," he commanded. "Where's the other case?"

I stood next to him, hanging my head and leaning on my knees. "What other case?"

Turning on me, he pushed me upright against the wall, both hands on my biceps. While his actions were intense, his voice remained low.

"Unless you want to end up like this deer, I suggest you start talking."

"Okay, okay," I answered hastily. "Cris took it."

"Cris who?"

"Cris Jiles."

He pushed me against the wall harder, lifting my feet from the floor, making us the same height.

"Don't lie to me," Joe grunted, the faintest annoyance entering his voice.

"I swear!" I squeaked, trying to raise my hands in innocence. "There's another Crispin Jiles."

He raised an eyebrow.

"He told me to meet here," I continued.

"Why?"

"Because I left a note!"

I watched my reflection in his wayfarer sunglasses.

"You have to believe me! You've got the wrong guy."

"I'm never wrong," he answered.

"Come on, man, I swear!"

"Then where is he?"

His grip tightened around my arms; they were small within his grasp.

"He said he was checking out or something."

Dropping me, I collapsed, unprepared for impact. I rubbed my arm, struggling to stand.

"Where were you going?" he asked again as I stood.

"I wasn't going anywhere," I cried.

Panic flooded my senses. I attempted to refer to Father's Rules, but nothing came to mind. I was small in Joe's presence. His rock-solid build was as threatening as Cris's gun to my head.

"You have to believe me," I pleaded.

His muscles tensed. A tsk escaped beneath his beard. "Give me a reason to believe you."

I reached into my pocket and pulled out the sticky notes. "Look! He told me to meet him here."

He analyzed the notes, scrutinizing the last one.

"How do I know it's not the other way around?" he asked gruffly. "Are you waiting for someone?"

"No, I swear!"

Joe checked his watch, the very watch he bought from me two weeks before. "It's not even noon yet."

My eyes grew wide. "I was early!"

He stepped to the briefcase, turning the number dials above the clasp. My chest tightened with every click.

The briefcase didn't hold the bills I expected. Instead, it held small plastic bags, each filled with a white powder that I hadn't seen in years.

CHAPTER 56
GUNS AT THE READY

I was twenty years old when I first saw cocaine. Adam had come home one morning from a party. I was about to head out the door for my landscaping gig when I saw him snorting the dust off the counter. I questioned him then, but he retaliated by saying I was *no fun* and needed to *learn to live*.

"Is someone meeting you to buy it?" Joe asked, pulling me from my memory, speaking in his calm, monotone voice.

"What? No! I couldn't open it."

"Why steal it if you couldn't get inside?"

"I told you it's not me!" I folded my arms. "Besides, if I wanted it open, I could have smashed it with a hammer."

He closed the case and turned back to me, removing his glasses to reveal his small, blue eyes. "Where's the other case?"

I snatched my hat from the ground. "How many times are you going to ask me this?"

"As many times as it takes," he said plainly.

My confidence charged the longer the conversation dragged. The lack of emotion in his voice and repeated questions got under my skin.

"Listen, Joe... if that even is your name—"

"Why wouldn't it be?"

"It's probably a—forget it! There's another Crispin Jiles, and he's been stalking me."

I paused as the realization struck me. *He freaking framed me!*

"I tried to meet with him, and then he must have run off or something. And how are you factored into this? Were they your cases or something?"

"Something like that," he said.

"Let me guess. For your *freelance* work?"

"Yes."

"Wait, so *you're* the one that's been blackmailing me?"

He didn't reply.

"But he was following me... and Mr. Zhang... and the shooting... This doesn't make any sense."

Again, he remained silent.

I threw my hands in the air. "You know what? Forget it, man. Take your case. I never wanted it in the first place."

He put a hand on my shoulder, his grip stopping me in my tracks.

"Did I say you can leave?"

Nervousness returned in an instant. I swallowed a lump in my throat, facing the door that seemed impossible to exit.

"Describe him."

His words caught me off guard. I faced him, meeting his eyes (although I preferred the sunglasses at this point).

I rattled off a list of descriptions. "Blood-scabbed lips, caucasian, white dress shirt, gold watch, black hair." I paused before remembering another detail. "He has a black Beetle. Maybe it's in the parking lot."

He walked me by the shoulder to the window.

We didn't see a black Beetle, but what we did see was a surprise to us both.

Police cars skirted to a halt one after another in the parking lot. Men in uniforms charged the building, guns at the ready.

"What the heck?" I muttered.

Joe returned his sunglasses to his face. "We've been conned."

CHAPTER 57
A SLAVE TO THE GAME

Joe grabbed the briefcase by the handle and threw it my way. It nearly knocked the air out of me as I caught it in the stomach.

"What do you want me to do with this?"

"Follow me if you don't want to get caught."

"Caught?" I choked on the word. "But I'm innocent."

"You won't be if you're found with that."

"You mean they're looking for *me*?"

I tossed the suitcase back on the bed; danger was imminent with it in my possession.

He peered through the peephole as he spoke. "Why else would half-a-dozen squad cars be at a hotel unless they were tipped that a murderer was in?"

"Murderer!?"

"Grab the case," he said with his back to me. "We're leaving."

"I'll leave it behind," I argued, using the bedsheet to feverishly rub off my prints.

"You're only more guilty leaving it here." He opened the door and peered back at me. "Follow me, or meet your fate."

How did this happen? My racing mind made it difficult to process. Had Cris Jiles lied to me? Was there even a warehouse? Was Joe lying? How was my past connected to any of this?

Joe scanned the hall before leaving. "Let's go."

He ducked out the door, turning to the right to take the fire exit. Not wanting to be found with a briefcase full of drugs (or suffer the wrath of Joe if I left it behind), I followed with the case in hand.

The moment the fire exit shut behind me, voices and running came from the hallway. We started down the switchback stairs, but heard multiple hustling feet coming from below. Joe spun around and rushed past me to ascend instead.

I followed him to the fourth floor. Joe looked out the door's window, scanning the hallway. He put a finger to his mouth as we waited.

Officers' boots and orders reverberated through the stairwell. We waited and listened for another few seconds, then Joe silently opened the door.

A couple, hand-in-hand, had exited their room, walking down the hall. Joe caught their room door before it swung shut. We slipped inside without a sound.

"We're just going to wait here?" I asked. "It's only a matter of time. What if they lock the building down?"

"They can't lock a building down under suspicion," he said in his monotone way. "You need a disguise."

"What?"

"You've been profiled. Check the suitcase."

Next to the bed was an unzipped suitcase on the floor. I flipped it open and grabbed the first hoodie on top, a large pink pullover with Disney princesses standing arm-in-arm with the famous castle in the back.

"That will work. Anything else in there?"

I tossed clothes over my shoulder. It reminded me of the times my father, brother, and I used to steal from Salvation Army bins.

At the bottom of the suitcase, I found an electric Wahl beard trimmer in a plastic bag.

"Lucky find. Ever buzz your own head?"

I touched the back of my ear. The last time I had my head shaved was nearly a decade ago. The more problematic things became, the more my life melded with the days of old.

I was a slave to the game. Innocent or not, the Devil had returned, put a shackle on my ankle, and considered me his own. I thought I had escaped the previous life I lived, but the more I tried to run, the more it became my reality.

"You need help?"

Joe lifted his hat, showing his experience.

"No."

I headed for the bathroom and removed my hat, taking one last look at myself so as to not forget the appearance of innocence.

CHAPTER 58

SACRED GROUNDS

"I like your sweater," said a young girl as I walked out the lobby doors. "Rapunzel's my favorite."

After shaving my head and flushing the hairy evidence down the toilet (Joe's idea), I threw on the princess hoodie, and we emptied a bookbag, shoving the briefcase inside.

"They might be looking for it," Joe explained when we left.

Interestingly, Joe left money and a post-it note on the bed, apologizing for taking the couple's bag and hoodie. During years of thieving activities, not once did I apologize for the things I had stolen.

My steps were stiff as we passed the policeman. Most of them were on the third floor, some stationed by the stairs, others checking the rooms. More uniformed men stood post in the lobby. Two of them made hot chocolate and coffee while others actually did their job watching everyone who entered and exited.

No one (other than the little girl) gave more than a glance or nod in our direction.

Once outside, I put down my hood, only to quickly return it. The quarter-inch buzzing guard didn't leave enough hair to protect my scalp from the midday sun.

Joe unlocked a blue Honda Civic and told me to get in.

"Where are we going?" I asked, throwing the backpack at my feet.

"I'm surprised you don't know," he replied.

"How am I supposed to know?"

"I gave you my address."

I thought back to our first conversation. "New Binghams?"

"1256."

Twenty minutes later, we were on the other side of town, in what was known as the historic district. We parked on the old Main Street, where Wilkes City began before the rest of the city outgrew the sacred grounds they left untouched.

The streets were narrow, some laid with decaying cobblestone and others with newly-replaced brick. Old decorative signs and posters with fancy calligraphy scattered the windows of shops and restaurants. Every building was brick, and most were connected, the only divide being the different splashes of paint. Exotic colors such as mint green, fuschia, and mustard made the decrepit buildings deceivingly vibrant and full of life.

The area had become more of a tourist attraction than anything else. Most of the apartments were Airbnbs. Nate, Sophia, and I walked the streets during a festival the year prior, but since then, the only time I came this way was for the occasional Uber pickups and drop-offs.

With Joe as my escort, we walked down an alley with murals of flowers along the walls and doors. He unlocked the door painted with daisies.

Upon entering, I met a one-room apartment with a kitchenette on the left wall of the living room and a bathroom door on the right. The high ceilings and steampunk pipes lining the corners made it feel larger than it was.

Joe pointed to the black couch, where I dropped the backpack and sat down. He grabbed a folding chair from the corner and, straddling it backward, sat across from me, folding his arms across the backrest.

He grabbed a paper cup from the coffee table between us, the logo reminiscent of the boba café I dropped him off at two weeks before.

His eyes were shielded by his shades, but I could only assume he was staring into my own. Silence crawled on as he sipped his drink, his face and posture never changing.

"Buzz cut suits you," he finally said.

"What?"

Feeling self-conscious, I tore off the hoodie and pulled my rooster-embroidered hat from the bookbag.

"By the way," he continued, "this watch you gave me is fake."

"I know."

"As long as you know," he replied. He sipped his drink again, then pointed at the cup. "They have good chai."

"What's this have to do with anything?"

"Nothing," he replied in his low tone.

"Why am I here?"

"I'm wondering the same thing, Crispin."

"I go by CJ."

"I thought you went by Tom."

I bit the inside of my cheek. "Okay, so I lied about my name."

"Why?"

"You were sniffing me out like a cop."

"But you didn't lie about anything else?"

"No."

"Hm." He sipped his chai. "Interesting."

"How did you know I lied?"

"I read your file at Private Rides."

I leaned forward. "Well, it was the wrong file because I never worked there, and if you weren't such a lousy blackmailer, you would've known that."

"Lousy?" He repeated with little expression.

"How could Cris Jiles also be following me this whole time and you never notice?"

"Who said I didn't notice?"

"Even worse!" I shook my head. "You knew and never suspected him?"

"I kept my focus where it was necessary and chose to intervene once I saw you with the briefcase."

I kicked the coffee table. "Well, you should've intervened earlier."

Joe remained calm, unmoved by my action. "My patience paid off."

"Tell that to my landlord," I said. "If you would have just met with me, he wouldn't be in the hospital."

"I did meet with you."

"When?"

"Two weeks ago I rode in your Uber."

"But you never mentioned your accusations then!"

"Because you lied to me," he said plainly. "But since you're ready to be honest, my name's Barry, not Joe."

"Why did you lie?" I asked arrogantly.

"Because you did," he said. "But like you, it was the only lie I told."

I crossed my arms. "So what now?"

"You still have my notes?"

I pulled the six notes from my pocket and dropped them on the coffee table. Barry took a moment to put them side-by-side. Seeing all six next to each other, I realized the difference in writing between the notes. The first five were the same thin, chicken-scratch penmanship. The final note that was a reply to my own was bold and in caps.

"So you were my blackmailer this whole time?"

Barry scanned the sticky notes. "Extortionist, technically."

"How is it possible that you've been following me as long as Cris and I never once noticed you?"

"I guess I'm not that lousy after all."

"You didn't do anything else?"

"Other than searching your apartment, no."

"Actually, you *trashed* my apartment!"

"I like to be thorough."

I rolled my eyes. "Why sticky notes? We could've had this sorted by now."

"To force a mistake."

"Well I didn't make any!"

"Mhm," he hummed, examining the last note.

"How did you know these things about me?"

"You told me, CJ."

I thought back to our conversation in the car, recognizing how much I gave.

"I also dropped clues to who I was. I guess you didn't catch on."

"Like what?"

He pointed to one note. "I asked you about baseball." He pointed to another. "You almost hit someone on the crosswalk."

A bit pedestrian, I thought. *How did I miss that?*

"Can we skip to the part where you explain what's really going on here?"

He placed his chai back on the table, speaking in his emotionless voice.

"Thursday, August 10th, 2:00 AM, a man was shot and killed in a Private Rides vehicle."

I should have known that was connected.

"The deceased was in possession of two briefcases—one held cocaine; the other held money. The murderer was believed to be the driver. I was asked to find him and recollect the cases. Process of elimination, everything led to you."

"So the briefcases aren't yours?"

"No."

"Who hired you?"

"Why does that matter?"

I tried to answer, but nothing came to mind. Instead, I said, "Why was there money and drugs in suitcases?"

He cocked an eyebrow. "Do I really need to answer that?"

"So what? The guy was a dealer or something? And Cris shot and robbed him?"

"Your words, not mine."

Like a flash of lightning, a name thundered through my mind.

"George Morris," I whispered.

Barry didn't respond.

"My brother told me," I continued, now speaking in a level voice. "Morris has some kind of drug subscription operation. Private Rides is in on it?"

He showed no expression. "I don't ask questions I don't need answers to."

"But why hire someone to find a thief? It can't be worth that much to someone like George Morris."

Again, Barry remained silent.

"Well, this proves I'm innocent, right?"

"Perhaps."

"What do you mean *perhaps*? He literally baited me to a hotel room, had the police called on me, and I had to freaking shave my head to get out. And yet you still don't believe me?"

"I didn't say that," he answered flatly.

"This is ridiculous." I stood from my seat. "You know I'm innocent. There's no other possible solution. I already gave you information on the other Crispin Jiles, and now that you know he has the same name, he shouldn't be too hard to find. Just leave me out of this."

Barry also stood, towering at least six inches over me. "If you try to leave, you'll force my hand."

"Force your hand to do what?"

He removed his sunglasses, revealing his steel blue eyes. "I haven't missed a deadline in years." His words came out as icy as his gaze. "I will not be missing this one."

"And what's that supposed to mean?"

He reached down and finished the last of his chai, letting out a sigh.

"I'm expected to apprehend a Crispin Jiles by tomorrow. I won't go empty-handed. Dead or alive, I will deliver a Crispin Jiles."

Chapter 59
Anonymous Tip Line

He zip-tied my hands and feet to the folding chair, not once, but twice.

I stood no chance against Barry. Fleeing physical altercations all my life made my combat skills nonexistent. I could possibly outrun him on the streets, but in close proximity, I was no better than a car without a battery.

He was *kind* enough to switch on the WCN channel before he left.

"Let me know if you learn anything useful," he had said.

Sure, meathead, after the way you coerced me into coming to your Airbnb and zip-tied me to this chair, I'd be happy to help you.

I leaned forward and pulled at the zip ties. The chair creaked as I shifted my weight, but the bands held strong. I pulled repeatedly, each time harder than the last, holding my breath with each attempt. The chair rocked on its front legs. Heat rose through my face; blood vessels threatened to pop. It was no use.

I tried moving my arms up and down to slice through the plastic ties. The only thing with wear and tear was my wrists, raw from torturous friction.

He had been gone for five hours, according to the news channel, with the time in the bottom right corner.

Night approached; the sunlight left the window. Hunger settled in my lower abdomen from going without sustenance since the Wendy's breakfast sandwich that morning.

Thoughts of every decision I made bedeviled my mind. I was so focused on searching for someone from the past and chasing the wrong guy, that I ended up falling into the hands of my worst enemy.

Or is Cris Jiles my worst enemy?

If Cris *did* in fact frame me for the crime he committed, then he couldn't have been telling the truth about working together. He lied about what was in the briefcase he gave me; I couldn't trust anything else he said.

Barry said the police were there for me. Cris must have called them. But how do I know I can trust him?

If it wasn't for Barry, I would be incarcerated. Maybe that would have been better than this—or worse. There was no way the police would buy my story.

Although, I was unsure if Barry bought it either.

News anchor Haley Thompson suspended my thoughts when a picture of my face appeared on the screen.

"Recognize this face? Wilkes City Police need you to be on the lookout for this man. Crispin Jiles—age 27 and height of five-eight—is wanted in connection with a shooting that occurred early morning on August 10th at the corner of Eagle and Cornwallis Street, and with new information brought to the surface by an anonymous tip, is potentially facing a felony charge of arson and assault. As of now, police have said he is a person of serious interest in their investigations and that he is possibly dangerous. Little is known about Mr. Jiles's whereabouts, but he was last seen at Blue Ridge Lodge in a gray v-neck and black hat. Wilkes City Police Department has asked for anyone with information on Mr. Jiles to call the Shooting Investigation Group or the Wilkes City Police Department Anonymous Tip Line at—"

"Arson?" I mocked. "They can't even get their facts straight."

I wondered if the police questioned Nate and Sophia.

What would they say? Would they tell about the blackmail?

The police probably questioned Mr. Zhang as well. However, Mr. Zhang hated everything that had to do with the government and believed anyone with a badge was racist, so I doubted he would say much.

I thought of my little friends and what they must think of me. I'd probably never be allowed to play street hockey with them again.

My mind then shifted to my brother.

If Barry is my blackmailer and Cris Jiles is the thief, Adam must be innocent.

While I was relieved by the thought, others shut down my ease in an instant. Adam was potentially in the same amount of danger as myself. If the police found him, who knows what else they'd find.

Or worse... If George Morris thinks I'm behind this and finds out Adam's my brother, he might beat the police to him. Would he be tortured? Killed?

Thinking about Adam made me desperate. I couldn't stay here. He definitely didn't watch the news; I doubted he knew I was missing. I had to warn him, tell him to run. He was good at that. We lived in the shadows for half our lives. If I gave him a head start, at least he'd have a better chance at survival.

"Please," I begged out loud, groping in agony, my wrists chafing from exertion.

In desperate endeavors, I tried again, now pulling and rubbing at the same time, but I leaned too far and fell on my face.

Shockwaves of pain spread through my skull. I rolled on my side, the chair attached like a shell. With one hand and leg suspended in the air, they ached from blood flowing out from them. Pins and needles filled my fingertips and toes.

"Help!" I screamed, hoping someone from a neighboring apartment would hear.

I listened, but no one yelled back. The only reply was a passing car's engine and a faint meow from somewhere outside.

I tried to move but made little progress. I searched the room for something of value that would alleviate my situation. The only thing nearby was the coffee table with the paper cup.

I had reached my end. I deliberately banged my head against the floor as tears flooded my vision.

I was a wanted murderer.

Adam was in danger.

Bound to a chair, the blackmailer planned to ship me off to the drug lord of Wilkes City.

Do I deserve this? Adam doesn't! He can't get caught in the crossfire like Pops.

Like a whisper fluttering through the air, Rodman's voice came to my ear. "You're still alive for a reason."

If Barry didn't kill me, there was at least an ounce of mercy within him (or a reason). My only hope was that his mercy wouldn't run dry before I was out of time.

CHAPTER 60

ONLY BELIEVE WHAT YOU SEE

Barry stood my chair upright when he returned. He cut my ties as well.

"You hungry?" he asked, a splash of kindness seeping from the words. "I assume you like pizza from where you live."

I caressed my wrists, feeling childlike as I nodded.

He dropped a pizza box on the coffee table and handed me a water bottle. He removed his jacket, revealing a tattoo on his bicep that read *esse quam videri* in cursive (whatever that means).

"You gonna sit?" He gestured to the cushion next to him.

It was an ironic moment, both uncomfortable and laughable.

Never thought I'd be sharing a pie with my blackmailer—or, my extortionist.

I sat next to him, keeping my distance as I hesitantly ate a slice.

"I brought you clothes, too," he said between chews.

"From my apartment?"

He tossed me a plastic bag of clean laundry.

"Shower while you're at it. Towels are in the cabinet."

He watched the TV as he spoke. I looked at him blankly, confused by the kind gesture (or maybe I smelled that bad). I considered making a run for the door, only to realize he inserted a travel lock between the door and frame, its release mechanism padlocked. I didn't have the energy anyway.

"Don't think about leaving," he said, following my gaze. "You won't get far."

After a long, overdue shower, I returned to find a sleeping bag laid out on the floor next to the pullout bed from the couch.

"You got me a sleeping bag?"

"No," Barry replied, taking off his hat and putting it on his knee. "It's mine, but I'm letting you borrow it."

"Why are you being nice to me all of a sudden?"

Seated on the bed, he caressed his beard and continued to watch the news, a rerun of the same announcement about me from earlier.

"I don't believe in cruelty."

"Threatening me with sticky notes is pretty cruel," I mumbled.

I stood next to the couch, taking a sip from my water bottle.

"So you believe me?"

"Believe what?"

"That I had nothing to do with this."

His antifreeze eyes seemed tired as they stared into mine. He was older than me, at least ten years, if not more. He had indented wrinkles around his cheeks and forehead. His shaved head and burly beard were beginning to gray.

"Karma has a funny way of catching up with you. We are all guilty of something."

I twisted the water bottle in my hand the same way guilt twisted the knife in my stomach.

"But you know I'm innocent of stealing the briefcase, right?"

He turned back to the TV. "Yes."

"So I can leave?"

He hesitated before answering. "No."

"Why not?"

"I don't fail, CJ."

"What's that supposed to mean?"

His voice remained toneless, almost robotic. "I don't have a choice at this point."

"But you do!" I pleaded. "You can go after the other Cris Jiles. You tracked me down no problem."

"It's not that simple finding a man hiding amongst half a million people," he said. "I was given two weeks. Tomorrow is my deadline."

"And what if you miss your deadline?"

"Not an option."

I paced the floor, throwing my hands in the air. "So, what? You're telling me I'm already dead."

He didn't reply.

"No." I shook my head with a lip-curling grimace. "No. This is not it. This is not how it ends."

"It would have been wise to tell me it wasn't you two weeks ago."

"How was I supposed to contact you?"

He faced me with a hint of mockery. "Maybe you could have left a note."

I rolled my eyes.

"Why didn't you?" Barry asked.

"Why didn't I *what*?"

"Why didn't you leave a note? It's an obvious decision to make. You knew I was watching."

"For your information, I didn't consider the idea until last night," I snapped. "And if you were such a good private eye, maybe *you* would have found the note instead of Cris. It's your fault my face is plastered all over the news."

"Why only consider the idea last night?"

"I don't know!"

My voice rose with my emotion; his stayed controlled. His composure increasingly made me feel small.

"I know why," he answered grimly.

I stopped pacing, his words catching me off guard.

"Something blocked the idea. Something else was on your mind." He paused, studying my face. "You are a thief, aren't you, CJ?"

I didn't answer. Lightheaded, I sat on the sleeping bag.

He interlocked his fingers on the back of his head, chuckling to himself. "Like I said, karma has a funny way of catching up with you."

"It was a long time ago," I muttered. "It's not who I am anymore."

Barry didn't reply.

I had to try something else. Every minute that passed was another minute closer to my doom.

"So what are you guilty for?"

"Pardon?"

"You heard me," I replied, neither of us looking at one another. "You said everyone's guilty."

He didn't answer right away, the only voice coming from the TV.

When I was about to ask again, he said, "I missed a deadline."

"What happened?"

I struck a chord, and for once, it was obvious from his facial expression. A mix of anger in his distant eyes veiled a buried memory.

While Barry's complexion filled with sorrow, he still spoke in his surly way. "I have no need to confess my sins."

"What are you afraid of? I'll be dead tomorrow, anyway. Who better to confide in?"

It hit me that I was speaking about death so flippantly, as if the door had already closed.

"Unlike you, I don't feel obligated to give personal information to strangers."

I rolled my eyes at the sideways comment. "Not really strangers anymore with everything you know about me."

"Why are you so sure you'll be dead?"

I laughed. "What kind of question is that? Do you not know who you're working for? Everyone knows George Morris is bad news."

Man, now I sound like Rodman and Adam.

"He's running a drug ring," I added. "Doesn't that say enough?"

"We shouldn't stereotype actions," he replied. "Your brother wouldn't murder, right?"

"How do you know anything about my brother?"

"I've been watching you, CJ."

"But you thought he was my friend."

"For a time, yes."

"Were you there that night?"

"Do you only believe what you see?"

"Could you stop with the games? Why are you asking if I think I'll die?"

"Just a simple question," he answered.

I took a sip of my water. "It bothers you, doesn't it?"

Again, he gave no answer.

"You know you're handing me over like a sheep for slaughter when I'm innocent."

He kept his attention on the TV.

"Why do you work for George Morris anyway?" I pressed.

"I never said I did."

"Oh, cut the crap!"

He remained silent. I stood in front of the pull-out bed to block his view.

"Come on, Barry. There has to be an ounce of morality inside of you. You can't do this!"

"Have a better option?"

I put myself in his shoes, considering what I would do.

"We could both run," I suggested.

Barry got a kick out of my idea, a titter leaving his lips. "And how did that work out for you?"

"Until you came around, it was working fine."

"But unlike myself, others wouldn't think twice about putting a bullet in our heads. Running is not an option."

"So you don't kill?"

"Only if necessary."

I walked the room, leaving the front of the screen. "Okay, so what if I help you finish the job?"

"Why would I allow you to do that?" he replied. "From my point of view, the job's already finished."

"By turning me in? What if I tell Morris I'm the wrong guy?"

"Your word against mine; I'm willing to take that risk."

I downed the last of my water bottle, crinkling it back and forth.

Think! Think! Think!

"You're still alive for a reason," echoed Rodman.

I dropped the water on the floor as the epiphany struck me like a car going seventy.

"Why didn't you turn me in?" I asked with my back to Barry.

He didn't reply.

"Where were you the whole time I was tied up?"

Still, no reply came, but the answer was clear, hopefulness erupting from within.

"The job isn't finished, is it?"

I turned around. He looked back at me with a slight squint in his eye.

"You need the other briefcase. You searched for it and couldn't find it, and you know you'll need me to help get it."

Barry turned off the TV and folded his arms. "Let's say I do need the other briefcase. Why would I need you?"

"It's obvious, isn't it?" I sat in the folding chair, bending forward with full investment to the conversation. "Cris framed me, but he hasn't run, right? He's been watching me. He must want me caught to make it look like I'm guilty. It's the only way his plan of getting away Scot-free works."

"Meaning?"

"Meaning he's still here in Wilkes City somewhere, and you know it. He wouldn't leave if I'm alive. You would have handed me over by now if you thought otherwise. He's waiting for the news to say I'm dead or arrested with a case full of drugs. That must be why he left it in my possession. He just wants the money."

"Except," Barry started, lowering his head and pointing a finger, "there's no way of knowing where the other case is."

"But there is!" I said. "I've seen it myself. He showed me the money. And if his plan is to run after I'm dealt with, he'll have it with him."

"That's to say we can find him," Barry replied.

"We won't have to look far."

"Why is that?"

"He'll come right to us. He hasn't killed me all this time because he wants to frame me. His master plan involves me going down guilty so he can get away without a trace."

Barry ran a hand over his bristled, graying hair. "And you think I need your help to find him?"

Father's wisdom returned in my moment of confidence.

Rule 13: Weakness is your greatest weapon.

"You're running out of time, Barry," I said, matching his deadpan voice. "You said it yourself—you won't kill me. You can't live with the idea of handing over an innocent man. To top it off, you're a case short."

Barry didn't reply.

"Face it. Without me, you'll miss another deadline."

He looked toward the door. "How do I know you won't screw me the moment I let you walk?"

Leaning back in my seat, a soft chuckle slipped from my lips. I wiped away a tear that escaped my eyes as my father's body materialized at my feet, but for the first time in my life, no guilt came from his presence.

"You were right. I am a thief. I've done things that aren't worth forgiving—things that have led to losing people I love." I clutched my hands tightly together. "But I'm not that person anymore. I want this over just as much as you do."

I then faced Barry.

"Without Cris Jiles, I'm a wanted man back on the run."

He took a deep breath. "Alright, CJ, I'm all ears. What do you propose we do?"

I gave a thin smile. "Ever been to Center Street Mall?"

CHAPTER 61
SAYING GOODBYE

Hidden by the brim of our hats, Barry and I sat in the parking lot, watching every car that passed. We were burning daylight, and not a single familiar car had arrived.

"You sure they'll be here?" Barry asked, looking at his watch.

"I'm sure," I replied.

Another half hour waned by, and Barry's patience became fickle.

"Might have a better chance driving around the places you've seen him."

"Come on, Barry. Shouldn't you be used to sitting around watching people and waiting for things to happen?"

"I'm more of a man of action when time is of the essence." He checked the time again. "If things go south—"

"I know."

Barry had made it clear what would happen if my plan didn't work. My heart sank at the thought, but this plan was all I had left.

Overcast clouds bent their wings across the sky. We cracked our windows to let the slight breeze tumble through the Civic. It was going to rain. I could smell it. The asphalt bled; its pores filled the air with dirt and dust.

In the corner of my eye, Barry checked his watch for a third time.

"Deadlines are pretty important to you, huh?"

He scowled. "Time is something that shouldn't be wasted."

"And it won't be if things go as planned."

"*If*, being the operative word here."

I turned to him, his eyes hidden by his sunglasses.

"Why are you always stone faced?"

"How do you mean?"

I shrugged my shoulders. "You're always so serious."

"In my line of work, I don't believe I should conduct myself any other way."

I gazed back at the entrance of the parking lot.

"So... you were late for something before?"

"No," he replied in a low voice, pausing before continuing. "Many things."

"And now you don't like being late anymore?"

"Yes."

"Did you miss something important?"

Barry put the car in reverse.

"Woah! Sorry, I'll stop asking questions."

He didn't reply; instead, he backed up.

"Come on, man. A few more minutes. They'll show."

"We don't have time for this," he retorted.

I pleaded as he reversed from the parking spot when a yellow Mustang came up the drive.

"There!" I pointed. "That's them!"

Nate pulled up to the curb of the hospital, which looked more like a prison with its gray walls and security guards posted at either side of the doors. The one waved at Sophia as she went inside.

Purposefully parked over the line to keep two spaces open, Barry pulled out, and just as we hoped, Rodman pulled into one of the spots. We rounded the opposite row of vehicles and pulled in next to him. Rodman dropped his window a quarter of the way when he saw me.

"How're you holding up?"

"Probably better than you by the looks of it," replied the silhouette, only his forehead showing above the dark tint. "You being followed?"

"Can't be sure, but playing it safe."

"Is that why you're meeting me like this?"

I nodded.

"We've been worried about you. Didn't think of calling?"

"I don't have your number memorized, and my phone was stolen."

"Ironic." Hostility rippled in his voice.

"The police talk to you?" I asked.

"Not yet, but I'm sure they will sooner or later." He sighed. "I hope this isn't your way of saying goodbye and asking me to lie about where you're headed."

"It's not."

"Then what is this?"

I looked to Barry, then back at Nate. "I need your help. One last time."

He ran a hand over his loose, yarny hair. "I don't know, CJ."

His head dropped in disappointment. I lost his trust.

"You were right, you know," I said. "The notes were talking about briefcases."

He stayed looking forward.

"And you were right about another thing—the stalker isn't my blackmailer."

"Extortionist," Barry mumbled under his breath from behind.

"And I should've taken your advice. I was chasing my problems without a plan. I was being reckless and I..." My voice dropped as the words fumbled out of my mouth. "I was selfish. I'm sorry."

His silhouette remained still.

"But I'm ready to end it. All of it. I have a plan."

He finally turned to me, lowering his window a little more for me to see his eyes.

"I'm guessing you have new information?"

I sat back in my seat. "Rodman, meet Barry."

Barry leaned over the steering wheel. Nate nodded in Barry's direction, giving him a flat smile. "And Barry is...?"

"My blackmailer."

CHAPTER 62

HEADS SWIVELIN'

Upon arrival, Adam greeted me by throwing his arm around my neck.

"My man! How we doin', CJ?"

"Thanks for agreeing to come. You weren't followed?"

"Don't believe so," Rodman replied, closing the daisy-painted door behind him. "Adam parked by the café like you told us to. We cut through Fisher Park, went through the art studio and out the back, then turned up New Binghams."

"I doubt nobody could follow the ways we took," Adam said, rubbing his hands together. "How'd you come up with sucha round'bout path?"

"Always prepared," Barry answered in monotone.

"And Sophia?" I asked.

"She took the day off to be with Mr. Zhang," Nate said. "He was adamant that he open the bar tonight, but Sophia said she'll try to get him to rest."

"Hopefully he listens to her."

Barry removed his jacket and tossed it onto the couch.

"To be, rather than to seem," Nate said.

"What?" I asked.

He pointed to Barry's bicep. "*Esse quam videri*—it's Latin. The origin is from Cicero, a philosopher right before the time of Christ. He wrote a lot about ethical behavior. It's quite fascinating, both Jesus and Cicero were killed by the Romans after standing in opposition to their power."

"You're religious?" Barry asked.

Nate shrugged his shoulders. "I consider myself more of an *areligious theist*."

Like any of us even know what that means.

"So you're the schema behind the notes, huh?" Adam said to Barry. "Man, you had our heads swivelin'."

"You tracked CJ from the Private Rides info?" Nate asked.

"Yes."

"Ha!" Adam laughed. "You were bamboozled like the rest of us."

"I suppose I was."

A stark contrast became prominent between Adam's enthusiasm and Barry's maturity.

"So what's the plan?" Nate asked, rolling up the sleeves of his quarter-zip sweater.

I looked at each of them. "It all began with a note; it will all end the same."

I gave them the details of the day prior and what Barry and I discussed the night before, handing them each a matching note.

"So basically what you sayin' is," Adam began, "we leave a note for him, lure him in, and Barry swoops in from behind?"

"Yup."

"Dang! I was hopin' I get to meet this guy."

"Doesn't he have a gun?" Nate asked.

"Yeah, but Barry will be watching the whole time. He'll have him before Cris is even near me."

"Why we not just grabbin' him when he finds one of these?" Adam held up his sticky note.

"Controlled environment," Barry replied. "We only have one shot at this."

"And we don't know where he is," I added. "If we leave notes at different places, we can cover more ground."

"Are you sure about this?" Nate asked me.

"Can't be too sure of anything, but he took the last note I left. I think it'll work."

He pulled me aside, keeping his voice low. "I don't like this, CJ. You might get killed. And how do we know we can trust this guy? You literally just met him."

I glanced over my shoulder at Barry, his arms folded across his chest, his graying beard and wayfarer sunglasses hiding his emotions.

"I trust him. I don't know why, but he doesn't seem like the big, scary ogre he puts off."

Adam talked Barry's ear off in the background, probably threatening Barry somehow (or telling one of his stories). Barry remained silent, unperturbed by the comments.

"What if Cris doesn't show?"

"He will. He left me alive at the lodge so he could paint me guilty of his crime. As long as I'm still walking free, his plan's incomplete."

"What if Barry double-crosses you? What if he takes you both?"

"He would've handed me over last night if those were his intentions."

"Clock's ticking," Barry interrupted from behind.

"What if this doesn't work?"

I thought about my agreement with Barry. Rodman would never go along with the plan if he knew.

"It will."

He hesitated, rubbing the stubble on his chin and looking away.

"Besides," I continued, "without Barry, I'm a wanted man." I put my hand on his shoulder. "Do you trust me?"

After a long pause, he matched me, putting his hand on my shoulder, too.

"I trust you."

CHAPTER 63
MUDSLINGING

We took our stations as the afternoon transitioned to evening. Adam stayed at his house; Nate sat at Harper's Diner; Barry drove around downtown; I sat on the fire escape above The Pizza Bar. We all patiently watched the sticky notes we placed, hoping one would be received by Cris Jiles.

I was nervous being home, knowing the risk of the police finding me, but I never updated my license, and the only place with my address on record was Private Rides. My hope was they hadn't gotten that far in their search.

On top of that, I didn't like the idea of Sophia being alone. Someone (other than Mr. Zhang) had to be at The Pizza Bar in case Cris showed up, and it only felt right for that to be me.

I checked the texts on the phone I bought earlier. No one had seen a black Beetle or Cris. Dark clouds snatched away any ray of sunshine left behind. Daylight faded; we were running out of time.

"See anything?" I texted.

Barry and Nate responded in a matter of seconds.

"Nope."

"Nothing."

My brother, as usual, didn't respond.

Freaking Adam probably fell asleep or his phone died.

Nate noticed his absence in the group chat and sent another text a few minutes later.

"Should I go check on your brother?"

I considered saying yes, but I thought Adam's house would be the least likely location to find Cris.

"Don't worry about it," I texted back.

A knock came from inside the apartment as I set my phone beside me. I looked through the window to see Sophia at my bedroom door. She climbed out the window onto the fire escape.

"No luck?"

"Not yet. How's Mr. Zhang?"

She sighed. "Finally lying down. Apparently, the cleaning company that restored the kitchen didn't put everything back the way he wanted it."

I pictured Mr. Zhang muttering Mandarin curses as he organized his pans and utensils.

"Haven't found Marrie?" she asked.

I had forgotten about Marrie. I didn't have a collar on her, so someone could have taken her in. Perhaps she had breathed her last breath somewhere on the streets. I didn't know her age, but by the way she moved, she was no kitten.

Hanging my legs over the edge, I tapped my feet together. "I haven't seen her."

"I hope she's okay."

I rested my chin on the railing. "I hope so, too."

A moment of silence passed (perhaps in reverence for Marrie's life) before Sophia spoke again.

"Are you sure he'll show?"

"I don't know. I would have guessed he'd be seen by now."

She dropped down next to me, crossing her legs and leaning back on her hands. "And if he doesn't?"

I gazed out at the brick apartments lining Bentley Street, unsure of what to say.

The streets were empty. An hour prior, the boys were playing street hockey as per usual on a Friday afternoon. Marcus crushed the boys with ease, as Ronny and Jamal's stand-in player was even worse than Davie. I wanted to join them but couldn't for obvious reasons. It broke my heart as I stared out my apartment window.

Jamal waited expectantly for my car to pull into The Pizza Bar parking lot. I hadn't missed a game in ages. Seeing his little face drop in disappointment only emphasized in my mind how much was on the line.

What kind of role model winds up dead or in prison? What would they think of me? What would their parents think of me?

Sophia's voice pushed the thoughts away.

"Will you run... again?"

Her ghostly skin glowed as shadows settled among us, her freckles darkening around her eyes.

I removed my hat and bent it in my hands. "I think—"

I stopped when she put a hand over her mouth in shock.

"What?"

She reached out, touching my head. "Your hair—it's gone."

Heat rose up my neck. "Oh, yeah, I guess I forgot to tell you. It probably looks dumb."

She gently ran her hand over my head for another second before pulling away.

"No," she smirked. "Buzz cut suits you."

I turned back to the street.

"So?" she said, rolling her hand in the air.

"So what?"

"Will you run?"

"Oh, right." I took a deep breath. "No, I think I'm done running."

Her cheeks rose, not into a full smile, but a face of reassurance. "I'm glad."

I continued watching the parking lot below, scanning the two streets that met at the flickering corner lamp where I left the Post-it note.

"CJ," she started softly, leaning forward and passing her thumb over her painted nails, "I want you to know... whatever happens..."

She stopped, dropping her hands in her lap.

"What is it?"

She raised her head just enough to catch my eyes. Her thin eyebrows rose with innocence. She sheepishly bit her lip, considering her words. Even disguised in shyness, I found her beautiful.

"I want you to know that I—"

My phone buzzed against the metal platform of the fire escape. Adam's name popped up on the screen.

"Sorry."

"No, no, it's okay. Take it."

Putting the phone to my ear, I heard heavy breathing coming from the other end.

"Adam? You good, man?"

"Oh, yes, Adam will be just fine, CJ." A sadistic laugh followed. "That is if you do exactly as you're told."

I looked over at Sophia. Her nervousness matched my own. She leaned closer, placing her ear against the other side of the phone.

"Listen here, you filthy—"

"Oh, save the mudslinging, CJ! I've received your message. Same time, but I'm thinking a more scenic location. Top level."

Adam yelled in the background. What he said wasn't clear, but with a thud, as if someone had switched off a car radio, nothing but silence came from the phone.

"One more thing," came Cris's voice, "don't forget the briefcase."

CHAPTER 64
GREATER LOVE HATH NO MAN

Nate pulled into the gravel parking lot of The Pizza Bar, Barry only seconds behind him. Their headlights illuminated the area.

"What do we do?" I shouted as they walked over.

"We meet him," Barry said firmly.

"I mean, that is what we wanted, right?" Nate said.

"We were never supposed to even get near him! Now Adam's life is on the line!" I threw my hat to the ground, my trembling limbs ready to give way. "And he changed locations. Does he actually want me to help him now?"

"Doubtful. He knows it was a setup," Barry said. "The top level will be too empty for me to get close."

"What if he kills my brother?"

"Do we think he'll do that?" Rodman asked.

"What else would he do with him?"

"But you said you didn't think he'd kill you."

"Yeah, that was when his plan was to pin the murder on me. Adam's a loose end! I don't know what his plan is anymore."

"Let's not wait to find out," Barry insisted.

Rodman put up both hands. "We should really assess the situation first. If he's trying to get away with a clean escape, we can only assume he's looking to make a trade."

I shook my head as I paced. "A trade for what?"

"Your life for your brother's," Barry explained.

"So he changed his mind? You think he'll actually kill me?"

"Or your brother. Can we go now?" Barry's voice was persistent. He pushed back the sleeve of his leather jacket to check the time.

"The plan can still work, CJ. We can—"

"No," I said, cutting Rodman off. "It's too dangerous. We need a new plan."

"Is it time to finally call the police?" Sophia asked from behind.

No one answered her.

Barry shook his head. "It's too late for new plans."

"Give me some time to think."

"No." Barry grimaced. "I've given you all day."

He clenched his hands into fists and started back toward his car.

"You can't be serious right now!" I shouted from behind.

He didn't stop.

"You're worried about missing your stupid deadline when my brother's being held hostage?"

"I'm not going to be late!" he barked.

It was the first time I ever heard his voice rise, his beard doing little to cushion the noise.

"What are you going to do? Go in guns blazing and hope Adam's not caught in the crossfire?"

"I'm not letting this rat get away with the money."

Everything froze in place. It had to come to this, didn't it? My father took a bullet to the chest. Whether I believed it was meant for me or not didn't matter anymore. I couldn't let Adam suffer the same fate.

As Barry opened the driver-side door, there was only one thing I could think of saying to stop him.

"Then take me!"

Barry stopped right before dropping into his car.

My breathing was stifled, my lungs restricted as the words crawled my throat.

"We'll go with your plan. If he gets away, you can take me."

"CJ, what are you saying?" Sophia took hold of my arm from behind.

I kept my eyes on Barry. He hadn't moved, his hand on the open door of the Civic. He still debated leaving.

"You said it yourself—dead or alive, you'll hand over a Crispin Jiles." I blinked away the tears. "I'll make the trade. If Cris escapes, turn me over to Morris instead."

A gasp left Sophia's lips. Rodman closed his eyes. Barry turned back, his face stoic as always, shrouded by his dark sunglasses. A streak of lightning reflected in their lenses followed by a roar of thunder.

A crippling moan left my lips. "Please, Barry," I whimpered. "Please!"

He raised his wrist to check the time again, then spoke to Sophia. "Call the police in twenty minutes. Tell them that Crispin Jiles is hiding at Center Street Mall's parking garage and someone's been hurt."

"There's a second plan?" Rodman asked.

"He'll probably have the case in his car," Barry continued. "CJ, you'll go meet Cris and buy time. I'll find the car, then come to you."

"What about my brother?"

"Stall, and we'll make sure he gets out alive."

Rodman furrowed his eyebrows. "What are the cops for?"

Barry wouldn't look at us. He turned back to the car, his baritone voice nearly too low to hear. "In case there's more than one body."

Sophia pulled me into a hug from behind, her tears wetting my neck. "Don't do this."

The pressure built too great for even the skies, releasing their own tears. I held her long and hard as the rain came crashing down.

"No matter what happens, take care of Mr. Zhang for me."

"You're not going to die, CJ," she whispered in my ear.

"And maybe you and Rodman can help Adam clean up his life."

"Stop talking like that."

I cleared my throat, trying to steady my shaky voice. "You've always had a special place in my heart."

"You can't die." Her voice cracked. She hugged me tighter. Her bergamot perfume filled my senses as she whispered, "I... I love you."

I didn't return the words, too afraid of torturing her more if I never returned. As we released, I held her face in my hands, etching her slender features to memory.

I then turned to Nate.

"He can't be serious going for the briefcase before Cris."

"It was already discussed. If my plan didn't work, I agreed to be bait so Barry can find the briefcase."

"Why didn't you tell me?"

"You wouldn't help me if you knew."

He shook his head. The disappointment said it all; he knew there was no other option. He closed his eyes, holding back the pain.

"I'll be there."

"You don't have to. You and Sophia should stay here."

"I'll be there to—" His voice hitched. "To make sure everything goes to plan."

I pulled him into a hug. "Just make sure Adam gets out alive."

His voice was raspy. "Greater love hath no man than to lay down his life for a friend."

I coughed a broken laugh as I stepped back, desperate to evade the reality of the situation.

"I can't believe you're quoting scripture at me right now," I said over the rain, a mix of bittersweet emotions rolling through me. "I guess my father was wrong."

He pushed back his caramel locks as the rain matted them to his face. "How?"

"My father's last rule—Rule 20: Fear stops you from living, not dying."

"More of a platitude than a rule."

Even with emotions trying to steal his voice, his dry, sophisticated humor remained.

I looked at Barry, who stood in the rain, listening, waiting.

I wiped away the tears and grabbed my hat. "You ready?"

He removed his sunglasses before answering. "Let's save your brother."

CHAPTER 65
A CRUEL REMINDER

Rodman parked on the first level of the parking garage, the whoosh of rain becoming a distant memory as we entered. We parked next to Barry's navy blue Civic. Already here, he lurked among the vehicles scattered above and below in search of the Beetle.

I stared at the note I gave to Rodman—the note I rewrote four times over the night before. He must have removed it from the diner window before meeting at The Pizza Bar.

I'm In. Meet Me.
Center Street Mall
Parking Garage
Bottom Level
10 PM

It was a strategic location, squished between the mall and a towering bank. There no street parking within three blocks, making it more likely he'd leave his car somewhere in the garage. The mall would be closed, so there wouldn't be any chases through JCPenney. The basement lot was filled with reserved parking spots; it would have been easy for Barry to sneak up on him.

Or at least... that *was* the plan.

"Are you ready for this?"

I sat motionless. "Feels like I'm walking to my death."

Nate pushed at the sleeves of his wet sweater. "Let's hope that's not the case."

I let out a short breath through my nose as I smirked. "Hope's a funny thing."

"If it makes you feel better, people that look for the positives in obstacles have a 30% greater chance of success."

I didn't reply, brushing the note back and forth against my leg.

Nate put a hand on my arm. "Sorry, not meaning to make light of this."

I nodded. "I know."

We took the stairwell in the corner. Rodman led the way, his flip-flops slapping his heels. My legs wobbled more with every echoing step. The briefcase hung low, threatening to pull my arm out of its socket. It felt like a bag of bricks, each stacking up to be a regretful burden.

My motivations were severed. I could run, never look back, leave everything behind. Forget Wilkes City; forget the briefcase; forget my friends; forget Adam.

But I knew that wasn't an option. Guilt doesn't allow omission; its claws sink deep into the mind, a cruel reminder of broken mistakes. I had already known from tragic experience that life governed by remorse isn't a life worth living.

As we reached the top floor, I tripped over the final step, catching myself with trembling arms. Rodman helped me to my feet.

"You should stay here," I said.

"I'll be right behind you."

"For all I know, he'll shoot me *and* Adam. Don't become a third victim."

He swallowed hard, nodding in agreement.

I turned to the door, looking out the small window with crisscrossing gridlines. Rain poured outside. A misty fog caused everything to blend. I couldn't see Cris, but I knew he was out there.

"Whatever happens, CJ, he won't get away with this. I promise."

With one final, free breath, I wiped my hands down my shirt, then pushed against the door, leaving Rodman in the stairwell.

The top level of the parking garage was dark, only lit by light poles in each corner, everything in between slithering with shadows. Reflections of the lights bounced off hoods and windows but did little to allow me to see through the heavy rain.

I looked over Center Street behind me. The bright lights of the living city and its bustling traffic below felt miles away from the deathly abyss I was in.

The mall was shorter than the parking garage, allowing for a full view of the city to the West. The bank on the other side pillared up another ten stories, blocking any view of the East.

In front of me, two lanes stretched at least a dozen parking spaces in length. The lot was only a quarter full, cars and trucks sprinkled throughout.

I walked down the center, rolls of thunder tremoring above my head, splashes of rain puddling beneath my feet. Rain dropped from the brim of my hat like a ticking clock, ramping up by the second as my racing heart synchronized with each drip.

Tire and musk filled my nose. A howling breeze whipped at my ears. My skin went cold as beaded droplets seeped into the scrape on my face, the scratches on my exposed arms, and the scabbed cuts on my knuckles. It put ice in my veins, freezing my bones.

The blistering environment immersed me into a new world, the city disappearing beyond its bubbled atmosphere. I entered a battlefield, a *mano a mano* royale with demons from the blackness cheering. Their breaths mingled with the roar of rainfall and the stench of death.

Each step clapped with a splash. A stream of water soaked my feet. My jeans and white shirt stuck to my body, making my movement feel weighted.

As I approached the other side of the parking garage, no sign of life was evident apart from my own. The lights from the corners only provided a small glow beneath them, their luminescence swallowed by inky midnight at the center.

A strike of lightning flickered through the sky, a spider web that brightened my surroundings. Two silhouettes materialized before me thirty feet away, disappearing with the flash. I took another few steps, until their forms came into full view.

"Adam!"

His head hung low. Another flash of lightning exposed a gash on his head.

Cris gripped the back of his wet shirt, holding him up with his silver gun pointed against Adam's side.

"Finally," Cris announced with an eerie grin. "We were beginning to worry you wouldn't show."

"Well, I'm here," I said, trembling. "Leave him out of this."

"I really took a liking to you, CJ. It's too bad we couldn't work something out."

"You screwed me!"

"Ah," he sighed with a devilish smile. "You were never going to work with me. I knew you'd run. Just like you've always done."

I tightened my grip on the briefcase and balled my other hand into a fist.

"We could've been rich," he continued. "A mere fifty grand won't go far."

"Then why'd you do it?"

His eyes, full of malice, gleamed with delight. "Because I hate Tooly, of course! You think I screwed you over? Wait until you get a load of this guy."

He laughed, shaking my brother as he did so.

"Tooly's business is built on the backs of his slaves. All the while, he rakes in millions from Morris. I haven't received a raise in five years!" He pointed his gun at the briefcase in my hand. "I've been shipping their precious cargo all over town, and for what? For the money? No! Because I had a gun to my head if I didn't."

His sadistic laugh intertwined with the rain. "You don't know what it's like, CJ. No one stands up against George Morris."

"So what is this? Some way of standing up for justice?"

"Don't you get it, you idiot? I'm making a difference!" Anger rose in his voice, offended by my ignorance. "The fleet of drivers are in a stranglehold to do or die. You can't quit. Any time away from the job is an opportunity to cry for help. They don't care about their people. Ironic that it would be their downfall. Tooly didn't even know me by name! They were stupid enough to fall for my ploy and go after you!"

"So you just off your coworkers?"

"The ones that deserve it."

"And I'm supposed to be okay with being your fall guy?"

The pouring rain swallowed my words.

"Don't make this about you, CJ. Your sacrifice is part of the plan, but it's only the beginning. Once you're out of the picture, they'll drop their guard, and I'll do it again."

I looked at Adam. He looked back at me in a dazed expression. The last time I remembered him mute was in the presence of our father, dead on that dirty floor. Whether it was the grip of fear or the amount of blood loss from the wound to his head, he seemed ready to give out at any moment.

Tossing the briefcase in front of me, I dropped to my knees, taking a stifling breath as they hit the concrete.

"Kill me then," I said. "Just let my brother go."

"Oh, no fight? No plea for mercy?" Cris mocked. "You've caused me all this trouble just to give up?"

He pushed Adam by the collar of his shirt, walking over to me. He pointed the barrel at my head, his crimson-scabbed lips smeared with a dirty smile.

"Are you ready to watch your brother die?" he said, a cynical muse slipping between each syllable.

I turned to Adam. Stricken with fear, he twisted his face away. I didn't blame him. He was about to witness it all again—a loved one dying before him.

I shut my eyes, accepting my fate.

The voice of the rain rose in volume. It was melodic—a rhythmic chant before a sacrifice.

With my eyes squeezed closed, I thought of the choices that brought me to this point and what I could have done to change the outcome. I wondered if I'd see my father on the other side, if Rodman's God could find favor in His heart for a couple of thieves.

Perhaps it was destiny for it all to end this way—a universal justice for my crimes.

I guess it's like Barry said—karma has a funny way of catching up with you.

The next thing I knew, a gunshot rang in my ears, and the roaring cries of the rain engulfed my senses.

CHAPTER 66
DISCO BALL

The rain blurred my vision as I opened my eyes, numbing the wound I must have endured. The ringing slowly died, beating me to the finishing line—or so I thought.

"CJ!"

A muffled voice rang out over the pitter-patter. I craned my neck, expecting it to be Adam. It was Rodman.

"CJ!" he said again, this time clearer as my senses snapped back into place.

I felt my stomach and chest. I next felt my head.

"I'm alive," I muttered. Then, I said it again, but terror filled the words. "I'm alive!"

Adam lay in a murky pool of blood, slowly mixing with the rain.

"ADAM!"

His stomach was warm. Thunder quaked the ground. Lightning ignited the skies. The flash illuminated my red hands pressing against the wound.

Adam gazed at me with glossy eyes. He reached up with a shaky hand, wrapping his fingers around the nape of my neck. He tried to speak, but nothing came from his lips.

Nate sat next to me, his hair sticking to his face. His hands joined mine on Adam's stomach.

"Get out of here! The cops will be here any minute."

"I'm not leaving my brother."

"You don't have a choice!"

"We need to take him to a hospital!"

"There's no time. An ambulance will be faster than us."

Adam's breathing came in short gasps.

"I can't leave him," I said, shaking my head.

"Can't you see? You have a case of drugs in your possession, and now Adam's the dead victim. It's how he'll get away with it." Nate pulled out his keys. "Get him before you lose your chance."

I pulled away from the wound, letting Nate take over. I stared down at the keys in my hands.

"Go!"

I looked at Adam one final time.

He spoke in a gurgling voice. "Rule 18."

I told him I loved him and grabbed the briefcase from the ground, darting back the way I came.

Vengeance led every stride as the rain rinsed me of fear. Reaching the bottom of the stairwell, I saw the lights of a car descending from the level above. Running behind it was a security brute with a beard.

I hopped in the yellow Mustang and fired up the engine, pulling forward to cut him off. The black Beetle swerved around me just in time, grinding the fender of a parked car on the opposite side before proceeding out the exit.

Barry jumped into the passenger seat. I froze for a moment, wondering if he had given up on the other Cris Jiles.

"What are you waiting for?" He slapped the dash of the car. "Go! Go!"

As we exited the parking garage, police cars and ambulances flew by.

"You're alive," Barry said between breaths. "How are you alive?"

"He shot Adam," I answered.

He shook his head. "Is he—"

"Not yet."

We raced down Center Street. I dropped it into second as we took a sharp turn onto Elm. We ramped up speed from thirty to forty to fifty, switching lanes as we caught up to the Beetle. I passed an old Sunfire with rubber ducks on the antenna, then a white Mazda with a skeleton hanging from the bumper. Horns blared on either side as I gained ground.

The tumultuous rain smacked the windshield like rocks with each heavy hit. Even with the wipers whipping at full blast, the road looked more like an abstract watercolor painting with city lights reflecting off every surface.

"Did you get the case?" I asked as I honked the horn and passed another vehicle.

He smacked his leg. "I didn't find his car in time."

Barry pulled out his gun, checked the chamber, and switched off the safety.

"Get right behind him so I have a clear shot."

I nodded, keeping my eyes forward. Only three cars back, I kept my sights on the little turbo diesel.

Dropping from fifty to twenty, we took another turn onto the main drag. The brakes screeched as the tires struggled to keep traction. We sped by Ricardo's Rum and Ribs, but there was no time to wave as we passed. The glow of the city glared in the rearview mirror as we headed into the suburbs, disregarding every light and stop sign as we went.

I pulled the e-brake as we came to a left, drifting through the turning lane median past a white van. As we slid, I caught the eyes of the woman driving the van, who looked at me like I was crazy. I dropped the brake and ripped the wheel in the other direction, continuing our chase.

The turbo Beetle zipped forward, gliding into the on-coming traffic lane to pass another vehicle. I did the same, causing Barry to hold the handle above the door as a car faced us, its beams of light swerving away right before impact.

We came to an on-ramp for the highway, but to my surprise, Cris didn't take it. He kept straight, heading for the country roads beyond the city.

"Where's he going?" I asked out loud.

"He'll try to lose you on backroads," Barry said.

Finally caught up, we stayed bumper-to-bumper for another two miles, the Beetle's back lights staring back at me. Mist kicked up from the back tires, making the already low vision dangerously blurry, but I didn't slow down. Instead, I went faster, coming within inches of his bumper.

The road became straight for a time, and we hit eighty. The Ford decal on the back of the Mustang animated in the rearview mirror. I heard the neighing, the galloping, the heavy snort of the horse as we flashed by barbed wire fields and distant windmills that blinked at us through the rain.

Barry put down the window. "Keep it steady," he yelled over the gale, his beard a tattered flag in the wind.

Instantly drenched, he sat halfway out the window, pressing his body against the top of the door. He fired a shot. The tail of the beetle swerved in surprise but kept pushing onward. Barry fired another, obliterating the back glass of the Beetle.

Before shooting again, the unfamiliar road descended into heavy foliage and windy turns. The red lights of the Beetle flashed in my eyes, and I slammed my brakes to avoid colliding. Barry slotted back through the window right before I took a turn too late, catching the guard rail. The Mustang shrieked in pain, but I kept control.

"You know these roads?"

"Not really," I admitted.

The lack of vision and foreign country drag made this chase more lethal than any pursuit of my past.

"We're coming up to an old bridge. You know it?"

"Vaguely," I shouted, struggling to keep up.

"Get up next to him when we're there, and when I say brake, you brake!"

Less than a minute passed before we came to the bridge. It was a historic tied arch bridge half a mile in length, passing over a deep valley between the mountains that guarded Wilkes City.

The bridge flashed in brilliance as lightning lit up the dark forest around us. We charged between two large wooden beams from its original construction. Steel beams replaced the others, soaring high into the sky with cables attached.

With no oncoming traffic, I did as Barry said and got in the left lane. I crept up on Cris Jiles's tail, but he ripped his car to the side before I was next to him. Slowing down, I returned to the right. He gradually moved back in front of me. I pressed the gas pedal to the floor, swerving back to the left and giving him no chance to cut me off.

The moment our front tires were even with his back, Barry leaned out the window and fired.

"Brake!"

Three loud bangs reverberated through the air, exploding the Beetle's back tire. I slammed the brakes, struggling to stay in control as we hydroplaned at sixty. Barry pulled himself through the window before the backend lashed to the side. We slid sideways, my door facing the action ahead.

Out my window, the black Beetle whipped out of control, the back tire ripping to shreds. Brake lights swung out of sight, replaced by high beams. The car spun like a disco ball. The front end rammed the median barrier before flipping on its head.

We fishtailed ourselves, doing a full one-eighty before I regained control. We skirted to a halt, the back fender only a few yards away from the Volkswagen.

Sitting motionless, the Mustang's idling engine blended with the sound of the showers. Barry and I shared a glance before opening our doors.

Barry led the way, his gun pointed at the vehicle, but there was no need. When he opened the driver-side door, Cris Jiles was already dead.

"Is it over?" I asked.

Barry reached through the broken back window, pulling out a silver briefcase lying inside the car.

"Yeah," he said, a small smile forming on his lips. "It's over."

I looked up, letting the rain freely fall on my face. My hat fell as I tilted back my head.

I put out my hands and cried out into the night.

But it wasn't a cry of fear. It was a cry of relief.

CHAPTER 67
THE SHAMISEN

I faked a pass to Jamal and took a shot. The soda can puck rattled off the trash can goalposts. Players jabbed at the flattened can that sat motionless in front of the defender's goal, barely moving as everyone slapped sticks.

Kaleb (with a *K*), the defending sandy-haired goalie, made contact, sending a clear pass to his new, lanky teammate. With a lack of experience, he quickly swatted the puck away to avoid being dispossessed.

I lunged forward with my broom-handle hockey stick, but Marcus bullied me to the side and maintained possession. He sliced down the lane and pushed past Jamal with ease, sending a blazer in Ronny's direction. Ronny's kneecaps collided as he tried to stop the shot, but it was too late.

"Through the legs and in!" shouted Timmy, his tunneled voice booming through the traffic cone. "That's the first goal by the Bulldogs, putting the overall score at three to one."

Hoots from the crowd filled the atmosphere. One boy drummed against five-gallon buckets to add to the noise. A girl clapped a metal garbage can lid against a building.

I gave a nod to my teammates. "Sorry, guys. That one's on me."

Marcus beat my friends in response. "No worries, old man," he jeered.

He strutted back to his side of the street with a showboat swagger, high-fiving his teammates with his hockey stick.

Jamal stuck out his tongue. "Shut up, Marcus!"

I put up a hand to say he wasn't worth it.

One of the children from the sidewalk tossed me the flattened Coca-Cola. I dropped it in the chalk-drawn center circle, facing the new Bulldogs teammate in the stand-off.

"Who's he callin' 'old man'? If only he knew I was the older brother."

I grinned at Adam, turning my hat backward. "They'll know soon enough—right after I dust ya!"

We hit the ground with our sticks, then brought them up to meet above the puck. After three rhythmic beats, we fought for control, the puck flying wayward as it pinched between our forces.

The game continued with fast-paced action, concluding after ten minutes with the usual supper bell. Mrs. Hopskey had made her famous lasagna.

"Ronny!" his mother scolded from the window above. "How many times do I have to tell you not to wear your dress shoes while playing? Come clean up!"

Kids giggled as they parted ways with Timmy's conclusion to the match.

"Bentley Bulldogs have defeated the Wilkes City Wildcats six to four. Will the Wildcats ever beat the new Bulldogs roster, or will Marcus lead his team to another long-reigned victory? My name's Timmy, and I'll see you next week at Bentley Rink."

Kaleb and Marcus dumped the prize pool jar in the street, handing Adam a five-dollar bill. He grinned from ear to ear holding it up to me with haughty laughter.

"Yo, CJ." Marcus strolled over, his gold chains bouncing against his sweaty skin. "Wanna thank you for inviting your bro. I'd take his lanky legs over Davie any day."

I smirked as we bumped fists. "Good game, man. See you next time."

Sophia and Rodman pulled into The Pizza Bar parking lot a few yards ahead of us. Adam ran past me, holding up his green.

"Winner, winner, chicken dinner!" he cried. "I beat 'em, guys. I actually beat 'em!"

They both laughed. Sophia glanced past him, meeting my eyes, her smile drawing me in.

Before heading over, I dropped my hockey stick in the alleyway, only to notice a yellow sticky note slapped to the dumpster's side.

"Come on, hockey pro," Rodman shouted.

"Just a minute."

The note had an arrow pointing to my left. I walked the sidewalk to the opposite end of the street from my friends, where a familiar leather jacket hid behind the corner.

"I could've used a sub, you know."

Barry chuckled beneath his beard as he leaned against the back door of his Civic, choking on a sip of his chai. "It's good to see your brother's recovering swiftly."

I peeked back around the corner as Adam danced around in the parking lot with his hard-earned money.

"Bullet went through cleanly, missing anything important according to the doc," I replied. "Actually, it worked out in his favor. Being in the hospital a few weeks has led to him being sober since the night of the accident."

"I hope it stays that way. How'd the hearing go today?"

"Went well. How'd you know about it?"

"I watch the news."

I rolled my eyes playfully. "The judge was generous. The only thing I got busted for was counterfeit jewelry since it wasn't connected to the case."

"They found out about that?"

"While Cindy Lou was at the body shop, I guess some cops went over to check for any missing evidence."

"Serves you right. My watch doesn't work anymore."

I held back a laugh. "Judge said I could have done prison time."

"But?"

I shook my head in disbelief of my fortune. "But he gave me a fine instead."

"Any other charges?"

"Everything was dropped. Rodman's voice recorder came in clutch. He caught most of the conversation from the parking garage, dropping all suspicions against me."

"Surprised he was able to get close enough. Sorry I wasn't there."

I shrugged. "You did what you thought was best."

"They say anything about the car chase? About the accident?"

"Nope. Story goes that Cris Jiles fled the scene and hydroplaned. Body was never found."

Barry sipped his chai as he nodded. "Interesting. Sounds like someone's pulling strings at the courthouse to keep things quiet."

"Nate said it's probably George Morris. His name came up during the hearing, Tooly's too, but it's a bunch of he-said-she-said, half of it coming from a dead guy on a voice recorder, so I don't think it'll result in anything. Speaking of Morris, he's not after me, right?"

"How would I know?"

"You worked for him."

Barry removed his wayfarer shades. "I never said I worked for him."

I gave a knowing grin.

"If you mean to ask if the owner of the briefcases thinks you're responsible—no, I made sure you were in the clear."

"Well, that's a relief. Why are you here anyway? I thought you would've left by now."

Barry pointed over his shoulder. "I have something of yours."

I tried to think about what it could be.

"Or someone, I should say."

He stepped away from the car and opened the back door. A calico cat leaped out onto the street, rubbing her head against my shin.

"Marrie!" I pulled her into my arms. "How? You mean you had—what?!"

Barry found my confusion amusing. "I didn't like the thought of hurting an innocent animal in the process of chasing you, especially when I presumed I'd be turning you in. I've been laying low the past month, so I haven't had the chance to return her."

"Where did you keep her?"

"Binghams Street. You think I'd risk only renting out one Airbnb?"

He reached back into his car. "And this."

Barry handed me the small frame with a picture of Adam and myself, our arms around each other's necks. The picture meant more than ever before.

"Thank you," I said. I pointed back toward my friends. "This would all be gone if it wasn't for you."

He turned toward The Pizza Bar. Sophia, Nate, and Adam were deep in conversation. Sophia rolled her eyes as Nate gave one of his *presentations*.

"She seems like a good girl."

I lowered my head to hide the pink in my complexion.

"There was a woman in my life once," he continued. "She reminds me of her."

His face was expressionless, but his heart beat loud and clear.

"What happened?"

"I was late." He chuckled, but it was short-lived. "I can't even remember what movie we were going to see."

After a pause, he went on.

"She was always upset when I was late— it had become a normal occurrence." He looked to his left at the downtown buildings in the distance. "But that night was the last time I was late for her."

I bit the inside of my lips, unsure of what to say. "She broke up with you?"

"She was gone. A coworker said someone else picked her up."

My heart dropped to my gut.

He shook his head. His lips remained flat as he spoke. "She left town. I never saw her again."

He straightened his posture and cracked his neck to the side, returning to his original demeanor. "But it's in the past. Can't let karma dictate your ways."

I scratched the back of Marrie's neck.

"To be, rather than to seem," I quoted.

He patted my shoulder. "It was good seeing you, CJ. Maybe see you again sometime."

"Wait," I said as he dropped into the car. He put down his window.

"Wanna join us for a few drinks?"

"As I said, I'm laying low for now. Another time." He put the car in drive. "But don't try to call. I got rid of the line."

"How will I reach you?"

He kept his eyes forward. A slight smirk formed on the side of his lips, cracking through his stoicism. "Leave me a note."

The blue Civic disappeared down the street. I shot it with finger pistols before it was gone.

I hugged Marrie closely before putting her down. "You and I have so much to catch up on."

I walked back to The Pizza Bar with the picture in hand and my cat following behind.

"You found Marrie!" Sophia shouted as I approached, pulling the cat into her arms. "I was so afraid she was gone forever."

"Well, no need to worry anymore."

We headed inside to enjoy our Friday night. Subtle incense filled the room. The shamisen played in the background. Mr.

Zhang stood behind the bar, already preparing a round of Dunkel beers.

Sophia sat next to me after bringing Marrie upstairs. "I'm glad things are back to the way they were before."

I turned to Adam and Rodman on my right, then back to her.

I took her hand. She blushed at the gesture, interlacing her fingers with mine.

"Things are better than before."

"So, Crispy." Nate knocked off my hat to get my attention, revealing my short, brown hair. "What's next, now that you're a free man?"

"I don't know." I shrugged my shoulders. "I guess I'll keep Uber driving for now."

"Ah! Get new job," Mr. Zhang said, tossing a tray of pizza in front of me. "You still owe money. You pay late again."

"Yeah, and you owe me for the repairs on my Mustang," Rodman teased.

"What happened to forgive and forget?" I fired back.

"Actually, while the principle is spelled out dozens of times in the Bible, the correct phrasing is 'forget and forgive,' derived from the Spanish epic, *Don Quixote*."

Adam slapped his beer on the dark cherry counter. "Well, forgive me, 'cause I just about forgot every word you said."

"Join the club," Sophia jibed.

We continued our banter through the evening, honest grins plastered across each of our faces (even Mr. Zhang's).

ABOUT THE AUTHOR

Michael Jaymes is an author, writing coach, and editor from Scranton, PA. His love for writing developed at a young age when a close friend passed away. In response to the tragedy, Michael wrote a poem that received an award in a state-wide fine arts competition. The admiration sparked a fire within him, and a passion was born.

In 2019, he pursued studying story structure and began his business, offering services such as outlining, editing, and consulting. In 5 years, Michael has served over 400 unique clients and delivered over 600 orders, with one client becoming an award-winning author and another going on to be a best-seller on Amazon.

Now residing in Greensboro, NC, Michael continues to write his own works and serve clients both online and locally within his community.

OTHERS BY MICHAEL JAYMES

Other published works by the author are a young adult horror, *Letters from Lily*, and a middle grade fantasy, *The Secret Fountain*.

www.ingramcontent.com/pod-product-compliance
Lightning Source LLC
Chambersburg PA
CBHW020523110726
47899CB00004B/1225